PRAISE FOR CAROLYN BROWN

The Wedding Pearls

"*The Wedding Pearls* by Carolyn Brown is an amazing story about family, life, love, and finding out who you are and where you came from. This book is a lot like *The Golden Girls* meet *Thelma and Louise*."

—*Harlequin Junkie*

"*The Wedding Pearls* is an absolute must read. I cannot recommend this one enough. Grab a copy for yourself, and one for a best friend or even your mother or both. This is a book that you need to read. It will make you laugh and cry. It is so sweet and wonderful and packed full of humor. I hope that when I grow up, I can be just like Ivy and Frankie."

—*Rainy Day Ramblings*

The Yellow Rose Beauty Shop

"*The Yellow Rose Beauty Shop* was hilarious, and so much fun to read. But sweet romances, strong female friendships, and family bonds make this more than just a humorous read."

—*The Reader's Den*

"If you like books about small towns and how the people's lives intertwine, you will *love* this book. I think it's probably my favorite book this year. The relationships of the three main characters, girls who have grown up together, will make you feel like you just pulled up a chair in their beauty shop with a bunch of old friends. As you meet the other people in the town you'll wish you could move there. There are

some genuine laugh-out-loud moments and then more that will just make you smile. These are real people, not the oh-so-thin-and-so-very-rich that are often the main characters in novels. This book will warm your heart and you'll remember it after you finish the last page. That's the highest praise I can give a book."

—Reader quote

Long, Hot Texas Summer

"This is one of those lighthearted, feel-good, make-me-happy kind of stories. But, at the same time, the essence of this story is family and love with a big ole dose of laughter and country living thrown in the mix. This is the first installment in what promises to be another fascinating series from Brown. Find a comfortable chair, sit back, and relax, because once you start reading *Long, Hot Texas Summer* you won't be able to put it down. This is a super fun and sassy romance."

—*Thoughts in Progress*

Daisies in the Canyon

"I just loved the symbolism in *Daisies in the Canyon* . . . Carolyn Brown has a way with character development with few if any contemporaries. I am sure there are more stories to tell in this series. Brown just touched the surface first with *Long, Hot Texas Summer* and now continuing on with *Daisies in the Canyon*."

—*Fresh Fiction*

The Barefoot Summer

The Barefoot Summer

CAROLYN BROWN

Montlake
Romance

Published by Montlake Romance, Seattle

www.apub.com

Amazon, the Amazon logo, and Montlake Romance are trademarks of Amazon.com, Inc., or its affiliates.

ISBN-13: 9781503941281
ISBN-10: 1503941280

Cover design by Laura Klynstra

Printed in the United States of America

In memory of my mother,
Virginia Chapman Gray Essary,
May 18, 1927–February 6, 2010

CHAPTER ONE

Black showed respect for the dead, so Kate Steele wore red to her husband's funeral that Saturday. It seemed fitting that she would bury him on the first day of July, the same day he'd come into her life fourteen years ago. It brought everything full circle—right back to the afternoon that she'd met him in the cemetery when visiting her father's grave. Six months later they were married. A year after that, the marriage went to hell in a handbasket.

Conrad Steele had definitely conned her, but she'd be damned if he would win.

Would the preacher go on forever? Maybe those other people sitting in the chairs at the other end of the single line appreciated what he was saying, but Kate had trouble listening to nice things about the son of a bitch. One thing for sure—that preacher didn't know jack crap about Conrad or he wouldn't be talking about him being among the angels in heaven. If he conned his way past Saint Peter at the pearly gates, then the angels best lock down those streets of gold.

Sweat streamed from her neck to puddle between her breasts. Not even with all Kate's money could she buy, beg, steal, or borrow a breeze that afternoon, and there wasn't a shade tree in sight. She eased a hand down beside her chair to fish out a few tissues to discreetly stuff into her bra. But she'd left her purse in the car. She brushed a strand of her shoulder-length blonde hair away from her sweaty neck and uncrossed her long legs. One little gust of wind to cool her thighs would be worth a fortune.

Her mother, Teresa, sat ramrod straight right beside her. No one could ever say that she wasn't a lady. Not even the Texas heat was a match for Teresa Truman. She'd face off with the devil on his best day. Legs encased in black panty hose, properly crossed at the ankles, a black silk suit tailored to her long, thin body, gray hair styled that morning, and a wide-brimmed black hat with only the hint of a thin veil dropping down from the front, she was a true force to be reckoned with.

Only God, Kate, and Teresa knew that the whole funeral was a show. Kate didn't care if they rolled him up in a used dog blanket and tossed him in a hole. Teresa insisted that they had an image to uphold, because, through Kate, his name was associated with the family oil company. And God—well, Kate would like to be a mouse in a corner when God got a firm grip on Conrad's soul.

An antsy feeling that something was wrong crept up the back of Kate's neck, making all the fine hairs stand on end. She glanced over her shoulder to see Detective Waylon Kramer standing behind a tombstone about ten yards to her left. The handsome detective had asked her to identify the body. He'd even told her right up front that the spouse was usually the first suspect, but she'd provided a rock-solid alibi. So why was he attending a funeral in the broiling Texas heat when he didn't have to? Did he think she'd throw herself on the casket and confess to having her husband killed because he was a bastard?

Since he was there, he could be a gentleman and move up closer. With his height and broad body, he could provide some shade for her. It would make him good for something other than suspecting that she'd had Conrad killed.

"Stop fidgeting," Teresa hissed from the side of her mouth.

"This is such a sham," Kate whispered.

Teresa shot her a dirty look from under that fancy little veil.

Kate sat up straight and pretended to pay attention. But with sidelong glances, she studied the four women and the child sitting at the other end of the row of folding chairs. Thank goodness for big sunglasses so she could stare as long as she wanted and not get caught.

Two women and a child who were definitely Hispanic hovered first in her peripheral vision. The older one was as stone-faced as a statue, and for a while Kate began to think maybe the old gal had succumbed to the terrible Texas heat right there in the cemetery. Just as Kate was about to yell at the detective to call an ambulance, the woman let out a long sigh. Kate could relate. She would have gladly doubled whatever the preacher charged the funeral home for his services if he would cut his sermon short and let everyone get out of the scorching heat. The minutes ticked off at the rate of one every hour.

The dark-haired lady beside the older woman must be quite a bit younger, most likely the mother of the little girl with big brown eyes who, for the most part, looked confused. Poor little thing probably would have rather been home playing in a kiddie pool or watching cartoons on television than sitting at a funeral in the middle of a Texas heat wave.

An empty chair separated that group of three from an older woman with gray hair sitting beside a very pregnant red-haired woman, maybe in her late twenties. The pregnant lady moaned and sobbed into a white hankie as the other woman patted her shoulder. At least Conrad had one acquaintance who would cry for him, or—Kate eyed her mother carefully—had Teresa paid a mourner to come to the funeral and weep over that man's body for appearances?

Kate leaned to the left and whispered, "Do you know those people?"

Teresa shook her head.

"Did you pay that redhead to cry?"

"Hush," Teresa hissed. "I would never do that. But he's dead, so we need to show respect."

Eight people at the funeral.

It all went to show that a con man did not have real friends. Were those women related to Conrad? He'd never mentioned sisters or cousins, but then if he had, she wouldn't have believed him. Not after she'd found out exactly what he was. She should have given him the divorce and the million-dollar settlement he wanted, and then she wouldn't even have had to be there that day with sweat trickling down her ribs. That young one, who evidently sincerely mourned the bastard, could have buried him and maybe even put flowers on his grave. A settlement would have been well worth the money if it had gotten Kate out of planning and attending the funeral.

She glanced down the row again. The little girl held her red rose as if it were a piece of delicate china. The expression on the face of the woman beside her left no doubt that she wanted to get this whole thing finished as much as Kate did. The pregnant girl had wrapped her wrinkled handkerchief around the stem of her rose and now wiped her tears away with the back of her hand.

"Let us pray," the preacher said.

Praise the Lord, Kate thought as she bowed her head, but she did not shut her eyes. She stared straight ahead at the shiny black casket with the reflections of the mourners, real or obligatory, right there before her. Their faces distorted in the casket's curvature, but what she saw was sorrow, disgust, confusion, acceptance, and something akin to indifference.

"Amen!" the preacher said, and Kate mouthed the word even though she had no idea what he'd petitioned God for that afternoon. He could have begged the Lord to open up the ground and swallow Conrad Steele's wife right there on the spot, or he might have read that week's grocery list, but she could definitely say, "Amen," if it got her out of the heat.

The preacher nodded toward her. "And now, Mrs. Steele, do you have any last words or something you want to say before we conclude the service?"

She shook her head, stood up, and hoped her slim skirt wasn't stuck to her sweaty thighs as she took the red rose the funeral director had handed her when she arrived and laid it on the top of the casket.

"Yes, I have something to say." The pregnant girl laid one hand on her baby bump and pushed up out of the chair. "Conrad was an amazing husband, and I cannot believe he's gone." She burst into another round of deep sobs.

"Sweet Jesus!" Surely the heat had fried Kate's brain cells. That kid couldn't be married to Conrad, and yet the scenario didn't change, no matter how many times Kate blinked.

The older woman quickly stood up and wrapped an arm around the girl's shoulders. "It's all right, Amanda, darlin'. Just give your flower to Conrad and please stop crying."

"I can't. He was such a good man, and now he'll never see our baby grow up," she wailed.

Kate's eyebrows shot up so high that it gave her an instant headache. Conrad had married without divorcing Kate and the woman was pregnant? She was still staring at the lady when the Hispanic woman popped up and her hands knotted into fists.

"You can't be married to Conrad! I am his wife."

Kate inhaled and let it out slowly, but then couldn't make herself suck in more air. Her chest ached and her hands went clammy as the scene played out in slow motion.

"You are lying!" Amanda threw off the older woman's arm and stomped up to the other woman until she was nose to nose with her. "I married him seven months ago. You might be his ex-wife, but you are not his wife today."

"I have the marriage license showing that I've been married to him for seven years. *With* no divorce, so if he married you last year, kiddo, you aren't even legally married. This child right here is his daughter." Her dark eyes flashed.

Kate's mother sighed. "I told you he was bad news."

"Holy smokin' hell!" Kate finally gasped.

"Okay, ladies." Detective Waylon Kramer stepped between them. "You can both take a step backward. Neither of you are legally married to Conrad. This lady right here"—he pointed to Kate—"is his legal wife of fourteen years."

"You can't tell me that. I have a marriage license. Amanda Hilton and Conrad Steele were married the last day of December last year," Amanda argued.

"So do I," the dark-haired woman said and poked herself in the chest with a forefinger. "Jamie Mendoza and Conrad Steele were married the last day of December seven years ago."

Waylon glanced at Kate.

She shrugged. "The last day of December fourteen years ago."

"You"—Amanda raised her voice to only an octave below what it took to break glass—"are his sister. And that old woman beside you is his mother. He showed me pictures of you awful people together—his mother liked you better and gave you most of the money. He only got a little bit from his trust fund, which would be mine if something ever happened to him. And I need it for this baby." Her hands went to her rounded stomach.

"Old woman!" Teresa gasped.

Kate bit back a nervous giggle. Nothing was humorous about anything that was going on, but that pregnant redhead had no idea that she'd just opened the cage to the scary Teresa Tiger, who could rip her throat out with nothing but icy words.

"I am his legal wife, and there is no trust fund," Kate said.

"Bringing up money at a funeral," Teresa muttered under her breath. "This is worse than *The Jerry Springer Show*. If I'd birthed that son of a bitch, I would have thrown him in the river before he was a week old. Old woman, my ass!"

"You are both wrong. Come on, Aunt Ellie. We're going home and we'll get a lawyer to sort this out." Amanda set her mouth in a firm line.

At least that annoying sobbing had stopped. Kate didn't give a baby rat's rear end about her late husband, and when that woman woke up and realized that she'd married a con man, she might change her tune.

"Your rose," her aunt Ellie reminded her.

Amanda laid it on the casket with her handkerchief. "Darlin' Conrad, take my rose and my tears to heaven with you, and someday we will be together again."

It might be funny if it wasn't so bizarre. Lord, this kind of fodder just might be good enough to make it to those tabloids beside the grocery store checkout counter. Kate shuddered as she pictured all three wives with sweaty faces lined up beside a picture of Conrad on the front page of a magazine. What would that do for her reputation as president of the oil company?

Conrad had three wives. At the same time. She held her hands to keep from counting them off on her fingers. Kate, Jamie, and Amanda, married seven years apart on the same damn day. At least he wouldn't forget his anniversary. It sure put new meaning to the seven-year itch.

"Did you know this?" she asked Waylon.

"I did yesterday." His sexy grin jacked up the temperature another ten degrees.

"And you didn't warn me?" She glared at him.

"I wanted to be sure that you didn't conspire together to kill him or have him killed. The second wife, Jamie, showed up at the precinct when she heard the news on the television. The third one, Amanda, arrived in hysterics worse than you saw today when she saw the article about his death in the newspaper," Waylon said.

"And what did you tell them?"

Waylon removed his cowboy hat, combed his thick dark hair with his fingers, and resettled the hat. "That the funeral was today, where it was and the time. And that his family was taking care of arrangements."

"And now?"

"I'm not ruling out a conspiracy, but you are still my prime suspect. Don't leave the state, Miz Steele," he said.

"How can she be a suspect? She was with me in a board meeting all day when Conrad was murdered," Teresa asked.

"That does not mean she couldn't have paid someone to do the job when she found out about these other two wives." Waylon tipped his hat to the two ladies and headed out across the green grass toward a pickup truck parked behind Kate's Cadillac.

"You killed Conrad?" Jamie confronted her, hands on her hips and brown eyes flashing anger.

"I did not." Kate took a step forward, jolted by her unexpected burst of offense at those words, and looked down on the shorter woman. As if she'd bother.

"You had him killed, then?" Amanda wailed as she made her way back toward Kate.

Kate quickly shook her head. "No, I didn't do that, either, but if either of you want to confess, I'll chase down that detective and we can get this over with right now."

Amanda took a step backward. "I would never . . . how could you even suggest . . . he was my husband."

Jamie stood her ground. Her eyes flashed anger, and her body fairly well hummed. "Well, he's damn lucky I didn't know about you or that other whiny pregnant hussy or I would have done the job myself."

❧

Jamie's heart beat so fast that she thought it might jump right out of her chest. And her high heels sank into the green grass all the way from the graveside to her seven-year-old van. That hoity-toity bitch back there was probably laughing at her trying to keep her balance. She made sure Gracie and her grandmother had their seat belts fastened and drove out of the cemetery ten miles an hour above the speed limit.

Rita Mendoza crossed her arms over her chest. "I told you that something was not right. No man leaves his wife and daughter and only comes home one week out of every month. I don't care what his job is—if he is within a hundred miles, he should come home. Now we know that he was staying with his other wives. But that leaves an extra week. Is there a fourth wife in the woodpile?"

"God, I hope not." Jamie gripped the steering wheel to steady her shaking hands.

"Mama, are they going to put my daddy in the ground? Was he really in that big black box?" Gracie asked from the backseat.

"Yes, baby girl, your daddy is gone and he won't come home anymore. But we will be fine. You still have your grandmother and me," Jamie answered through clenched teeth.

"How do we know he was really in there?" Gracie asked.

"I'm sorry that you won't see him again, sweetheart"—Jamie had to work at keeping her voice calm—"but he was really in the casket."

It wasn't a lie. She was sorry that Gracie wouldn't see her father, but Conrad was lucky that someone had shot him before Jamie figured out why he only came home one week during each month. How dare he turn his back on Gracie and marry that girl! She wasn't a day over twenty. She might not even be old enough to buy a shot of tequila, and Conrad was past forty. Did Kate have children with him, too?

Gracie nodded seriously. "Can we go to McDonald's now?"

Rita laid a hand on Jamie's shoulder. "Let it go. Don't sugarcoat the truth when she asks, but don't say too much. He was a good father when he was around."

"I. Am. So. Angry." Jamie emphasized each word with a slap of the steering wheel.

"With damn good reason, but it will pass," Rita said.

"I'm starving." Gracie folded her arms over her chest. "I hate getting all dressed up. My shoes pinch."

"I'm hungry, too, baby girl." Rita smiled. "We'll get a burger and a milk shake, and we can eat it in the playroom. Afterward you can go down the slide as many times as you want."

A picture flitted through Jamie's mind. Conrad had taken her and Gracie to a McDonald's in a different part of Dallas. He was, or had been, tall, dark haired, blue eyed, handsome, and when he walked into a room or even a McDonald's all the women in the place eyed him. When he flashed a bright smile, they would stumble around at the privilege of being in his presence—just like she did when they'd met at the teachers' party that year.

"Mama, can I have a big hamburger instead of the little kids' meal?" Gracie asked. "I'm really, really hungry."

"Of course," Jamie answered. She dreaded going back to her house. Family pictures were everywhere—from a collage on the wall behind the sofa to the credenza in the foyer. One of the two of them on their wedding day was on one nightstand, and on the other side was the three of them in the hospital the day Gracie was born.

Seven years of her life, and it was all a deception. She was mentally throwing pictures at the walls when she reached McDonald's and pulled into a parking spot. She put her head on the steering wheel and groaned.

"What now? He can't be killed twice," Rita said.

"Pictures. Finances. Life. All of it. But I'm too mad to talk about that right now."

ⅆⅆ

Amanda sat in the passenger seat of the small Chevrolet truck, seat belt around her bulging stomach, crying into tissues that she kept tossing behind her when they were too soggy to use anymore.

"This is a nightmare, Aunt Ellie. I'm going to wake up and Conrad will arrive tomorrow and we'll go to the cabin for our summer vacation," Amanda said between sobs. "This cannot be happening. What about our baby and . . . oh, my God, what am I going to do?"

Her aunt Ellie kept one hand on the steering wheel and shook a long, bony finger at her with the other one. "You are going to shut up that carryin' on and get a hold of yourself, girl. You will do exactly what you've been doing the past six months—live in your apartment, help me run the store—and in two months you will have a baby. You were a single mother anyway. He was only home a few days a month."

"Do you think he was really already married to those other two women?" she finally asked.

"Yes, I do." Ellie pushed back a strand of salt-and-pepper hair behind her ear. "Why would they attend the funeral and why would they lie? Be thankful you didn't have to pay for that ceremony. I bet the casket alone cost a fortune."

"Do you think"—Amanda hesitated, not wanting to even utter the words—"that he slept with them when he wasn't with me?"

"Most likely," Aunt Ellie said.

"You aren't any help at all." Amanda pouted. "He might have married them, but there are divorce papers somewhere. They will show up, I'm positive of it."

"You are acting like a dramatic teenager. Shit happens. Men are sometimes bastards. You had six months of bliss. Count that a blessing and be glad that someone shot that fool, because I would be tempted to get the pistol out of my purse and do it if they hadn't," Ellie scolded. "You were going to leave tomorrow for your vacation time. I suggest you take the week off and get yourself together."

"I hate those other two," she said.

"I don't expect there's much love in their hearts for you, either." Aunt Ellie turned north on Highway 287 toward Wichita Falls. "Put the seat back and rest your eyes. I'll wake you when we reach the city limits. Wanda will have closed the store by the time we get there, so I'll take you straight to your apartment," Ellie said.

Amanda obeyed her aunt's orders, but she couldn't sleep. Conrad was dead. Really dead. She'd seen the article about his death in the Dallas newspaper yesterday and laughed at first, thinking she would tease Conrad about there being two of him.

What appeared to be a robbery had gone bad in a well-known flower shop in Dallas. Conrad Steele had been fatally shot. The owner described two people who came into the store wearing masks. He'd given them the money without an argument, but then they'd both turned their guns on Conrad. One blew his face off with a shotgun and the other shot him in the groin with a pistol before they ran out of the store and sped away in a black late-model SUV.

She'd called the Dallas police station and talked to a detective, who verified that Conrad Steele was dead. She wanted to go see the body, but he told her that the family had decided on a closed casket under the circumstances. Kate Steele, a member of the family, was taking care of the arrangements. He was kind enough to give her the name of the funeral home and the time.

That was yesterday, and she had barely had time to buy a decent black dress and make arrangements for their part-time help to run Ellie's Boutique so that she could go to the funeral. It was all so surreal—no one buried a person that fast. Three days was the minimum. Conrad had been shot on Thursday afternoon, and he was already in the ground and it was only Saturday. There'd been no wake, no family night for friends to come and console her for her loss, not even a church luncheon after the funeral—nothing but a short graveside service. There was no closure in that.

Amanda needed something to hang on to, anything at all to replace the fact that Conrad had three wives—at the same damn time!

CHAPTER TWO

*E*motions should have been swirling around Kate on Sunday afternoon when she opened the door into Conrad's bedroom. She expected the memories to bring back something—anything. Something in the room should cause a flutter of love, anger, sadness. But there was nothing.

She'd been depressed when she met Conrad, and he'd made her happy for the six months they'd dated and for nearly a year following their marriage. Surely she could latch on to one happy memory. But any happiness had been drowned the day that she lost their baby and the doctors said she'd never have any more children. Depression had set in, and Conrad began to hound her for a divorce and his money. Anger joined depression when he became mentally abusive.

Now he was dead, and she should feel something . . . relief? Even if he had been nothing more than a con artist who had lived in her house a couple of days a month for more than a decade, he was still her legal husband. She dug deep into her heart, but there was nothing—she would have had a bigger rush of emotion if one of the janitors at the oil company had died.

Teresa pushed past her into the room. "I told you that you should have divorced him years ago. Now you have to deal with all this, plus his business affairs. Thank God you can use the company's legal department or you'd be out thousands in lawyer fees."

"Let's just get this packing done with," Kate said.

"At least it's over." Teresa went to the dresser and picked up a man's wedding band. "What's this all about?"

"He took it off years ago. I'm surprised he didn't hock the damn thing." Kate took it from her mother and tossed it into the bottom of the black garbage bag she'd brought with her.

"You could get something for that in a pawn shop," Teresa said.

Kate shook her head and opened the first drawer. Without checking pockets or even going through pajama pants, shirts, and the rest of his things, she threw them into the bag with the wedding ring. Then she slid open the closet doors. He used to have a packed closet, but now there were only a few suits, dress shirts, and slacks in front of her.

"I told you not to buy all those fancy things for him when you were first married," Teresa said. "Now they are hanging in one of those other women's closets. They'll take them to a consignment shop and make a fortune on them."

"I don't care if they burn them and dance naked around the flames. I just want this thing settled. I never want to see those women again." Kate shoved it all into the bag.

"Well, this isn't going to take long." Teresa reached for a box on the shelf. "Are you even going to look in this or do we just put it in the bag, too?"

More to appease her mother than anything else, Kate flipped the lid off onto the bed. His last five years' tax returns were there, but no will, which might have simplified things. The deed to the cabin he owned up by Lake Kemp, along with the taxes and insurance papers concerning the cabin, were tucked into a big manila envelope. She flipped through the federal business—no dependents, married but filing separate, with her listed as his spouse, and very little return for any of the five years. They'd been prepared by an accountant whose card was stapled to the front of each copy.

Kate set the box aside. "I'll take this to the lawyers tomorrow. Looks like that cabin where we went on our honeymoon is his primary asset, so I'll have to deal with it. I'll get in touch with his accountant tomorrow to see if he has kept the utilities paid."

"How many times did I tell you that man was trouble?" Teresa sighed.

Kate didn't answer. Arguing with her mother was like fighting with a tornado—lots of wind and noise with only mayhem and destruction remaining at the end of the argument. It wasn't totally unlike fighting with Conrad these past thirteen years, but at least he didn't start every other sentence with "I told you so."

Teresa glanced around the room. "Anything else?"

"I don't think so." Kate looked down at the bag. Fourteen years all neatly tied shut with a red plastic drawstring. Nothing remained but a few phone calls and selling a cabin located two and a half hours north of Fort Worth. "I'll take this out to your car and put it in the trunk."

The mistake she made fourteen years ago was finished and over. He wouldn't appear at her house once a month and rant about a divorce.

"Nothing else in the rest of the house?" Teresa put the lid on the box, picked it up, and followed Kate out into the foyer.

"Not one thing," Kate said.

She'd long since gotten rid of pictures or anything that might remind her of him when he was gone. What he had was contained in a room she hadn't set foot in since she came home from the hospital after losing the baby. That was the first time he'd asked her to divorce him. Emptiness was worse than any emotion that she could imagine, but that's the only thing she felt as she carried the trash bag out.

"Okay, then, I'll drop the bag by the charity donation center at the church. I'm going to the office an hour or so this afternoon, so I'll put this box on your desk," Teresa said as they made their way out to the curb where her car was parked. "You could come home for a few days if you don't want to be alone."

A sweet offer, but Kate would rather ask her housekeeper to come over and stay a couple of days as spend time in a house with her mother. "No, thank you. I'm fine." Kate tossed the bag into the trunk and slammed the lid shut. "I'll deal with the accountant and start proceedings for probate on the cabin tomorrow." She didn't need or want sympathy that day. She wanted to be alone—period.

"If you change your mind, just give me a call." Teresa slipped into the driver's seat and started the engine.

Kate waved over her shoulder as she slowly walked up the sidewalk to the big two-story house in one of the elite sections of Fort Worth. God, she hated that house and had for the past thirteen years. She'd loved her little two-bedroom bungalow set back on a wooded five acres south of Fort Worth, but Conrad wanted a big house, and in those first few months, he got whatever he wanted. Thank goodness she'd had the foresight to leave his name off the deed.

She opened the front door, went inside, and slid down the back of the door. She drew her long legs up and wrapped her arms around her knees. She would sell the house and either build or buy a smaller place down around Aledo, where she'd lived before. She liked that little bedroom community.

Her phone rang while she was making plans. Figuring her mother forgot something, she rolled up on her feet, fished the phone out of her purse without even glancing at who was calling, and hit the "Answer" button.

"What did you forget?" she asked.

"Lots of things. Can we meet tomorrow?" a masculine voice asked.

"Who is this?" Kate snapped back.

"Detective Waylon Kramer. This is Kate Steele, right?"

"Yes, it is, and I've already answered your questions," she said.

"This is a murder investigation, and there will be new questions coming up every week. May I talk to you tomorrow morning?" he asked.

"I don't have my calendar with me, but you can stop by the office at ten and I'll try to work you in," she answered.

She didn't want to talk to him anymore. She'd told him everything she knew. Her mother and a dozen people in the office had told him that she was there all day. There was no more to say, and she did not like the way that his sexy grin affected her.

"I've got a couple more stops to make, so I'd rather be there at nine," he said.

"Can't do it. It's ten or it'll have to wait until Tuesday or Wednesday," she told him. She could rearrange her schedule, but Detective Waylon was not going to call the shots.

"Then I'll be there promptly at ten," he said.

"You could ask me whatever you want to know right now and save a trip."

"I do not do interviews on the phone." Without a *good-bye*, *have a nice day*, or *kiss my butt*, he was gone.

She tossed the phone onto the sofa and headed up the stairs to change from her cute little peach suit and high heels into something more comfortable. She had nothing to hide, so the detective could interview her every day for the next year, but by damn, he would do it on her terms. If he thought he could just pop into her business any old time, then he'd better bring a sandwich and a cup of coffee, because he might spend a lot of time in the waiting room.

With her Sunday outfit hung up and her shoes put back in the right box, she flopped back on her bed and stared at the ceiling. Maybe she wouldn't sell the cabin. If it didn't harbor bad memories when she went up there to take care of all the legal matters, she might just keep the thing. It was big enough, with three bedrooms, to use as a weekend company getaway. The lake provided fishing and swimming. She could envision a spreadsheet where employees could write in days for either weeklong or weekend vacation time. That way the place could be a company tax write-off.

Cold air from the ceiling vent chilled her body, so she swung her legs off the side of the bed and slipped into a pair of pajama pants. Pulling a chambray shirt on over a tank top, she made her way back down the stairs, picked up her phone, and carried it outside to sit beside the pool.

"I hate you, Conrad Steele." She threw her hand over her eyes to block the setting sun. "You could have waited another year to get killed. Mother is retiring in December, and I'm up to my eyeballs in work. I don't have time for this crap right now."

Her phone rang, and she was careful to check before she answered this time. If it was the detective again, she planned to let it go to voice mail.

"Hello, Mother," she said.

"I think you should take some time off," Teresa said. "No one at the firm knows about the situation, but the news will break, and when it does . . ." She let the sentence hang.

"I'm going to be a big black spot on the company's immaculate reputation, right?"

"Something like that."

Kate counted to ten. "I'm not running away. That makes me look guilty."

"It's only taking part of the three months' worth of vacation time you've got built up. It's not running," Teresa argued.

If she'd asked for a long weekend a month ago, Teresa would have gone up in flames higher than a Texas wildfire. But now that it was to do with the business, everything had changed quicker than the blink of an eye. Kate wasn't going anywhere.

"You are retiring. I'm trying to get things lined up to step into your office. I can't take time off."

"Yes, you can." When Teresa got an idea, she went at it like a hound dog chasing a coyote. "If we get into a bind, you can work from wherever you are. Go to that cabin and take care of the business involved with that so you'll be finished with everything outside of the company when I'm gone. You can work from the computer if we have a problem. And if something really serious happens, you can be here in less than three hours."

"I told you"—Kate smiled at how slickly those words came from her mouth—"that I'm fine. This whole thing was over years ago."

"If you don't take some time now, you will be too busy after I'm gone to get away. Don't argue with me. Come into the office tomorrow, spend the week getting things lined up, and then go," Teresa said.

"But . . ." At forty-four years old, she didn't need someone to tell her what to do. But then she was also amazed. Her mother had never suggested that she take even a few days off. Was Teresa Truman, president of the Truman Oil Company, getting soft in her old age?

No, Teresa would be hardheaded and -hearted until the day that they crossed her arms over her chest in a coffin. This had nothing to do with Kate's emotional well-being and everything to do with company image.

"I've been running this company since I was thirty years old. The one thing I regret is not taking vacations," Teresa said. "If it did not involve business, I didn't see the need for it. Don't get to be seventy years old with regrets, like I'm doing now."

"I'll think about it," Kate said.

Regrets, my naturally born white ass! The only thing that you might feel sorry about is not buying out Texas Red when it was a small company or maybe letting me buy stock in this company through the years. Now I own thirty percent, which is only slightly less than what you own.

"Good. That's at least a baby step. See you in the morning. I'm leaving the office now and going home to get a few laps in the pool before dark," Teresa said.

"'Bye, Mother," Kate said and hit the "End" button.

She visualized her mother's smile, the one that made her eyes twinkle, the one that she pasted on her face when she won a big deal.

She eyed her own pool for a minute, then stood up and stripped down to her underwear. The water enveloped her in its coolness when she dived in and started swimming from one end to the other. One hundred laps later, Kate had made up her mind to take a week of her vacation time. Surely it wouldn't take a day longer than that to get things settled with the cabin.

⌘

A cute little lady in a dark suit made a phone call and gave Waylon a visitor's tag to clip on to his sports jacket that Monday morning. She pointed toward the elevators and told him to go to third floor. As she said, the waiting room would be to the right and Mrs. Steele would send her assistant for him when she could see him.

A wall of glass at the end of the waiting area provided a view of downtown Fort Worth. Current magazines occupied orderly rows on the coffee table in front of the sofa where he'd slumped down. He couldn't get comfortable—the seat was too short for his tall frame, and the back hit him at a place between his shoulder blades that had been sore for weeks. Finally, he left the sofa behind and watched the traffic down on the street from the third-floor glass wall.

God, he hated the city. Time was when he loved it and everything about the Dallas/Fort Worth area, but lately his heart was back in Mabelle, Texas, on the ranch that his folks had left him. He was tired of chasing the bad guys and doing paperwork. He wanted to sweat in the hay field rather than in a jacket, white shirt, and tie.

He checked the time on his phone every thirty seconds, and finally, at ten minutes past the hour, someone said his name. He turned around to find a short gray-haired lady with a no-nonsense expression motioning for him.

She'd made it with five minutes to spare. He did not wait more than fifteen minutes for an appointment—doctor, dentist, or suspect.

"If you are Detective Waylon Kramer, Mrs. Steele will see you now."

He followed her into an outer office, through a set of double doors into a bigger room with the same view out the window on one end. Mrs. Steele was sitting behind her desk and did not get up or extend a hand. He removed his cowboy hat and laid it on the edge of her desk.

"Please sit," she said. "Could we get you something to drink? Coffee? Water?"

"Coffee would be nice. No sugar or cream. Just black," Waylon said.

"Millie, make that two coffees and two glasses of water," she told the gray-haired lady. "Now what can I do for you today, Detective?"

"You've given me a complete rundown of where you were on the day your husband was killed. Could I have something on paper, like your schedule and who you were meeting with on that day? And I'd like access to your financial records," he said.

"Okay, I will have Millie run a copy of my schedule that day. I believe you came to the office at three, so I suppose anything prior to that would be enough? And if you want my phone records or my financials, get a warrant."

"I want you to tell me in your own words, but I would like a copy. I can get a warrant if it's going to be a problem," Waylon said.

"You bring the warrant and I'll grant you access. Am I still a suspect in Conrad's murder?"

"We always look at the spouse first, especially when there is an insurance policy involved," he answered.

"And is there an insurance policy? I don't have a copy of one. Maybe one of the other wives bought the thing."

"You took it out on him and you pay the premiums," he countered.

She inhaled deeply and let it out in a whoosh. "I forgot about that."

Waylon bit the inside of his lip to keep from grinning. So he could fluster the ice queen. That made the ten-minute wait worth every second.

"Which leads me to believe maybe you forgot about something else," he said.

"It's only for twenty-five thousand dollars, for God's sake, and I had the premium set up for automatic payment. I figured if he died out there on the road it would pay for his funeral expenses. It's damn sure not enough to kill him over," she protested.

Her tone had gone an octave higher, and her body language said she was even more rattled. "Hell hath no fury like a woman scorned. Did you find out about those other two women before he died?"

Millie brought in a tray and set it on the desk. "Anything else?"

"No, that's all for now," Mrs. Kate Steele said.

Millie shut both doors behind her as she left. Waylon reached for coffee, and Kate picked up a glass of water, downing a third of it before setting it back down—in his books a sign that she was guilty as hell in some way and her mouth was dry from her lies.

Kate hit a couple of keys on her computer and brought up her calendar. "I told you all this before, but if you want the minute details, here they are. I arrived at work at eight thirty. I came in thirty minutes early to get my files in order for a meeting with the acquisitions department concerning buying out a smaller company. I went from my office to the conference room at nine o'clock. I did not have time in that five-minute ride in the elevator to dash down to the flower shop and kill my husband," she said. "We were there until noon, hashing out the finer points of a buyout. Millie had lunch delivered, and we took a forty-five-minute break. I didn't leave except for ten minutes in the ladies' room, and there were at least two other women in there at the same time I was. We were back at the table at one o'clock and wrapped it all up by two. I went back to my office to make phone calls. I did not kill Conrad or have him assassinated."

Waylon took out his notebook and wrote down the timeline as she talked. Most of the time folks got real antsy when he made notes in his book. It didn't seem to affect Kate Steele as much as he wanted. She sat across the desk from him sipping her ice water as if he were no more than a gnat that she would squash with that glass paperweight any minute. He put his pen and notebook into his pocket and finished off his coffee.

"You got anything else you want to say this morning?" he asked.

"Only that if I'd wanted to kill Conrad, I would have done it years ago and I would not have hired someone to do my dirty work," she said curtly.

"Don't leave town. I might have more questions. Thanks for the coffee." He rose up out of the chair slowly and settled his hat back on his head.

"I am leaving town next weekend, but I'll still be in the state," she said. "You have my cell phone, and before you accuse me of murder again, why don't you pull your head out of your butt and do some real detective work? Who was he sending flowers to? They damn sure weren't for me. And if there are three of us, there might be another wife in the wings. Find them and see if that person has a gun to match the bullets that killed dear old Conrad."

Waylon nodded. "Good day, Mrs. Steele."

"Think about what I said." She raised her voice slightly as he left.

"Dammit!" he muttered as he pushed "L" on the elevator.

She'd brought up two good points that he was already investigating. Was she covering her own tracks by throwing him off course, and why was she taking a vacation right now? Hiding evidence?

Chapter Three

On Tuesdays the trash man picked up the garbage, but since that particular day was a holiday, they wouldn't get it until Wednesday. Still, Jamie was determined to get rid of anything in her house that had belonged to Conrad. She did leave one picture of Gracie with her father in her daughter's room. Even though Conrad had been a son of a bitch, he was still her father.

Was it something in the genes? Jamie's mother hadn't had a lick of sense with her relationship, and Jamie had been the result. She twisted her black hair up the back of her head and held it with an oversize clamp, dragged two bags out to the curb, and returned for a third big black one that held their actual garbage for the week. It would be ready for the trash man when he came the next day, and it would damn sure be out of her house.

Her grandmother had suggested giving his things to a charity, but Jamie was a little superstitious. She sure didn't want another man to put on one of Conrad's shirts or even his socks and feel the urge to become a con artist. The trash truck rumbled down her street before she even made it back to the porch of the small three-bedroom house that she and Conrad had bought together the week after they'd married. They'd planned on at least two children—a boy and a girl was what Conrad wanted. Moving from a small one-bedroom apartment, she'd felt as if she had bought a mansion when she first moved in. Now it seemed small, because memories lurked in every corner and every damned one of them fueled the red-hot anger inside her.

She would sell the place and move into an apartment. There was no way she could make the mortgage payment, pay taxes and insurance, and keep up with all her other bills on her teacher's salary. He might have been a bastard, but he did give her the money for the mortgage every month.

"Unless I can sell the cabin and put the money on the house." She sat down on the porch, propped her elbows on her knees, and put her chin in her hands. "That has to be Gracie's inheritance, since she is his oldest living blood kin. As her guardian, I could sell it and pay off most of this house. I'll make a will leaving this property to her, which I would have done anyway."

"Who are you talkin' to, Mommy?" Gracie plopped down beside her. She smelled faintly of cinnamon from the french toast they'd had for breakfast, but the rest was sweaty kid that had been playing jump rope in the backyard.

If anything could ease the feelings inside Jamie that day, it was love for Gracie. She hugged her up next to her side. "I was talking to myself, trying to get things figured out. How would you like to go to the cabin for a few weeks?"

Gracie jumped up and clapped her hands, her black ponytail flopping up and down in excitement. "Yes, yes, yes! We can swim and go to the snow-cone stand down by the store and will we be there for the festival? And Daddy can share cotton candy . . ." Gracie stopped and tears filled her eyes. "Daddy won't be there, will he? Do you think he's in heaven like the preacher said?"

Jamie pulled her down on her lap and buried her face in Gracie's hair. "Only God knows that."

"Maybe Mama Rita will know. She talks to God."

"You'll have to ask her." Jamie smiled.

Gracie wiggled out of her mother's embrace. "Can we go to the cabin today?"

"We've got some stuff to take care of first, and tonight we have to go see the fireworks display with Mama Rita. How about this weekend? That will give you time to get your toys packed and decide which outfits Barbie will need to take." Jamie smiled.

There would be memories at the cabin, but they only spent a week there each summer. It would be a far better place to figure things out than sitting in the house all summer, and besides, Gracie loved it there.

"I think I left one of my Barbies there last time we went. I bet she's lonely." Gracie sighed. "I will miss Daddy. We never been there without him."

"I know, sweetheart, but we'll have a good time, and maybe you can turn some balloons loose when we leave. They can rise right up in the sky and he might even see them." Jamie fought the desire to cross her fingers behind her back.

"Okay," Gracie said with a serious nod. "Now I'm goin' to start packin' my Barbies and their clothes. They'll need bathing suits and I'll have to take Snugglies or I won't be able to sleep." She disappeared into the house in a blur, leaving the sound of a slamming screen door in her wake.

An official-looking black vehicle slowed down as it passed her house, then backed up and pulled into her driveway. She shaded her eyes with her hand and hoped to hell it wasn't more bad news. That detective from the funeral got out, shook the legs of his jeans down over cowboy boots, and tipped his hat toward her. Tall and dark haired, he shot a winning smile her way and swaggered over to lean on a porch post.

"Mrs. Jamie Steele?"

"That's me," she said.

"Could I come inside and ask you a few questions?"

"No, but you can sit on my porch with me and ask anything you want," she said.

The hat and clothes might make him look like an innocent cowboy, but she'd been conned by a professional for seven years. Detective Waylon could barely be classified as an amateur in the field, even with his winning smile and those sexy eyes.

"Hot one, ain't it?" He sat down on the top step and rested his back against a porch post.

"I've never expected snow in July," she said. "Let's cut to the chase. What do you want to know?"

He pulled out a notebook and a pen. "You are a schoolteacher, right?"

She nodded.

"Are you angry right now?"

"Not that it's a bit of your business, but hell, yes, I'm mad. I just found out my husband is a polygamist and he's got at least two other wives. Have you found more?"

"Not yet, but I'm still investigating." Waylon smiled.

Might as well pack that grin up in your shirt pocket, because it's not going to win you any favors in my court.

"Then why are you here?"

"I want to know where you were on the day he died, from early morning until after three," he said.

"Why until then? Why not until midnight?"

He looked up from the notepad. "He died instantly at three o'clock in the flower shop."

"And who were the flowers sent to? They damn sure didn't come here," Jamie said.

"It's an ongoing investigation, so I can't tell you that."

A new rush of pure old mad flowed through Jamie. Conrad never sent flowers to her, not one time. When they were courting, he'd brought her a bouquet of wildflowers in a quart jar, and on their first anniversary he showed up with a box of chocolates that he'd bought on the half-price after-Christmas sale shelf. At the time she'd thought it was sentimental. Now that she knew he was shopping at an expensive florist, it was just downright cheap.

"Did that son of a bitch spend money for flowers on those other two hussies? He never sent me a damn thing, or Gracie, either, for that matter," Jamie fumed.

The detective poised his pen over the notebook. "I told you I can't answer that. But it will help if you can tell me where you were all day."

"Thursday, I spent the morning with my grandmother. We went to a farmer's market and bought vegetables. At noon we stopped by a burger joint down near Desoto, and then we went came home and put away the produce, had waffles for supper, and I heard about the murder on the television that evening. My grandmother and Gracie were with me all day. Do you think I killed him?"

Was the detective mentally challenged? If Jamie had killed him, she would have been standing on the roof of that flower shop shouting to the whole world. She was not a woman to run and hide, and Mr. Detective could write that in his little notebook.

"We are covering all bases," he said. "Tell me the truth. Did you find out about those other women before or after he was killed?"

"If I'd known about those other two wives, he wouldn't have been alive on Thursday to be buying flowers in that shop. Now let me ask you something. He owns a cabin up near Lake Kemp. Since Gracie is his oldest living blood kin, won't she inherit that?"

He put his notebook and pen back into his shirt pocket and got to his feet. "I have no idea about property. You'll have to talk to a lawyer if you want to get into it with his first wife."

"Surely that hoity-toity witch won't end up with the cabin, since he has a child," Jamie said.

"She is his legal wife unless one turns up from before fourteen years ago, but a lawyer will have to help y'all with the property thing." He started to walk away and then turned back. "Don't leave town. I'll have more questions as the investigation continues."

"I'm not guilty of jack shit, and I'm going up to that cabin this weekend. It's Gracie's, and nobody is taking it from her," Jamie declared.

❧

Amanda heard the squeak of the door to her tiny one-bedroom apartment open and didn't need to open her eyes to know that her aunt had stopped by—again. She could hear her in the kitchen putting food in the fridge, right along with what she'd brought the past three days. Very little of it had been touched.

Amanda hugged her wedding picture closer to her chest and curled up around it on the sofa. She couldn't eat. She couldn't sleep in the bed they'd shared last week. She could barely look at the bassinet with the cute little airplane mobile above it. Conrad was dead and those other two horrible women were telling lies about him. He might have been married to them, but he'd divorced them long before he even met her. And that little girl didn't look anything like him, so she couldn't be his child.

Conrad loved her with his whole heart, and he would have told her if he'd had another child. He talked all the time about the excitement of his first baby with her. She frowned. Or had he said his first son? She couldn't remember, but still, he would have told her.

She opened one eye to peek at the picture and then snapped it shut as the hole in her heart grew bigger and bigger. She vowed that there would never be another man in her life. She'd given all her love to Conrad, and he'd taken it to heaven with him.

"You might as well open your eyes," Aunt Ellie said. "This has gone on long enough. Today you are going to take a shower and get dressed, and you will leave this apartment. We are going to the store and you are going to do your job. You've had three days past the funeral to wallow around in sorrow."

"I can't," Amanda whined.

"You will or I will drag you into the bathroom and put you in the shower. This is not good for that baby," Aunt Ellie said with enough conviction that Amanda opened her eyes and sat up.

"I loved him so much," she said with a long sigh.

"I reckon he was good at making the women love him." Aunt Ellie pointed toward the shower. "Go. I'll be right here when you get back. Put on makeup and something nice. You're not going to the store looking like hammered buzzard shit."

It took an hour to shower, get dressed, and put on enough makeup to cover the circles under her eyes, but when she finished, Aunt Ellie nodded in approval.

"Now eat," she said. "I made bacon, eggs, and toast. Your plate is in the microwave. Coffee is in the pot. You've got fifteen minutes, so don't argue."

Amanda wanted to revert to her old rebellious days, flip off her aunt, and curl up back on the sofa with the picture for the rest of the day. But she'd promised Jesus when she accepted him into her heart that she would put her wild ways behind her, and so far she'd kept her word. Besides, Conrad had told her repeatedly how much he loved her sweet goodness and that she was going to make a wonderful mother to their son. She could not let him down, not even if it meant eating food that would taste like sawdust.

"I want to start my maternity leave next weekend," she said.

"Fine by me, but you are not holing up in this place with the curtains pulled and the lights turned off," Aunt Ellie said.

"I'm going to the cabin. Conrad said he was leaving it to me, and I can spend time on the deck looking out over the lake. We were supposed to go up there next week anyway. I think I can find closure there. Maybe I'll even stay longer," Amanda said.

"I can agree with that," Aunt Ellie said. "But a week before the baby's due date, you should come on home. Your doctor is here."

"And I will make all my appointments." She laid a hand on her baby bump. "I'll take good care of this little guy. That's the least I can do for Conrad."

❧

Waylon arrived in Wichita Falls right at noon, so he stopped at a pizza place advertising an all-you-can-eat buffet and had lunch. He'd found out this morning that the florist had no idea where Conrad was taking the dozen yellow roses he'd bought that day. He hadn't signed a card before he was slain. He had only just been in the process of paying for the roses, which he'd had in his hands when the two men in masks burst through the door and shot him.

Mr. Drummond, the florist, let Waylon look at the record of Conrad's purchases. At least once a week for the past three months, he'd bought yellow roses on Thursday. In the past year, he usually bought flowers right after the first of the month, and that order varied from daisies to orchids. The store owner was too eager to help, which meant he was probably hiding something big. Waylon made a note to call him later or go back to see him in a week or so. Maybe he'd deleted a couple of orders to protect someone?

Waylon couldn't manage to keep one wife at a time happy. How in the hell did Conrad keep three on the hook and still have time to buy flowers for other women? He had to have had a date book or a calendar somewhere. Waylon made a note to go through all the evidence they'd found in his van. He had to be a smart man, so he would not have kept it in any of the three wives' houses. The only other place it could be was in his van, with that load of clothing he was peddling across the state. If he didn't find it in the evidence boxes, he'd tear apart the van, one piece at a time.

He snagged the last parking space in front of Ellie's Boutique that afternoon. He left his cowboy hat and sunglasses in the car but pasted on a big smile when he opened the door.

"Whew, it's a hot one. This cool air feels good." He spotted a lady with two little girls looking at children's clothing in one area and an older woman flipping through hangers on the other side of the store.

"What can I do for you?" the woman who'd been sitting beside Amanda at the funeral asked. "You look familiar. Have we met?"

"Yes, ma'am, we have. At Conrad Steele's funeral. I am Detective Waylon Kramer." He showed her his badge. "I came to talk to Amanda, if she's available."

The woman crossed her arms over her chest. "She's not."

Amanda rounded the end of a rack of clothing. "I'm right here, and I have questions for you, Detective. Follow me back to the office." She led the way past the checkout counter and into a small room, where she pointed at an old straight-back wooden chair. "Have a seat right there. Would you like a soft drink or a cup of coffee? We've got both."

"Something cold would be nice." Waylon sat down in a chair that was more uncomfortable than the sofa in Kate's fancy office.

Amanda took a Pepsi from a small refrigerator and twisted the lid off before handing it to him. "Did you find out who killed my Conrad?"

"Not yet."

"Then why are you here?" she asked.

"I need a play-by-play of where you were all day Thursday," he said.

"Good Lord! I didn't kill him. I wouldn't. I couldn't. I love him." She threw a hand over her forehead in a dramatic gesture. "I would never"— her eyes welled up with tears that spilled down over her cheeks—"kill the father of my baby." She reached for a tissue and dabbed at her face.

"And if you do your job, you'll find that he divorced those other two women."

"We've been looking into that since his death. It appears that there are records of him marrying all three of you, but no divorces on file. Could you please just tell me where you were on Thursday?"

She pointed down at her stomach. "Did either one of those masked people who shot my Conrad have a belly like this?"

"They did not," he answered.

"Okay, then, take me off the suspect list. How could I? And I have dozens of people who were in and out of this store all day Thursday who will testify that I never left the place. Opened at nine and didn't close until after five that day. We had a pre–Independence Day sale going on," she said. "Besides, it's three hours to Dallas. There's no way I could have gone there and come back without being missed."

"Can you tell me who might want him dead?" Conrad pulled out his notebook.

"Probably one of those other two who have burned the divorce papers," she said.

There was enough venom in her voice that Waylon had to fight the urge to make the sign of a cross over his chest. "You think they might have conspired together to kill him when they found out he was a polygamist?"

"He is not." Her tone shot up so shrill that it could have cracked glass. "They did something with the papers. I'm his only wife. That rich bitch could have hired someone to kill him, but she wouldn't get her hands dirty with the job. The other one looked mean enough to me to have done it herself, just like she said. Your job is to find the divorce papers so my baby won't be a bastard." She shook her forefinger at him.

"My job, ma'am, is to find who killed him," Waylon said. "I'll have more questions later, so don't leave the state. I'll need a number where I can reach you."

She handed him a business card with her cell phone number on the bottom. "When you find out who did this, I want to be the first to know."

"Thank you for taking time to talk to me and for the cold drink." He straightened up and extended his hand.

"You will find these people, won't you?"

"I hope so. I'm retiring before long, and I don't want to leave an open case on my desk." He smiled.

"And you will let me know?"

He nodded. "You have my word."

He would tell them all when he closed the case, starting with Kate, the legal wife, and working his way down to Amanda. After the hysterics from her at the funeral, he'd expected to find her still weeping and whining. Maybe it was all for show and they were in it together after all. If so, he'd see them all behind bars before he left the precinct for good.

Chapter Four

Fourteen years hadn't changed the old cabin much. Five mismatched rocking chairs awaited her in a line across the wide front porch. The one on the end with the wide arms sat a little higher than the others, and she'd claimed that as her chair on her honeymoon. Kate would wrap a big quilt around her body and bring her morning coffee out to the porch. There she would listen to the soft laps of the lake as it rolled up on the shore.

Her high-heeled shoes sank into the soft green grass as she pulled two suitcases up onto the porch. She parked them on the porch and sat down in the rocking chair. Nothing happened. No peace, no memories. Just a hot wind, like that on the day of the funeral, blowing across her face and making beads of sweat pop up under her nose. She pushed up out of the chair and found the spare key hidden under the flowerpot shoved up in the corner.

Twenty-nine steps off the deck out back led straight down to the boat shed where the pontoon used to be housed. Conrad had used it in one of his schemes a few years back and bragged about it to her, so now there was just an empty shed down there. She opened the front door and wheeled her suitcase and briefcase inside. She expected the musty scent of a house that had been closed for a long time. But the aroma of something sweet, like a scented candle or potpourri, lingered. Had someone been there recently? Kate parked her suitcases in the middle of the floor and went straight to the thermostat, turning it down from seventy-eight to seventy degrees. And then she eased down on the sofa and covered her eyes with the back of her hand.

Coming to the cabin might have been a bad idea. She could have gone anywhere in the world for a few weeks, and this was the very last place she should be. But after her mother suggested that she get away for a while, all she could think of was the quiet happiness that she'd known sitting in that rocking chair on the porch. And she did need to get all the legal matters settled before her mother retired.

With its log walls and Western decor, the interior of the house was as rustic as the outside. The front door opened right into a great room—living room and country kitchen separated only by an archway. A panoramic view of the lake spread out before her from the sliding glass doors that opened up to the wide deck where Kate had watched beautiful Texas sunsets every evening for a whole week.

She was there and she didn't plan to leave, so all that was left was to unpack. She rolled her luggage down the hallway toward the master bedroom, but she couldn't make herself go into the room. She'd known he'd had other women, but did he bring them here? Did he have sex with them in her honeymoon bed? There was no way in hell she could sleep in that room. The therapist would call it love-hate, what she experienced as she stood there, her feet glued to the floor. She'd loved him. He'd tricked her. She hated him. All those feelings finally hit home and rolled up into a hard ball in the middle of her chest. They did not make for the happy, peaceful feeling she'd hoped for.

She crossed the hall to a second bedroom and noticed a furry paw sticking out from under the bed. Startled, her first reaction was to run until she realized it wasn't a mouse but a stuffed animal. She crossed the room and raised the bed skirt to find a little toy bunny no bigger than the palm of her hand and a Barbie doll wearing a bathing suit. The doll's black hair was frayed, giving testimony that it had seen lots of time in the bathtub. No doubt about it, Conrad had brought his daughter and her mother here.

Kate made her way to the second guest room. Judging by the dust on the dresser, no one had been in this room in years. Evidently the wife with the little girl only dusted and took care of the part of the house that they used.

Which makes this room perfect.

She set her briefcase at the end of the dresser and parked her suitcases in the middle of the floor, went back to the car, and rolled in a case with her laptop and printer/fax machine. She took it straight to the room and parked it beside the dresser. A queen-size bed with a split rail–type headboard, flanked on both sides with nightstands and lamps fashioned from horseshoes, a six-drawer dresser with a mirror above it, and a nice-size empty closet waited for her. A gold velvet rocking chair had been shoved into a corner. It looked comfortable and well worn, as if someone had used it a lot in the past.

"No bad auras here," she mumbled.

That room, with its rustic charm, felt right. She stripped down the bed, carried the sheets and the quilt to the utility room, and shoved as much as she could into the washer. She found a dust cloth and a can of spray cleaner in the cabinets over the washer and dryer and returned to the bedroom. While she was dusting, she thought she heard the squeaky hinges on the front door but attributed the noise to the washer and kept right on cleaning her new bedroom. She'd come to the cabin to get away from everyone, and no one even knew she was there.

"Hello?" a thin voice yelled.

Kate stepped out of the room to find a wide-eyed Amanda standing in the hallway not five feet from her.

Amanda tucked her chin and glared. "What are you doing here?"

"I own this place. What are you doing here?" Kate asked.

Before Amanda could answer, another voice called out, "Who's here? Show yourself."

Kate recognized wife number two—Jamie, was it? Amanda whipped around as fast as her big belly would allow and stomped into the living room with Kate right behind her.

"Get out! Both of you, get out! This is my cabin," Amanda shouted and waved her arms around. "Conrad told me when he brought me here for my honeymoon that he was leaving it to me in his will. So get off my property and don't ever set foot on it again."

Jamie took a step around the suitcases in the middle of the floor. "And he promised me and Gracie the same thing. You can leave. I'm staying right here the rest of the summer and there's not a damn thing either of you can do about it."

"Just for the record, I'm the first wife and this property is mine unless there *is* a will. So far there's nothing filed in Fort Worth or the surrounding counties," Kate said.

"He's only been dead"—Amanda winced at the word—"nine days. Give it time and it will turn up, just like his divorces from both of you, and when it does, you are both leaving my house."

Jamie crossed her arms over her chest. "And if it's my house, then you two can get out of it. How long will it take to figure this out?" She frowned at Kate.

"I have no idea," Kate answered. "Why would either of you even want to stay here?"

"It's where Conrad brought me last December on our honeymoon. We started off the new year right here on the deck and watched the fireworks display out on the lake," Amanda answered.

Jamie drew her eyebrows down in a frown. "And I suppose he said he'd bring you back here for a week out of every summer?"

Amanda nodded. "We were supposed to arrive tomorrow, and now"—she sniffled—"I'll have to just imagine that he is here with me."

Gracie tugged on her mother's shirttail. "Mommy, are they really going to live with us?"

"Looks like it, because we aren't leaving." Jamie grabbed the handles of two suitcases and rolled them down the hallway.

Kate wrapped her arms around her body in a hug, but it didn't help. Her blood still ran cold through her veins. Conrad had been a smart con. He kept his stories straight by keeping them the same, starting with her. Or did he? Was there another wife out there who was even older than Kate?

A week in the same house with those two was not the peaceful time she'd been looking forward to, but there was no way she was backing down from the challenge. Whether she wanted to be or not, she was the real wife at the time of his death. She'd paid for his funeral, and it would cost her a lot of money to get all this crap cleared up, so she was staying right here.

Amanda tilted her chin up a notch. "I'm having the master bedroom."

"I don't want it," Jamie said. "Gracie and I were planning to use her room anyway."

Kate shrugged and turned around, her high heels sounding like a BB gun on the hardwood floor. Jamie's cowboy boots echoed like shotgun blasts as she stomped down the hallway. Amanda's blinged-out flip-flops reminded Kate of a series of slaps as she stormed toward the master bedroom.

Two doors slammed before Kate eased hers shut. She fell back into the rocker and closed her eyes. Evidently, Amanda had kicked off her flip-flops, because Kate heard bare feet pacing from one side of the room to the other. Jamie had shut the door to her room, and although Kate couldn't understand a word of the rapid-fire Spanish, there was no doubt that she was ready to blow.

I'm going to stay until I get all this stuff settled, not only with the cabin but with the investigation. I'm not going back until everyone knows that I was not responsible for Conrad's death.

A hard rap jerked her into an upright position. She opened the door so she could discern between the noise of the washing machine and maybe someone knocking on the door. The second rat-a-tat-tat assured her that someone was at the door.

She headed that way, wondering the whole time if wife number four might be standing on the other side. If so, she was shit outta luck unless she wanted to sleep on the sofa or out on the deck, because the honeymoon cabin had no vacancies.

Kate found Waylon Kramer standing there, cowboy hat tilted back so she could see his blue eyes, a smile as big as a happy Cheshire cat on his face.

"Miz Steele," he said.

"How did you find me?" she asked.

"Easy. I called your office and your mother told me where you'd gone. She's as eager as I am to get this solved. Am I right in assuming that all three of the wives are going to spend time together in this house? Are you sure that you never met any of those women before the funeral?"

"I guess that's what's about to happen. And I'm very sure I never met them before then."

"Did y'all plan to be here at the same time?"

"Hell, no," she said.

He chuckled.

She crossed her arms over her chest. "What's so funny?"

"A cussword coming out of your prim and proper mouth."

"I don't think you can arrest me for cussing on my own property, can you?" she asked.

"No, ma'am. But I'm beginning to think maybe you all three did find out about the others and planned a perfect murder. You've all got alibis, but one of you had to come up with the money, and I'll bet that person was you. And honey, I will close this case," he answered.

"You drove all the way from Dallas just to tell me that?" she asked.

"No, I have a small ranch in Mabelle, so I was close by. But if you'd like to confess, I brought my recorder." He patted his shirt pocket.

"I have nothing to confess, and just so you know, I did not know those other two were coming up here. If there's nothing else, I've got unpacking to do," she said.

"When this all comes out in court, you'll wish that you'd come clean. We could probably make a deal to take the death penalty off the table if you didn't make us use up man-hours and resources. The jury might even have mercy on you when they hear what a scoundrel Conrad Steele was."

"Good-bye, Detective Kramer. You have a nice day, now. Do drive safe—I wouldn't want folks saying that you ran off the road and blaming me for your death." Kate shut the door in his face and slid down the back side. Her skirt hiked all the way up to her panty line when she drew her knees up and wrapped her arms around them. Tears stung her eyes, but she refused to let them flow. She would not cry, not one single tear, no matter how crazy things got.

She wasn't aware anyone was in the room with her until Jamie's daughter laid a hand on her arm.

"I'm Gracie. You are Kate, right? Daddy showed me a picture of you and said you was his sister. Does that make you my aunt?" Her big brown eyes bored into Kate's. "You have blue eyes. How can you be my aunt?"

"I'm not your aunt, Gracie. I was married to your father before he married your mama," Kate explained.

"And that other one, the fat one, was she married to Daddy, too?" Gracie asked.

Kate held the giggle inside. "Yes, she was."

"Like *Sister Wives* on television?"

"Your mama lets you watch that?" Kate asked.

"No, but my babysitter watches it and I know that there's one daddy and lots of wives, like now, huh?" Gracie asked. "Only y'all didn't even know you were sister wives, did you?"

"Gracie, where . . ." Jamie stopped both walking and talking.

"I'm right here talking to Kate." Gracie grinned.

"Who was at the door?" Jamie glared at Kate.

"That big man who was at Daddy's funeral," Gracie answered.

"What did he want?" Jamie frowned.

Amanda pushed her way past Jamie. "I heard a truck and looked out the window, hoping both of you were leaving. What did he want?"

"He thinks we have conspired together and paid someone to . . ." Kate looked down at Gracie. "You know."

"Is he insane? I told him I would never . . ." Amanda puckered up again. "I loved him too much . . ." She threw up her hands and hurried to her room.

"You better believe I told him I would have," Jamie said bluntly. "In a split second, if I'd known for sure."

"For sure?" Kate asked.

"Oh, yeah, I had my suspicions this last year when he started arriving late and leaving a day or two early. Import, export, my behind," Jamie said.

"Mama, can I take my toys out on the deck and play?" Gracie asked.

"Yes, but you can't go to the lake or even down the steps without me. Stay on the deck." Jamie nodded. She turned to Kate. "So exactly what is import, export? I never got a straight answer."

"He was a jobber. Do you know what that is?" Kate asked.

Jamie shook her head.

"He was an independent buyer of clothing and jewelry from stores after they had finished their seasonal sales. He would give the store ten cents on the dollar for all that was left and then sell it for twice that to discount clothing stores. He exported stuff out of those stores and imported it into other stores," Kate said.

"He made it sound like a fancy job." Jamie melted into a chair. "God, I feel stupid."

Kate rocked up onto her knees and used the door handle to help her go from there to standing. "You mentioned doubts?"

"A wife knows when a man is having sex outside of his home. Surely you did."

"I didn't give a damn after the first year," Kate said.

"Then why didn't you divorce him?"

"That's none of your business." Kate's hands were shaking when she went to her room, closed the door, and kicked off her high heels. She sat down on the edge of the bed. What if one of those other two did kill him? If so, then she might be next in line. They both sure seemed to be in a hurry to lay claim to the cabin, and she was the only one standing in their way.

"Stop it!" she scolded herself. "They want this place, but they did not kill Conrad. Not even a Hollywood actor can put on an act like they did at the funeral."

Still, a shiver ran down her back as she opened her suitcases and filled the empty dresser drawers, hung up shorts and shirts, and neatly placed her sandals on the floor of the closet. She'd brought two sundresses in case she decided to go to church and two bathing suits for swimming. Other than that, it was strictly casual summer clothing.

She unzipped her straight business skirt and removed the matching short-sleeved jacket, hung them on a hanger together, and then pushed the straps down from a full-length slip, letting it slide off her slim body and puddle up around her feet. No panty hose, no slips, no enclosed shoes—not until she went back to Fort Worth.

Dressed in khaki shorts, a bright-orange knit shirt, and her favorite brown leather sandals, she picked up her Kindle and headed toward the deck. Halfway there she remembered that Gracie was playing out there, so she steered for the front porch instead.

She settled into the rocking chair again. It would be a good place to sit and read until supper time, when she intended to eat the sub sandwich she'd tucked away in the refrigerator. Those other two hussies better not touch it. They had shared a husband and they might be sharing a house, but by damn, that sandwich was hers, and they'd do well to keep their hands off it.

Tomorrow she would drive down to that grocery store in Seymour and buy what she wanted for a week. They could starve or fish for their food. Frankly, Kate didn't give a damn what they did, as long as they stayed out of her way.

She hadn't sat there more than ten minutes before she got thirsty and went back to the kitchen to make a pitcher of tea. But there was no tea, no sugar, and not even a jar of peanut butter in the pantry. The only edible thing in the house was her sandwich, and she'd have to drink tap water. Fourteen years ago the water had had a strange taste to it. It was fine for laundry and not bad for showers, but drinking was impossible. She filled a glass, took a sip, and spit it out. The years had not changed the water one bit.

She headed toward the tiny utility room and switched the sheets over to the dryer and then tossed the quilt in the washer. Right then, she would gladly pay triple for a Starbucks coffee or a McDonald's sweet tea. Neither was available in the tiny little town of Bootleg, Texas. It had a convenience store, a post office, a tiny bank branch set up in a portable building, two churches, and a liquor store. And that was at least half a mile down the dirt road in front of the cabin.

There had to be more than what a convenience store offered. She made a quick trip to her bedroom, exchanged the Kindle for her purse, and headed out of the house without telling anyone where she was going. These were her acquaintances, not her friends, and she didn't care if they needed or wanted anything in the way of groceries. When the dust settled and they realized that their marriage licenses weren't worth the paper they were printed on, they'd leave and she'd put the cabin up for sale. Until then, they were three strangers sharing a house.

Still, even with that little pep talk, Kate was very glad there was a lock on her bedroom door. Those women were about as stable as nitroglycerin in the middle of an F5 tornado, and she didn't trust either of them.

She turned on the radio and headed south. "And now for your Texas news and weather," the DJ said in a deep voice. "Weather through the week is more of the same heat we've been having. It looks like we'll have days in the triple digits through Wednesday as least."

Kate passed a fireworks stand on the side of the road. It had closed up after the holiday the week before, but she could imagine the scent of firecrackers and that put a smile on her face. When she was a little girl, her father let her pick out her favorites every year. After the big display put on by the company after the all-day picnic at her childhood home, he would take her down to a grassy area near the pool and they'd have their own fireworks show. Her mother hated the noise and the smell of sparklers and bottle rockets, but Kate always associated them with her dad.

I wonder if there are certain things that Gracie remembers about Conrad. Did they come to the cabin on the Fourth of July and set off fireworks on the lakeshore?

"This is Denise Winters with your Texas news." The voice on the radio had changed. "In statewide news, there are still no solid leads in the shooting death of Conrad Steele, the victim of a robbery gone bad in downtown Dallas on Thursday, June 29."

Kate's whole body stiffened as she waited for the next sentence to be that it had been discovered that Conrad had three wives at the same time and that none of them were aware of the other two. That was sensational news—the kind of thing that those magazines beside the cash register at the grocery store checkout counter always had plastered

on their covers. The headline, in big red lettering, would say, Oil
Company Heiress Suspected in Polygamist Husband's Death!

The lady went on to other news, talking about the new political
front since the election and how gasoline prices were on the rise, but she
didn't mention Conrad again. Hopefully, pretty soon they'd stop even
mentioning him, and it would just be another shooting that slipped
into the cold-case file. At least she hoped that was the case. Maybe
Waylon Kramer's supervisor would put him on more pressing cases.

Fifteen minutes later, she was inside the small grocery store in
Seymour, Texas. She pulled a cart loose from a long string of others and
stopped at a display with all kinds of cookies, cakes, breads, and pastries.
She was trying to decide between iced sugar cookies or pretty little
miniature cupcakes when she felt a presence behind her. She whipped
around to find Detective Kramer so close that she could have slapped
him without even stretching.

Seeing him in the grocery store, for God's sake, was like throwing
gasoline on a bonfire. Was he going to show up in her shower stall next?
That put a picture in her mind that shot the temperature of the store
up twenty degrees.

"What are you doing here?" She looked up into his eyes and
visualized taking the top off the cupcake package and smashing the
whole dozen into his face to get the picture of him naked in the shower
out of her mind. Would that be considered assault?

"I might ask you the same thing. You are a long way from Fort
Worth." Detective Kramer grinned.

"A woman has to eat. Are you stalking me?" she asked. "Don't
answer that. I don't even want to know. Did you find out who Conrad
was buying flowers for that day?"

"You know I can't tell you anything about an ongoing investigation.
He had two more wives. Did you have an open relationship? How many
men am I going to find in your little black book?"

She looked him right in the eyes. "First you have to find the black book."

"From what I can piece together, y'all didn't have much of a marriage. No kids. No joint property. Why didn't you divorce him?" Waylon asked.

"Keep piecing it together," she threw over her shoulder as she walked away from him.

It was a damn good thing that Kate did not have a weight problem, because when she was angry she had a voracious appetite. She ripped open the cookies and ate the whole dozen as she loaded her cart. Twice she passed Waylon on an aisle, but she didn't speak and neither did he. She did sneak a peek at his purchases and was surprised to see flour, sugar, and staples that most folks bought if they were planning on preparing meals from scratch.

Where was it he said that he lived? It was a woman's name, like Marysville. No, Mabelle. Didn't they have a market there? Maybe he really was following her. Did that constitute harassment?

Back behind the steering wheel with the AC running full blast, she checked the statistics on Mabelle, Texas. Population at last census was nine. That wasn't big enough to be considered a community, much less a town. It was about nine miles southwest from Seymour and maybe five miles from Bootleg, which sat on the edge of Lake Kemp.

"I guess this is the closest grocery store, so at least he's not stalking me," she said as she started the engine and pointed her car north toward Bootleg.

CHAPTER FIVE

Kate let the engine run, keeping the vehicle cool, while she studied the lineup in the rocking chairs on the front porch. Jamie sat closest to the door, with a strange lady with short, curly hair a faint shade of purple beside her. Gracie was in the middle chair, bare feet dangling about halfway to the porch. Next to her, an old gentleman with thick glasses and a rim of gray hair around an otherwise bald head nodded as she chattered nonstop.

Neighbors? Grandparents? Friends? Hopefully, they weren't there to spend the night, or they'd have to pull out the sofa bed. She'd decided to treat this whole thing like her freshman college-dorm days—a building full of rooms with a single kitchen and lobby/living room. She turned off the engine and hit the button to open the trunk. By the time she got around the car to unload her supplies, the old gentleman was lifting out two bags of groceries.

"I'm Victor Green, and I'm your neighbor to the left." He nodded over his shoulder. "That's Hattie Bell up there on the porch, and she's your neighbor to the right. We know Gracie and Jamie from their week in the summer, but we ain't seen you."

"I was here about fourteen years ago, but only for a week," Kate said.

"So you'd be the oldest wife?" Victor asked.

Ouch, that stung, even if he didn't put emphasis on the word or even act surprised that they were all there at the same time.

"I might be," she answered.

Hattie followed them inside and unloaded the bags, setting the food on the table while Victor went back to the porch. "Jamie told us what happened with Conrad. I'm not a bit surprised. I told Iris when she married him that he was a shyster and just out to get her money. A year later she was dead and he owned this house, plus he had all of her savings. Her poor daughter didn't get a thing, not even the wedding rings that her father had given Iris. Poor Iris was only fifty-five when she had that heart attack." Hattie lowered her voice to a whisper. "I always suspected that he had something to do with it. And"—she narrowed her eyes until they were mere slits in a bed of wrinkles—"I wouldn't be surprised if he hadn't done the same thing before Iris."

"Is the daughter still alive?" Kate asked.

"Oh, no, she died in a car wreck about six months after her mama."

"And Iris was fifty-five?" Kate opened the refrigerator to find her sandwich gone.

"That's right. Conrad said he was twenty-eight, but I always thought he was younger than that. He was a charmer, all right. Iris was a fool to think he was in love with her and not what he could con her out of," Hattie said.

"Why are you telling me this?" Kate put away milk, cheese, and lunch meat.

"So all three of you understand that you weren't the first, and if he'd lived, you wouldn't be the last," Hattie said. "And besides"—she giggled—"I'm nosy. I want to know what happens with the three of you living in this house together. You got to admit it could be a reality show. Maybe something like *Hostile Sister Wives*. Me and Victor have a ten-dollar bet going as to which one of y'all killed that son of a bitch. In memory of Iris, I'll take whoever did it to dinner."

A smile spread across Kate's face as she put on a pot of water to boil for tea. "Did you see him—I mean, Conrad, very often? Did he come here and stay a whole week with anyone else other than Jamie and Gracie?"

"Honey, he showed up here all the time, but I never paid much attention to them. I did see him last winter with the redhead, and they stayed a week. Most of the time he'd slink in here with a different woman over weekends. He knew we didn't like him, so we all ignored one another," Hattie said.

"He came near the end of each month?"

"Oh, yes. How'd you know that?"

"Just a lucky guess." She dropped four tea bags into the boiling water, covered the pot, and set it aside. While they steeped, she ran water into a plastic pitcher until it was half-full, added a cup and a half of sugar, and stirred it until it dissolved.

"Just the way I make tea. Your mama taught you well," Hattie said. "Would you look at the time? Thirty minutes until Sunday night church services. Y'all are all invited anytime you want to attend. It's the little white church on the north side of town. The one on the south side has been closed down for a couple of years now. We usually have a potluck after Sunday morning services, so bring along a covered dish if you want to join us for that."

"Thank you for your help, Hattie." Kate smiled.

"Anytime. Me and Victor will be popping in to check on you girls." She grinned. "Like I said, I'm nosy, and besides, I'm old. That means I get to ask rude questions and say what I want."

"Then I can't wait to get old," Kate said.

"'Bye, now." Hattie waved as she crossed the room to the door and disappeared.

Kate removed the tea bags, squeezed all the water from them, and then poured the tea into the pitcher. When it was stirred well, she took a glass down from the cabinet, filled it with ice and tea, and carried it to her bedroom. She gulped down a third of the tea, set it on her dresser, and reached for her laptop. She opened a new folder and typed:

Information about Conrad:

Conrad came home at least one day toward the end of every third week. He would meet with his accountant to discuss his business and sign any tax papers or forms that she needed him to take care of. He'd draw out his monthly paycheck at that time, and he'd be at the house when I got home from the office. The conversation was always the same. He wanted me to divorce him. I refused. He'd have his evening meal in the dining room and I'd take mine to my bedroom. My house was simply a free hotel for the night.

She closed her laptop and drank the rest of the tea. When she went back for a refill, there was not one drop left in the pitcher. Her sandwich was gone and now her tea—it was the old proverbial straw that broke the camel's back. She marched out to the porch to find Jamie and Gracie sipping away at a glass each and Amanda on the other end of the porch chomping on the ice pellets left in hers.

"What's your problem?" Amanda asked.

"That was my tea and it was my sandwich in the refrigerator," Kate said.

"Well, pardon me," Amanda said with a head wiggle. "I was hungry, and it was the only thing in the house. Conrad never said I couldn't eat something that was left in the refrigerator. And I was thirsty, so I had a glass of tea. What do I owe you?"

"Being the first wife don't give you the right to get all bitchy over a glass of tea," Jamie said.

"Conrad is dead, so what he said in this house does not matter. And I'm not the first wife. I'm just likely the oldest one alive today. Didn't Hattie tell you about Iris?" Kate propped a hip on the porch railing.

"Who is Iris?" Amanda asked.

Kate told them the story, continuing, "I have started a file with things I can remember, like how Conrad only came home a day a month to talk to his accountant—or maybe I should say he came to my house. If you'll do the same, maybe it will help that detective to see that we aren't guilty of conspiracy to commit murder."

"I'm not doing one blasted thing," Jamie said.

"Then if he finds us guilty, you'd better get your affairs in order as far as Gracie is concerned, and you'd better have someone designated to raise that baby, Amanda."

"You are just trying to scare me." Amanda frowned.

"No, she's not. She might have money, but . . ." Jamie stopped.

Gracie picked up a couple of dolls. "I'm going to my room where it's cool. When is supper, Mama? I'm hungry." She slammed the screen door on the way inside.

Kate almost smiled as she remembered how she used to get into trouble from every single nanny she'd ever had for slamming the back door at her house in Fort Worth.

"But what?" Kate shook away the memory and glanced over at Jamie.

"Do you have children?" Jamie asked.

"No, I do not," she answered.

"Then she has less to lose than we do if that detective makes a case against us," Jamie said. "And she's not trying to scare you. I can prove the days that Conrad was with me and Gracie with my credit card accounts. I charge everything to get the points and then pay it off at the end of the month. Until the past eight or nine months, he came home on Sunday night and we always went to McDonald's for supper, and every evening after we had supper at home, we went to Culver's for an ice-cream cone. He said it was his way of spoiling Gracie since he didn't get to be with her all the time."

Kate set her mouth in a firm line. "He was spoiling her, but you paid for everything, right?"

Jamie shook her head. "He took care of the taxes and insurance on the house and paid the mortgage."

"No!" Amanda slapped the arm of her rocking chair. "I wanted to buy a house instead of living in an apartment, but he said we had to pay off this cabin first. I've been giving him five hundred dollars a month to make an extra payment on this place."

"He inherited this place and it's paid for," Kate said bluntly.

"Then where was my five hundred dollars going?" Amanda asked.

Kate shrugged. "Maybe to buy lots of flowers for other women."

"Mama"—Gracie poked her head out the door—"I'm really hungry."

"We'll have to go to the store. Maybe we'll get pizza," Jamie answered.

"There's sandwich stuff in the refrigerator," Kate offered.

There was no way she was going to let a child go hungry, not even for the length of time it took to drive into Bootleg and get a pizza from the deli part of the convenience store.

"Oh, so she can have some of your food, but I can't?" Amanda shot a dirty look toward Kate.

Kate ignored it and sat down in her favorite chair.

"Go on and play five more minutes," Jamie told Gracie. "And then we'll see about making sandwiches."

"Okay, Mama. Can I get a glass of milk until then?"

Jamie looked at Kate.

"Of course, she can have milk. I'm not a monster."

"Yes, you may," Jamie said and waited until the door slammed again. "I teach school in inner-city Dallas. Shall we set down some classroom rules here, since we are all living in the same house?"

"Maybe I'm sorry that I didn't ask before I ate the sandwich or drank the tea, but rules or no rules, I'm staying right here until September," Amanda declared. "Aunt Ellie says I need to get my head on straight."

"Apology accepted," Kate said, ignoring the latter part of her statement.

"I vote that we each take care of our own space, keep things picked up in the living area, buy our own food, and do our own cooking. Any leftovers that go in the refrigerator are up for grabs unless we put our name on them," Jamie said.

"Fair enough. Where's the nearest store?" Amanda asked.

"About six or seven miles south in Seymour," Kate answered. "Open until nine every evening. Hopefully the whole thing will be settled by the end of summer."

"The business part might be all done and finished by summer's end, but I'm scarred for life," Amanda whined.

"Stop the dramatics. Think about him in bed with a fifty-five-year-old woman," Jamie said.

"Yuck!" Amanda's nose wrinkled in disgust. "My Conrad wouldn't do that. He might have married her, but he didn't go to bed with her."

"Or all those women he brought up here toward the end of the month? You stupid enough to believe they weren't screwin' like minks?" Jamie argued.

"How do we know Hattie isn't lying or just sayin' those things because Iris was her friend?" Amanda asked.

"It'll be easy to verify," Kate said. "I can check his bank records as soon as the lawyers get this straightened out. I bet we see where he deposited your money, Amanda. There are probably receipts where he bought gasoline right here in Bootleg at the end of every month."

"How could he do this to me?" Amanda whispered.

"You? Do you think you are the only one? He was cheating on all of us outside of being married to us," Jamie said. "Grow up. How old are you anyway?"

"Twenty-eight," Amanda said defiantly.

"Then stop acting like you are sixteen."

"And you?" Kate looked over at Jamie. "I'm guessing you are about thirty-five?"

"Thirty-six," Jamie said.

"I'm forty-four," Kate said. "We were all about thirty when he married each of us."

Amanda's chin popped up two inches. "He married you for your money and Jamie to get a kid. He married me for love."

Kate shook her head slowly from side to side. "Wake up and smell the bacon, girl. Jamie, how much is your mortgage?"

"Four hundred eighty-nine dollars and fifty cents a month," Jamie said.

"Amanda"—Kate pointed at her—"your five hundred made her house payment so he could use his money to look around for rich women to fleece."

"No! He wouldn't do that," Amanda declared. "If you are so smart, then why didn't you divorce him? Oh, wait! Because he divorced both of you. When the papers show up, you'll both feel like fools."

Jamie pushed up out of the chair and stretched. "I'm tired of this crap. If you were serious about us using your food for tonight, I'm going to make sandwiches for our supper."

"I was serious, and Amanda, he would never divorce me," Kate said.

"Why? You are old," Amanda said.

Kate took a couple of deep breaths. "Because the prenup said that if he divorced me he only got what he brought into the marriage, and that could fit into a suitcase. If I divorced him, then he was entitled to a lot more. He said on the day that he signed it that he loved me so much that he would never leave me. A year later he vowed to make my life so miserable that I would divorce him and give him what was legally his for marrying someone no one else would have."

"And?" Amanda pressured for more.

"I inherited my mother's stubborn streak," Kate said as she headed inside the house.

CHAPTER SIX

Kate spread an old quilt out on the ground and sat down. The past two days had been a time of cool adjustment, sometimes a bit awkward, most of the time simply learning to stay out of one another's space. She'd already said more than she'd intended to ever share with these women, and she'd given them permission to use her tea and her food. That was enough.

It would take more than listening to the gentle waves lapping against the grassy shore to comfort her that day. She wished that she was back in her office, where the carpet was every bit as plush as the soft green grass beyond the quilt. Once this was over, she would go home, put it all behind her, and never deal with those two snippy women again.

Gracie's giggles drifted across the slight breeze—she had the spirit of an angel and the smile of an imp. It would take a heart of stone not to be even a little charmed by Miss Gracie. She skipped around the edge of the lake, running back and forth to the lawn chairs Jamie had brought up from the old boathouse for Hattie and Victor.

Kate smiled at the child, and a weight lifted from her soul for a moment.

Jamie sat at the end of the dock with her bare feet in the water. Amanda had propped her swollen feet on a chaise lounge up on the deck. If Kate turned her ear just right, she could hear country music coming from an old boom box that had been in the house fourteen years ago. At least she liked the same kind of music Kate did and not that hard rock stuff.

The hair on Kate's neck prickled, and a chill chased down her spine in spite of the heat. She glanced up to see Waylon walking down the hill carrying sunglasses by one stem, the brim of his cowboy hat obscuring his eyes. Maybe, just maybe, he was going to tell her that the whole thing had been solved.

"So you are all still here?" He sat down uninvited on her quilt and stretched out his long legs. His short-sleeved, pearl-snap shirt hugged his body and biceps like it had been tailor made. "I figured one or all of you would last about twenty-four hours and then go scampering back to your own places."

"I don't scamper." Kate's smile at Gracie's antics disappeared, taking the happiness with it.

He chuckled. "But you still aren't best buddies?"

"Sure we are. We're as close as sisters. That's what happens when you plan a murder together," she said sarcastically. "I hope you came to tell me that you found out who killed Conrad and that you won't be showing up here anymore."

"Your wishes and hopes aren't coming true this week."

She didn't know if it was a physical attraction brought on by that confident swagger that jacked her pulse up several notches or if it was anger that he would even entertain the asinine assumption that she would be involved in a crime.

He set his straw cowboy hat on the quilt and tossed his sunglasses inside it. "The sun was still bright when I left Dallas," he said. "So, have you always worked in your family's oil business?"

"I'm sure you have checked into my job, my alibi, talked to my mother, and know where I got my education and that I do not have children or pets," she answered.

"A little prickly tonight, are you?"

"Wouldn't you be if someone accused you of murder?"

"Maybe."

Gracie's dark ponytail flipped back and forth, and her bright-colored shorts and shirt flashed in the moonlight as she ran from the edge of the lake toward the dock. When she passed Kate's quilt, she stopped.

"Kate, guess what? I just stuck my toes in the water and Mama said if it ain't cold we can swim tomorrow." She threw herself down on the quilt, barely missing Waylon's hat and sunglasses. "And guess what else? Hattie says we need to go fishin'. Did you know about the festival? It's got a carnival and rides and a Ferris wheel and funnel cakes and it's all got to do with fishin' so we need to practice?" She inhaled and went on. "I'm going to catch the biggest fish for little kids this year and get the prize. Hattie says it's four tickets to Six Flags and I want to go. Daddy said he'd take me someday, but now he's gone away and Mama will have to take me, but we will get some extra tickets so you can go with us if you want to."

"Wouldn't that be fun?" Kate smiled up at her, pausing the entertaining monologue.

"Gracie!" Jamie yelled from the dock.

"I gotta go. 'Bye." Gracie ran as hard as her little legs would carry her toward the dock.

"Cute kid."

"Yes, she is."

"Ever wish you had a couple of children?"

He had no idea how much his question stung. She'd always wanted children, especially a daughter. But a miscarriage six months after she'd married Conrad had ended that dream. The doctor had said that the possibility of ever conceiving a child was a million to one and carrying one to term would have even slimmer chances.

"Do you?" she shot right back at him.

"I married my career and lost two wives because of it. No children. I'm too old to start now," he said.

"And that is?"

"Forty-five. By the time I got one through college, I'd be pushin' seventy." He pointed at sky over the lake. "Look at that moon and the way it's reflected in the water. Gorgeous, ain't it?"

The lake was indeed acting like a mirror, but she didn't give a damn about the moon. She wanted him to either tell her that she wasn't a suspect or get up off his butt and go find the real killer.

"You didn't answer my question," Waylon said.

"I don't intend to," she said. "What are you doing in Bootleg in the middle of the week?"

"I told you that I have a little ranch in Mabelle. My folks owned it. My dad died several years ago and my mother last year. So I spend most weekends here and come and go pretty often through the week when I can get away from the desk. It's not a long drive from Dallas," Waylon answered.

"So you grew up in this area?" Kate asked.

He nodded. "Went to school right here in Bootleg. Know everyone in this town and quite a few in Seymour."

"Hattie and Victor?"

Another nod. "Yes, and I knew Iris, too. So I already knew the scuttlebutt on Conrad Steele. And before you ask, there was not a shred of evidence that he caused Iris to have that heart attack."

"I wasn't going to ask. Conrad was smarter than that. If he had anything to do with her death, you would never catch him. Did you ever meet him?"

"No, but my mother told me about the little wedding reception at this cabin when they married."

She'd been conned by Conrad with his compliments and pretty face. Waylon couldn't begin to work his charm on her.

"How long are you staying in Bootleg?" she asked.

"A couple of days this time, but I'll be around pretty often. How about you?"

"Until you tell me that I'm not a suspect."

"Fair enough," Waylon said.

Fair?

If life had been fair, Conrad Steele would have never entered her life.

☙

Amanda dabbed at her eyes with a tissue. She was doing better. This was the first time she'd gotten all misty eyed that day, but the sunset reminded her of lying on the deck in Conrad's arms the last evening of their honeymoon. Tonight Conrad was supposed to be sitting beside her, his hand on her baby bump, smiling every time their son kicked. The only thing that made her happy was the decision she'd made about his name. When the boy was born, he would be Conrad Jonathan Steele Jr., and she would call him Jonathan or maybe Johnny.

She would raise her son to know that his father was a hero who'd tried to stop a robbery, and she would never tell him about the other two wives or about Iris. He would have to grow up without a strong male role model in his life. Amanda had not had a father figure in her life, either, just Aunt Ellie, but she'd survived. This baby would have a mother who loved and wanted him very much. She swiped at a fresh batch of tears.

She laid her hand on her stomach. "I wanted more for you, baby boy. I wanted you to have the storybook daddy who played catch with you and taught you how to throw a football."

Aunt Ellie's ringtone startled her. She didn't want to talk to anyone right then, but she answered the call. It was Aunt Ellie who'd saved her hide on more than one occasion, so she couldn't be rude.

"I'm on my way home from work and thought we could chat while I drive," she said. "We had a great day. Wanda and I went for the buffet down at the pizza joint on our way home to celebrate."

"I'm watching the sunset from the deck. Don't talk to me about pizza. I'm craving it, and all I had for supper was an omelet and toast."

"You sound depressed. Are you okay? If that place and those two women are upsetting you, it's not good for the baby. Come on home. Wanda has said she'll help me out in the store the rest of the summer so you won't have to come to work every day, but you'd be close to your doctor and you'll be near the people who love you."

Amanda managed a weak smile. "I'm only an hour away from you and my doctor, and I'm fine right here, where Conrad and I spent the happiest time of our marriage."

"And those other two?"

"We're staying out of one another's way for the most part. Jamie and Gracie spend a lot of time down near the lake. The deck is mine unless Gracie decides to play out here, but she's a good kid. She doesn't bother me much. And the front porch is Kate's."

"Well, I hope you find some closure," Aunt Ellie said. "I'm driving into my garage. Talk to you later. Love you, kiddo."

Amanda flipped through the pictures of her and Conrad on her phone, taking time to touch his face on every one. He'd said his "sister" Kate called him Conrad but he hated that name. He'd always wished that their mother, Teresa, would have called him by his middle name, Jonathan, but his father's name was Jonathan James Steele, so he had to be Conrad.

She rolled over to the last picture of them together. Aunt Ellie had taken it in the shop right before he had to leave the last time she'd seen him. His smile was genuine, and his eyes were twinkling. Yes, Conrad loved her. He might not have divorced those other two women, but she would never believe those stories about Iris or about him bringing other women to the cabin. Iris had probably only loved him like a son. If he was here, Conrad could explain the women that Hattie thought she saw at the cabin. They were most likely clothing store owners that he was trying to cultivate to sell him their sale merchandise at the end of every season.

Are you an idiot? a voice in her head shouted. Strange, but it sounded exactly like her best friend, Bailey, who had served as maid of honor at Amanda's wedding. *You should be throwing a hissy at that bastard, not moonin' around after him.*

She sat up a little straighter. Bailey was in Germany, stationed there with her husband, who was in the service, and Amanda hadn't told her about the situation. Still, that was exactly what she would say if she knew.

Just to be sure, she sent a text to Bailey: Call me when you have time. Lots I need to tell you.

The phone rang before she could lay it back on the table beside her. Amanda hit the screen and answered. "Bailey, what are you doing awake at this hour? It must be four o'clock in the morning there."

"It is, but I'm having one of those sleepless nights. Catch me up," Bailey said.

"Conrad was killed," Amanda said and went on to tell her the rest of the story.

"I knew there was something hinky about that man. I wouldn't say anything only because you were so much in love with him. He had shifty eyes and wandering hands. I steered clear of him. What a mess."

"I thought you'd support me." Amanda pouted.

"Support you, yes. Listen to you defend a son of a bitch like that, no, ma'am. You need to wake up and smell the coffee or the roses or whatever the hell it is that you smell when you wake up. Take a lesson from those other two you told me about. Get an I-don't-give-a-damn attitude or I'd-like-to-kill-him-again one, but stop feeling sorry for yourself and see him for what he was, and that's a con man," Bailey told her.

"He loved me," Amanda declared.

"No, he did not. He didn't love anything but the game," Bailey shot right back. "I'm going to hang up now, and you think about the fairy tale you're telling yourself and then think about the reality. Call me in a day or two when you figure out which one is really right. Good night."

"'Night," Amanda said, not bothering to hide her upset.

She hefted her weight off the lounge, stomped barefoot into the house, and went straight to her bedroom. She eased down on the bed and curled up around a pillow, pretending that it was Conrad's back and he was there with her. A dozen pictures flashed through her mind, starting with the week she'd met him, the whirlwind romance, the small but pretty church wedding, the honeymoon in that very room, and then the shiny black casket at the graveside service.

Then the pretty things all disappeared and she could see a line of faceless women, all with numbers in their hands, lined up from the bedroom door, through the house, down all those steps and out to the lake. There was no counting the women that Conrad had slept with in this very bed. Her eyes popped open as reality hit her smack in the face. She slung the pillow across the room. Anger set in. She wanted to hit something, kick holes in the walls, burn down the cabin—anything to get the misery out of her heart.

"Damn him for doing this to me."

Feeling as dirty, as if she'd been violated, she went straight to the bathroom and took a long, cool shower, washing her shoulder-length hair twice and lathering up her belly three times. "I will not name you after that man, my son. You'll have a good strong Irish name, like Liam or maybe Desmond, and I will think of something else to tell you about your father. It won't be that he was a hero. And you will not have any of his looks or ways. *I'm* your mother."

She felt a little better once she finished and was dressed in a baggy T-shirt that came halfway to her knees. But when she went back into the bedroom, she could not make herself even sit on the bed. She paced around it a few times and finally turned her back, closed the door, and went to the living room, where she pulled the cushions from the sofa. She tossed them to one side and pulled out the hidden bed. It might not be comfortable, but it would be a place that Conrad had never used. Or was his name even Conrad? Maybe that wasn't even the name on his birth certificate at all.

How do you know that? Bailey's voice was back in her head. *He might have used all the beds, including the sofa.*

"Because the one thing that I can believe that he told me was that he hated to sleep on sofas. It reminded him of his childhood," Amanda answered out loud as she went out to the deck, picked up her phone, and found a message from Aunt Ellie.

Rather than sending a text, Amanda called and ranted for half an hour about the bed. When she finished her aunt Ellie was laughing so hard she had the hiccups.

"Now there's the red-haired fireball of a niece that I raised. I wondered when that wimpy woman that had taken over her body would be banished. Welcome back, real Amanda Hilton." Ellie chuckled. "I will bring you a bed tomorrow. There's an extra twin-size one in storage in my garage. I'll be there by six, so be on the lookout for me."

"Thank you, Aunt Ellie. It will be more comfortable than the sofa, I'm sure. And bring a five-gallon can of gasoline with you."

Ellie gasped. "You will not set fire to a mattress in town. Those damn things burn forever, and the smoke would be awful. Besides, after all the women he's had on the thing, the fumes might be toxic. We'll talk about it when I get there."

"Thank you, but I intend to burn it or take it to a landfill. I won't have that thing in my cabin," Amanda said.

"See you tomorrow. Anything else you want me to bring?"

"A loaded sub sandwich with cold cuts and lots of Italian dressing," she said.

"You got it," Aunt Ellie said.

She laid the phone to the side, picked up the remote, and turned on the television, but before she could flip through the channels, the sliding doors out to the deck squeaked open. Gracie didn't pay a bit of attention to Amanda but headed straight to the bathroom with Jamie right behind her.

Jamie stopped in her tracks and raised an eyebrow.

Amanda narrowed her eyes and shook her head. "I don't want to talk about it. I'm not sleeping in that bed another night. Aunt Ellie is bringing me another bed tomorrow after she closes the shop. Good night."

Jamie giggled.

"What's so funny?" Amanda asked.

Jamie stopped and looked back. "It took you long enough to figure it out."

Kate smiled as she came in the front door. "She's young and slow."

Amanda shook a finger at Kate. "Just because you are old doesn't mean you are so smart. You married him, too."

"Yes, I did. But I did not spend one night in that bed."

"Me, either," Jamie yelled from the hallway.

"And I won't spend another one," Amanda declared.

CHAPTER SEVEN

It was one of those days when if something could go wrong, it did. Even if there was no way something could go wrong, it did anyway. Kate started out the morning by burning her breakfast toast, spilling coffee all over her favorite pajamas, and killing a spider on the kitchen counter. She'd just put the ingredients for a smoothie into the blender when someone knocked on the door. On the way to open it, she stumbled over Amanda's flip-flops and almost fell face-first across the living room floor.

"What in the hell is Waylon doing here this early?" she mumbled as she slung open the door.

"Good mornin'," Hattie said cheerfully.

Kate frowned.

"I'm here for Gracie. Jamie said I can have her the next three mornings for Bible school down at our church. Is she ready?"

Kate shrugged.

"You haven't had your morning coffee, have you? I'm an old bear until I get my two cups, too. I'll just see if they're out on the deck and you go get a cup poured," Hattie said.

Kate stepped aside and let her enter the cabin. Hattie stopped in her tracks when she saw Amanda on the sofa. "Why isn't she in one of the bedrooms? That can't be good for her back."

"She wanted the master bedroom but changed her mind last night," Kate explained.

Jamie slid back the doors out onto the deck and smiled at Hattie. "She's ready. We were having breakfast burritos while we waited."

Gracie's dark ponytail was held up with a bright-red bow that matched her red-checked sundress. Her white sandals showed wear, but Jamie had taken time to polish them. Gracie tiptoed across the floor and put her hand in Hattie's.

"I'm ready. You will be my teacher, right?" Gracie slipped her hand in Hattie's.

Oh, to be as trusting as a child, Kate thought.

"Yes, darlin' girl, I will keep you right beside me all day," Hattie said. "I'll have her back by one. We feed them lunch before we turn them loose."

Jamie bent down and kissed Gracie on the forehead. "Have fun. When you get home, I want to hear all about your new friends."

"I'll try to remember all their names."

Jamie handed Hattie a piece of paper. "Hattie, here's my phone number in case she wants me to come and get her before the Bible school is done."

"I'll get that programmed into my phone," Hattie said. "And Gracie, I can't wait for you to meet Lisa." Hattie led her out of the cabin, talking the whole way.

Jamie followed Kate to the kitchen and started to dump what was left in a skillet into the trash, then paused with a frown as she stared at Kate's burned toast and the mixture in the blender. "The toaster runs hot. You got to stand over it and watch it like a hawk or it will burn the bread every time. It's so old it doesn't have a setting on it. Whatever you've got in that blender looks like ground-up grass. There's enough egg mixture left for a couple of burritos. You want it?" Jamie asked.

"If she doesn't, I do," Amanda said from the sofa.

Kate set the blender in the refrigerator and nodded. "They do smell good. I could eat one."

"Well, rats! I could eat them both." Amanda padded barefoot from the living room to the kitchen. She went straight to the microwave and put a cup of water into it to heat. When it dinged, she stirred instant decaf into it, added sugar and milk, and took a sip before she carried it to the table.

"Too bad. I'm having one," Kate said. "How did you sleep last night?"

"Horrible, but better than if I'd been in that bed," she said honestly.

Jamie whipped up two burritos in a few seconds, put them on a plate, and set them in front of Kate and Amanda. Then she poured herself a cup of coffee and sat down at the table with them. "Y'all ever hear of the seven steps of grief?"

Amanda bit the end off the burrito. "I thought it was twelve steps. I went past denial into anger last night."

"It's five," Kate said.

"I'd expect someone as old as you to know," Amanda said.

Jamie cocked her head to one side. "Age can knock the socks off youth any day of the week, so be careful. There are two of us older than you." Jamie shook her head. "Back to the stages of grief. Tell us what happened to make you leave that bed. You whined for that room like a two-year-old wanting a cookie. So what changed your mind?"

Amanda swallowed and took a sip of coffee. "I talked to my friend Bailey, who was my maid of honor when I got married. Let's just say she started to open my eyes, and then I went into that room and I could see all those women who'd been there before and after me. It was not a pretty sight. I went from denial and shock straight to anger."

"Pain and guilt is step two," Kate said.

"I tied that up with denial." Amanda laid a hand on her stomach. "He's kicking. I wish he'd been a girl now, because I don't want him to grow up like Conrad."

"You really did do a turnaround, didn't you?" Jamie laughed.

"I honestly did. Now tell me what to expect on the rest of this grief crap. Have y'all hit the second stage yet?"

"Oh, honey, I started with anger in the cemetery," Jamie said.

"I finished the whole process thirteen years ago when Conrad asked for a divorce the first time," Kate said. "How did y'all meet Conrad?"

"I'm not sure I want to talk about personal things with either of you," Amanda said with a sniff.

Jamie rolled her eyes toward the ceiling. "Get over it, Amanda."

"Don't tell me what or what not to do," she smarted off. "How'd you meet him, anyway?"

"I was at a beginning-of-school pool party at the principal's house. He was the superintendent's date but spent most of the night flirting with me. He left with my phone number, called, and asked me out the next week. We were married the last day of the year, and I got pregnant soon after. But when Gracie was born, there were complications, so we knew she'd be an only child."

"Makes sense. I had a miscarriage, and the doctor said I couldn't have children," Kate said.

"Why does that make sense?" Amanda asked and then clapped a hand over her mouth when she realized what it meant. "He wanted a son, so he married me to get one, right? He only married me because I'm young and he might have a son with me."

Kate shrugged. "He was a con artist, so who knows, but that would be my guess."

"He was a jobber who came into our store to see if we wanted to buy from him," Amanda said. "We set up an account and he flirted like crazy, asked me out that next weekend, and we went on a picnic to the park. Very romantic, under the stars. That was late summer, and like y'all, we were married on the last day of the year. I was about four weeks pregnant at that time, and we were both ecstatic that he'd have someone to carry on his family name."

"If that is his name," Kate said.

"He did marry all of us with the same name, Conrad Jonathan Steele, right?" Jamie asked.

Kate and Amanda both nodded.

"And you?" Amanda asked.

"I was at the cemetery putting flowers on my father's grave, and he was there putting flowers on his mother's grave. Her name was May Smith, and she died in 1995. She's buried pretty close to my father. For the first year of our marriage, I kept flowers on her grave as well as my dad's," Kate said.

Jamie chuckled. "He told me his mother's name was Julie Smith and she was buried in Louisiana where he was raised. He had that southern drawl, so I never doubted him. I bet May Smith's family thought she had a secret admirer that whole year."

Amanda slapped the table. "He told me that you were his sister and your mother was also his mama. And that you had control of the money. What a mess!"

"Julie Smith is probably the name of one of those women that he conned," Kate said. "He bragged about how stupid women were. In his mind, with a wink and a few compliments, he could have any woman in the world falling into bed with him."

Amanda's hands went up to cup her face as her eyes bugged out. "He talked to you about his women—about us?"

"Not about you two specifically, but yes, about his other women. He was trying to make me mad enough to divorce him so he could have a lot of money."

"Well, we were all duped by the same rascal," Jamie said. "The next thing is what are we going to do about it?"

"Step number five is an upward turn," Kate said. "You'll see the light at the end of the tunnel and start to realize that you can have a normal life."

"Do I have to get over the anger before I can go to that one?" Amanda asked.

Kate picked up her coffee and sipped it. "Yes, you do, and also the depression."

Amanda sighed.

"Do you really hate Conrad?" Kate looked across the table at Jamie.

"Right now I do, and that's not healthy. So when I leave here at the end of summer, I want to be indifferent and ready to move on. How could he do this to Gracie? He could have divorced me. There was no prenup between us," Jamie answered.

"Even if he did divorce you, there would still be the Kate marriage. And he probably didn't want to get lawyers too close to any of the marriages," Amanda said. "Who knows what happened before Iris. There might be an even earlier wife out there who will hunt me for this cabin and whatever else he had in his bank account."

"When was his birthday?" Kate asked in an attempt to divert their attention from the ownership of the cabin.

"November 28, 1972, was on his driver's license," Amanda said. "That made him forty-four last fall."

"That's when we celebrated it, too," Jamie said.

"The birthday and the wedding dates are the same for us all." Kate pushed back her chair and headed to her room.

"Where are you going?" Amanda asked.

"I'm writing this down, like I told you. I may hire my own private investigator. If they find a living wife before me, then she will be in line for this property. If it's not mine, then I'll go home and let her worry with the legalities of the thing," Kate said. "I want to know the truth, and once I know that, I can truly have closure."

"Know the truth and the truth shall set you free," Amanda whispered. "But I will fight anyone to the death for this cabin."

"Quoting Scripture? Are you religious?" Jamie asked.

"Oh, yes, I am," Amanda said. "Conrad and I went to church every Sunday when he was home . . . Dammit!"

Both Jamie and Kate giggled.

Amanda frowned. "It's not funny. He was sitting in church with me, pretending to be all righteous when he was . . ." Tears filled her eyes and spilled down over her cheeks. "I can't believe that he even conned God."

Kate smiled. "A touch of depression is setting in, right?"

Amanda nodded. "He doesn't deserve to make me sad. I'm more depressed with myself than anything, because I was so gullible."

"That's what con men prey on," Jamie said. "Do you think I wasn't gullible? Or Kate? And honey, you can fight, but I've got a legal claim on this place that you can't unseat. Gracie is his oldest child, and she will inherit this place."

"We'll see when it all comes out that there are divorce papers hiding somewhere and that I'm his wife. And gullible? You might have been, but not Kate!" Amanda shot a glance toward Kate.

With a sigh, Kate turned around and returned to the table. "Of course I was. I'd spent my entire life working on my career. I was thirty when we married, which isn't old, but I was established in the business, had three degrees, and was working on my doctorate at that time. I have a level head on my shoulders until it comes to men, then all my common sense flies right out the window," Kate admitted. "And on that note, I have to go write down details before I forget them. Thanks for the breakfast, Jamie."

"You are welcome," Jamie said.

Kate changed from pajama pants and a tank top into shorts and a T-shirt. She wrote down every single thing that they'd discussed, and then she folded her shirt and pajama pants. When she tried to open the dresser drawer to put them away, it hung about halfway. She tugged on it, but it wouldn't budge. She tried to push it back in, but that didn't work, either.

Finally, she dropped to her knees, and with her face on the floor, she peeked under it to find the corner of a thick piece of paper jamming up the works. She needed something long and thin to slip under there. But if she removed the two top drawers, then she could reach under the back side of the bottom one and pull the paper out.

All it took was one little yank and the envelope was free. She tossed it onto the bed and shoved the drawer back, but just before it closed all the way, something else fluttered underneath. It didn't give her a problem to pull the drawer all the way out and set it on the bed with the other two.

"Good grief," she muttered at the sight before her. At least a dozen envelopes had been hidden under there. She gathered them all up and laid them on the bed with the others and then put the drawers back. Curiosity made her pull out the bottom drawer on the other side of the dresser, and she found a dozen more.

When she was sure she had everything, she sat down on the bed with letters in unsealed legal-size envelopes stacked up in front of her. Dates had been written where a stamp should have gone, starting with June 1 and ending with July 3. Nothing to indicate a year, but from the yellowed look of the paper, they'd been written a long time ago.

She held the one dated June 1 in her hand. They could have a bearing on who killed Conrad. Besides, she wanted to know more. She pulled the paper out, gently unfolded it, and gasped when she saw the first line:

My dearest Darcy,

I know you will find the new will and the letters I'm leaving you because this was your favorite hiding spot for treasures when you were a little girl. I must be a very strong woman in the coming days, because Conrad has threatened that if I don't do what he wants, he will divorce me, take his half of everything your father and I worked for all our lives, and then he will seduce you into marrying him. He can be very charming and I cannot bear the thought of you being taken in by that man.

Though he is very sweet when we're out, when we are alone he is mentally abusive. After the first two weeks of marriage, I moved into your old room, and he seems fine with the situation.

I love you, Darcy, and I'm very sorry for this terrible mistake I have made. There is a will in a sealed envelope. From what I found out, it had to be signed in front of two witnesses and the seal unbroken to be valid. Take it to our lawyer. He knows my handwriting and my signature. And the key taped to the bottom of this letter is to my deposit box at the bank. Conrad does not know about the box. What's in it belongs to you as well as this cabin where you grew up and whatever money that Conrad has not blown through.

Love you,

Mama

Kate laid the envelope with WILL written on the outside on the dresser and opened the next one in the stack. When she'd read through half of them, she lay back on the bed. Her heart weighed heavy for Iris, but why hadn't the woman mailed the letters and the will? Why had she left them hidden to be found after her death?

The next one answered her question. If Darcy knew what was going on, she'd do something about it, and Conrad had promised retribution. Evidently he'd convinced Iris that he would hurt her daughter, or worse yet, seduce her, if she breathed a word of what was happening, so she wrote letters with the hopes that Darcy would find them as soon as she was dead. She would be warned about what kind of man he was and she'd fight him for the property.

Kate laid the letters aside when she'd read them all. Iris damn sure had some grit. What should she do now? Darcy was dead, and if she had a will, how would it affect the cabin? If she didn't have one, what then? Should she share them with Amanda and Jamie? Should she give them to Waylon?

"I'll call the lawyers at the company first," she said. "But first I've got to think."

According to a report from a private investigator Iris had hired after she and Conrad had married, he'd been married twice under a different name, Swanson. One of those women died in a suspicious car wreck, and Kate would bet dollars to doughnuts that he got insurance money on the death as well as a settlement with the divorce. A copy of the full report was there. Conrad's birth certificate name was Cain Smith and he was born in New Orleans, Louisiana. Mother was listed as Linda Smith. Father was unknown. He was raised in foster homes because his mother had been an alcoholic—or maybe still was, if she was still living, but the detective could not find her.

Kate's blood ran cold in her veins. Maybe none of the three of them were married to him, since there wasn't anything in the report about him legally changing his name. Now wouldn't that be a royal kick in the butt?

She heard the crunch of gravel and then a vehicle door slam. She hurriedly gathered all the letters, plus the will, into a pile and shoved them into her suitcase.

Waylon was in the living room when Kate arrived. His biceps filled out every bit of the sleeves of a blue chambray work shirt, and bits of straw and hay stuck to his jeans. His sunglasses had slipped down on his nose, probably due to the sweat she could see at his hatband. He removed them and hung a stem in his shirt pocket.

"What are you doing here?" Kate asked.

"My partner called from Dallas. Do any of y'all know an Estrella Gonzales?"

Kate shook her head. "Is that who killed him?"

"Name sounds familiar. Does she live in Wichita Falls?" Amanda asked.

"There's a little girl in Gracie's class room named Estrella Gonzales. That's a really common name," Jamie said.

"Why are you asking?" Kate asked Waylon. "It must be important for you to leave the farm and come here to ask us when you could have called."

"I wanted to see your expressions, and I was coming through town on my way to Seymour for a load of feed anyway," Waylon answered. "The name Estrella Gonzales came up in the investigation when my partner went back to talk to the florist again. I thought he was holding something back, and he finally confessed that Conrad sent flowers to the woman at least once. I wanted to know if she might be a friend, especially of yours, Jamie."

"Why?" Jamie narrowed her eyes. "Because of the Hispanic name? You think all Mexicans know one another?"

Waylon took a couple of steps backward. "Just puttin' together a case. Y'all have a nice day."

Victor and Hattie stepped up on the porch with Gracie between them at the same time that Waylon opened it to go outside.

"Hello, Waylon," Victor said. "Looks like you been hard at work on the ranch today."

Hattie gave him a smile and a nod.

"Mama, guess what?" Gracie skipped across the room. "I got a new friend and her name is Lisa and guess what, I got a mommy and she's got a daddy. My daddy is dead and her mommy is dead. And guess what? Her house burned down. She lost all her Barbies and it made her sad, so I told her that she could come and play with mine anytime she wants to. Is that all right?"

"Of course it is, sweetie. I'm glad you made a new friend, but I'm sorry she's lost her house and her mommy." Jamie pulled Gracie close for a hug.

Gracie giggled. "And guess what else, Mama. Lisa is the same age as me."

"That's wonderful." Jamie beamed.

"I've got to go tell Snugglies all about my friends." Gracie danced down the hallway.

"Snugglies?" Amanda raised an eyebrow.

"The teddy bear that she's slept with since she was a tiny baby," Jamie explained.

"Got any new stuff on the murder? We really need a name so we can send the person who done it a thank-you card," Victor asked Waylon.

"If they get convicted, I'll take them a chocolate cake to whatever jail they are in once a year on their birthday," Hattie said.

Waylon chuckled. "Y'all keep talking like that and you'll go on my suspect list."

"We'd have as much right to be there as these three women," Victor told him.

"Be seein' you." Waylon tipped his hat and left.

Kate motioned Victor and Hattie into the kitchen. "Y'all want a glass of sweet tea?"

Victor removed his snap-bill hat, tossed it on a rocking chair, and followed her into the kitchen. "I would love one. Jamie, we've known Lisa since she was born, and she'll be a good friend for Gracie. They hit it right off. Lisa lost her mother last year after a six-month battle with cancer. Her daddy is the vo-ag teacher at the school."

"And I babysat her before she started school." Hattie bustled about in the kitchen, helping fill glasses with ice.

Kate made a fresh pitcher of tea and set it on the table. "Victor, do you or Hattie know an Estrella Gonzales? She might have come to the cabin with Conrad recently."

"Or maybe she lives around here," Jamie said.

Victor pulled out a chair and slumped down into it. He downed half of his tea before he came up for air. "Never heard that name, and I know everyone in these parts. Kids get younger every year and I get older. And believe me, they ain't all as well behaved as Gracie and Lisa."

"It's a different name. If I'd heard it I would remember," Hattie answered. "And Victor, quit your complainin'. We both love to be a part of Bible school, don't we?"

"Yep." Victor nodded. "Who is this Estrella Gonzales?"

"All Waylon would say is that her name came up in the investigation when they talked to the florist," Amanda said.

"You know Conrad didn't associate with none of us. Kept to himself after Iris died." Hattie sipped her tea. "He might have had this woman up here, but we never heard no names. Poor Iris. She'd turn over in her grave if she knew all this stuff."

"No, she wouldn't." Victor laughed and pointed at the ceiling. "She's so happy, she's doing a jig on the golden streets right now. And I bet Darcy is dancin' with her."

"Darcy?" Amanda asked.

"She was Iris's daughter who died not long after Iris," Hattie said.

"Did Darcy have children?" Kate asked.

Hattie shook her head. "Poor little thing never married and never had kids. Iris wanted grandbabies so bad. Me and Victor tried to share ours when they came to visit, but it wasn't the same."

"So you and Victor have lived here your whole lives?" Kate asked.

"Yep, and been best friends since we was little kids in the church nursery. We've been fightin' and tellin' each other our secrets for over eighty years," Hattie said proudly.

"And you never dated?" Amanda raised her eyebrows.

"Lord, no, darlin'. I wouldn't date this old fart."

"And I couldn't date her. She knew too much about me. Wouldn't be no fun in that." Victor laughed. "Thanks for the tea, but we got to get going. Got to get my lawn mowed this afternoon. Y'all want me to ride my mower up here and take care of yours?"

"How much do you charge?" Amanda asked.

"Well now, I reckon if you'd make up another pitcher of tea and maybe if you brought out some homemade cookies that would be plenty of payment." He grinned.

"You make the tea, I'll bring the cookies, and we'll have a front porch visit," Hattie said. "Say about three o'clock?"

"Sounds great to me, but do you have to ride yours up?" Jamie asked. "Maybe there's a mower here."

"There's not," Victor said. "Conrad had it done by someone out of Seymour, but now that things have changed, I'll be glad to take care of it for you this summer."

"He's got a new riding mower. One of them zero-turn things and the new ain't wore off yet," Hattie teased. "You know what the difference between men and boys is?"

Kate thought they were the same, especially the ones she'd met.

"What?" Amanda asked.

"The price of their toys." Hattie giggled.

CHAPTER EIGHT

Kate almost didn't answer the phone, hearing a ringtone she'd rather avoid. But on the fifth ring, she relented. "Hello, Mother."

"I hate to do this to you as you are trying to get all this crap sorted out, but there's one small project that you were working on that we can't finish without a couple of hours of work from you. If I e-mail it, can you—"

"Yes," Kate butted in, "I'll take care of it." She paused a moment. "I probably should tell you that both of his other wives showed up here the same day I did."

"That's horrible. Why haven't you left?" Teresa's voice went all high and squeaky, but by golly, not a single *I told you so* came out of her mouth.

"Conrad brought all three of us here for our honeymoons, and we're trying to find some closure," Kate answered.

"That pregnant redheaded one is liable to kill you in your sleep. You can see it in her eyes. Even after all the theatrics, my money would be on her as a suspect in the murder. She might not have done it and she might be sorry about it, but I bet she knows something. Now I'll worry about you," Teresa said.

Kate held the phone out from her cheek and stared at it. Where was her mother and who had taken over her body? Kate's father had worried about her, but Teresa? Never. She barely had time to acknowledge that she even had a daughter. A savvy business partner, yes, for sure. But a daughter that she worried about?

"Are you there? Did we lose the connection?" Teresa yelled.

Kate put the phone back to her ear. "I'm fine," Kate said. "And I would love to work from home on whatever you need done. Just send it to me and I'll get right on it."

Teresa chuckled. "We're workaholics. I'll tell Joyce to send it over to you, and maybe it will keep you from killing off the other wives for one day. But if you get really bored, I could send work every day."

"It might keep them from killing me if I get bitchy from boredom. I'm not sure I want a daily regimen, but if I change my mind, I will let you know." Kate laughed.

"I haven't heard your voice that cheerful in years," Teresa said.

"Crazy, isn't it?" Kate said. "I'm in a situation that borders on bizarre and I'm actually kind of content. Tell Joyce hello for me, and I'll have the work done by quittin' time today."

"It's on the way. Keep me up-to-date on this soap opera. I never had time to watch those things, but then my daughter wasn't starring in one."

"Will do, and thanks," Kate said.

Kate picked up her laptop and carried it to the front porch, propped her feet up on the railing, and settled down to work. It wouldn't be difficult to work from home in conditions like this. Plenty of sunshine, sweet tea beside her, barefoot, no constricting clothing, and her blonde hair in a ponytail—a really nice change from her usual office attire and four walls.

A gentle south breeze brought Gracie's squeals from the dock to the porch, and Kate heard the occasional splash and remembered enjoying the pool in their backyard when she was Gracie's age. Her father would sit in a chair grading papers, and she'd squeal and splash all she wanted. Sometimes her mother would join her in the pool, but when she did, it was all business and exercise. Teresa would swim to one end, kick off, and repeat the process until she got her desired number of laps for the day. Then she would get out, wrap up in a white terry robe, and kiss Kate's dad on the top of the head on her way inside to get dressed for dinner.

"I hadn't thought of that in years," Kate said as she opened the folder Joyce had sent, and in seconds she was engrossed in finishing a project she'd started a month before.

∽

Amanda sat on the deck all afternoon with a romance book in her hands. Her back hurt from two nights on the sofa. Aunt Ellie had found mice had eaten into the one in the garage, so she'd had to go out and buy a new full-size bed for Amanda. Tonight her aunt and her new bed would be there.

More than reading, she'd spent time watching Gracie and Jamie down on the dock. Oh, how she wished that there was no such thing as ultrasound equipment that could tell parents the sex of their child. She would have loved to at least hope for a little girl like Gracie. The little girl was such a bundle of joy and happiness all rolled into one that just watching her run up and down the shoreline was delightful.

She expected any moment to wake up and find that this whole past week had been nothing but a horrible nightmare. Everything was so overwhelming that she wanted to crawl into a closet and not come out for at least a year. By then maybe she could digest all that information Kate had told them while they'd made lunch together.

After finishing off a bottle of water, she eased up off the chaise lounge and went inside to the bathroom. On the way back outside, she picked up two more bottles. How twenty ounces of nothing but water could make her have to go to the bathroom at least three times was a mystery.

She stretched back out on the lounge, pulled a big floppy straw hat down over her eyes, and wished that all love stories could have a happy-ever-after like she read in romances. In a few seconds, she was sound asleep, and she didn't wake until she heard her aunt's voice right beside her.

"Hey, girl, are you going to sleep all day and night, too? Or are you going to come on inside and have that sub sandwich you ordered?" Aunt Ellie asked.

"No and yes." Amanda stretched. Then reality reminded her that her life was nothing like the romance novels, and she sighed. Life would never be the same.

Aunt Ellie, God love her heart and soul, had been Amanda's savior most of her life, and though she was past fifty, her aunt was still taking care of her. She looked plumb worn out that evening, but then she'd worked all day and then driven an hour to bring the bed to Bootleg.

"You look tired. Sit a spell and let's visit," Amanda said.

Ellie shook her head. "I want to get home before dark. I'll stay while you eat, but then I'm leaving." Ellie extended a hand. "I stopped by that barbecue joint that you like and brought ribs. You can save those for later."

Amanda put her hand in Ellie's. "Thanks for everything. I've missed you." She slung an arm around Ellie's shoulders, and they went inside together. "Let's eat and then we'll move the old bed out and the new one in. We do share food around here, so we'll put the ribs on the stove and if the others want some, then fine. If not, I'll have the leftovers for breakfast."

"Barbecued ribs for breakfast?" Ellie frowned.

"I'm pregnant." Amanda patted her shoulder.

Jamie yelled up from the bottom of the stairs, "Is that ribs I smell? You didn't tell me you were cooking supper, Amanda."

She and Gracie appeared. Jamie picked up a T-shirt from the back of a kitchen chair and jerked it on over her bright-orange two-piece suit. Gracie wore a cute little bathing suit with Cinderella on the front, and she kept right on going down the hall.

"She's going to change into something dry." Jamie held out her hand to Ellie. "I'm Jamie, and you must be Amanda's aunt Ellie."

Ellie shook hands with her and nodded toward the table. "Amanda has no idea how to make barbecue, but I know where to buy it."

"Thank you. I was going to make us a sandwich, but that smells so good. Nothing like a whole afternoon in the water to build an appetite," Jamie said.

"Hey, Jamie," Hattie yelled from the front door. "Are you here?"

Jamie quickly crossed the deck and went inside. "Right here. We were just coming in from an afternoon swim."

"I wondered if I could steal Gracie to help me at the church. I've got to get things set up for tomorrow's Bible school. Lisa is going to help me, so I thought maybe Gracie might like to go along," Hattie said. "I could have called, but I was driving right past anyway."

Gracie shot out of the bedroom wearing nothing but panties and a T-shirt. "Please, Mama. I want to go see my new friend."

"How soon?" Jamie asked.

"About twenty minutes. I've already got Lisa out in the car, but I need to pick up treats for tomorrow at my house, so I'll get Gracie on the way back through. Just grab her booster for me." Hattie nodded toward Ellie. "Hello. I'm Hattie Bell from next door."

"I'm Ellie Hilton, Amanda's aunt. Pleased to meet you," Ellie said.

"Hey, Hattie." Amanda waved. "Where's the nearest dump ground?"

"What are you throwing out?"

"The king-size bed in the master bedroom," Amanda answered.

"Would you mind donating it rather than tossing it? You remember Gracie's friend Lisa whose house burned down? Her dad could probably use it," Hattie said. "They live in the second house down from the bank. It's yellow with white trim. Belonged to his grandma, and she let him use it until he can settle up with the insurance company."

"Be more than glad to donate it," Amanda said. "But it's a bed and, well . . . you know."

"It does have a mattress cover, right? And it's washable?" Hattie asked.

Amanda nodded.

"That's wonderful. I'll call them and let them know. They have a pickup truck, so if you'll just set it out on the porch, I'm sure they'll come by and get it. His name is Paul Terry. Someone donated a bed for Lisa, but he's been using an air mattress and I know he'll be real happy to have a bed."

"Even with the history?" Ellie asked.

"Honey, once it goes out of this house, the history is wiped clean." Hattie grinned. "Gracie has time to eat, and I'll have plenty of cookies so she and Lisa can have some later."

"Can I go out to the car and see Lisa now?" Gracie bounced up and down like a windup toy.

"No, you can eat your supper and then get on some shorts. She doesn't have to be dressed up tonight, does she?" Jamie asked.

"Play clothes is fine." Hattie started toward the door. "I'll call Paul soon as I get to the car."

❧

In the middle of getting Gracie settled at the table, Jamie heard someone knock on the door. It was too soon to be Hattie, so it was probably that detective. Where was Kate? She was the one he usually had questions for.

"I'll get it." Jamie wiped her hands on a paper towel.

She was expecting Waylon to be on the other side of the door, but it was three younger men, none of them over thirty. "Can I help you?" she asked out of caution.

"I'm Paul Terry, and these are two of my buddies from the church. Hattie called and said you had a bed to give away. We thought we'd come help you tear it down and put up the new one for you. It's the least we can do." Light-brown hair, some crow's feet around the hazel eyes—a man that wouldn't turn many heads until he smiled, and then bushels of charm came out.

Jamie opened the door and motioned them inside. "Come on in. The bed is in the last room on the left, and the new one is out there on the back of that pickup."

"And the bassinet? Does it come into the house, too, or is it leaving?" Paul stopped in the middle of the room.

"It's arriving," Amanda called from the kitchen.

Jamie heard Aunt Ellie say something about how having it there would help Amanda get through the hard times.

"If you'll bring it in, too, it would be a big help," she said.

Paul smiled again. "You got it. To get to sleep on a real bed, I'd move a whole houseful of furniture."

Amanda yelled from the kitchen again, "Hey, Paul, you can have all the bedding, too, but you'll have to wash it."

"Thank you." Paul raised his voice, but his eyes were on Jamie. "This is the answer to a prayer. I am very grateful." Then he nodded toward Jamie. "You are Gracie's mother, right?"

"Yes, I am." Jamie nodded.

"She's all Lisa has been talking about." Paul's smile got even wider at the mention of his daughter.

"Well, Gracie is quite taken with her new friend, too." Jamie was reluctant to return to the kitchen.

I'm not going to propose to him. I just want to get to know him better if his kid and mine are going to be friends, she argued with the voice in her head.

Kate pushed open the sliding doors into the kitchen and raised an eyebrow at Jamie. "What is going on?"

"We're giving away the bed. You got a problem with that?" Amanda answered quickly.

Kate shook her head and yawned. "I do not. What time is it?"

"Six thirty, and barbecue is on the stove if you are hungry," Amanda answered.

"Good grief! I was working down on the dock and time got away from me," Kate said.

The guys came out with the bed and loaded it onto their trucks. Then they took in the new bed and a bassinet filled with cute baby things. Ellie wanted to get home before dark, so she hugged Amanda and hurried off while Jamie finished getting Gracie's plate ready.

"I would have helped tear down and unload for this supper." Jamie held up a rib.

"Mama, I got barbecue on my shirt. Does that mean I can't go to church with Hattie?" Gracie whined.

"It will wash. And you sound pretty tired to me to be going somewhere again tonight. Bible school until after lunch and then more than four hours of swimming and playing in the water?" Jamie laid a hand on her shoulder.

"Please, Mama, I want to see Lisa," Gracie begged.

"And she's looking forward to seeing you," Paul said on a trip back out to his truck. "Hattie loves to have the kids around her, and she told me she'd only be half an hour."

Suddenly a picture popped into Jamie's mind of Paul drawing her into his arms, brushing her hair back with his big hands, and then tipping her chin up for a kiss. She had to blink half a dozen times to erase the sight. Jamie could not remember the last time that she blushed, but a slow burn started at the base of her neck and shot around to her cheeks. The crazy thing was that not one thing had happened that should cause the hot little crimson circles but her own thoughts. Dammit! She was a widow of only a few weeks, and she had no right to even be thinking about another man, much less one she'd only met that moment.

Jamie nodded at her daughter. "Okay, but on one condition. When you get home, you go straight to bed."

"Deal." Gracie grinned.

೧

Amanda's breath caught in her chest. Conrad used to say that word with exactly the same inflection. Would her son turn out to be like his father? She had to put it out of her mind or she would lose her appetite.

"I believe I saw a few sparks in this room when y'all shook hands," she whispered for Jamie's ears only. "You are blushing."

Kate overheard and whipped around from the stove. "There *is* a lot of color in your cheeks."

"I am not blushing," Jamie protested. "I've been out in the sun too much today. And y'all would do well to remember that we've all only been widows a few days."

"I saw what I saw." Amanda shrugged.

Kate carried her plate to the table. "I thought we were taking the bed to a dump ground."

Amanda pulled a paper towel from the roll in the middle of the table. "Remember hearing about Gracie's little friend's house burning? I gave the bed to her daddy. They offered to take it away and put up the new one for me."

"Pretty good trade-off, but I would have been glad to help with the moving-out and moving-in business," Kate said.

Jamie finished her second rib and wiped her hands. "Conrad would be livid about this, you know?"

"Good," Amanda said. "I hope he is twisting and turning in"—she glanced at Gracie—"in the place where I'm pretty sure he is suffering from the heat."

"That's a change of heart from that whimpering girl at the funeral a few days ago," Kate said.

"The veil has been lifted from her eyes." Jamie took Gracie by the hand. "This little girl needs to get a clean shirt on."

Amanda laid a hand on her stomach as the men brought the smaller bed into the house and carried it down the hallway. "I wonder if women in a harem feel like this," she said.

"Not in your wildest dreams," Kate said. "They know they aren't the only ones in the lives of their master or husband or whatever he is to them. Conrad taunted me with constant reminders about how I was too damn ugly to hold a man's attention. But Jamie only had suspicions, and you were completely in the dark. So, no, it's not like a harem. They all know one another and know exactly what is going on."

"He told you that? But you are beautiful and smart and so prim and proper that I feel like a country bumpkin around you," Amanda said.

"And I feel like a big, ugly sunflower in the middle of a beautiful rose garden when I'm around you and Jamie," Kate said.

Amanda's eyes grew huge when the guys hauled out the mattress. "Kate, will I be in trouble for giving away something that goes with the cabin?"

"I don't think so. When the probate stuff starts, they'll count every bed and every spoon in the kitchen," Kate said.

Chapter Nine

When Kate was at home in Fort Worth, she and her mother had a standing date every Sunday. They attended church and then had dinner at a restaurant. One week Teresa made the reservations, the next week Kate did. After they had spent an hour and a half together over lunch, Kate would go home and do nothing but relax. In the summer she swam in the pool, usually doing laps like her mother did when she was a little girl. When it was too cold to get into the pool or when she wasn't in the mood, she watched recorded episodes of her favorite television shows.

If Gracie hadn't begged them all to go see her Bible school program that morning, Kate would have used the excuse that she had to get some last-minute work done. But she could not stand to think about disappointing Gracie. However, it did make her nervous to step outside her comfort zone and attend a church other than the one she'd been christened in as a baby and had gone to her whole life.

So there she was, standing in front of the mirror in a bright-orange floral sundress she'd bought on a whim when she had been looking at cruise brochures. Her mother would be so speechless that she wouldn't be able to utter "I told you so" if she could see Kate dressed like that. A lady wore appropriate clothing to church. She had an image to uphold, one that included a tailored suit, panty hose, and high heels. The image did not have time for a casual sundress and sandals.

She ran a brush through her shoulder-length blonde hair one more time, reapplied lipstick, and picked up her purse. She found Jamie and Gracie already in the living room and breathed a sigh of relief. Jamie wore a cute little denim skirt that skimmed her knee and a sleeveless chocolate-brown knit shirt—and cowboy boots. Gracie was in one of her sundresses and white sandals. Her hair was pulled up into a side ponytail with a big white bow at the top, and Kate wanted to pick her up and swirl her around the room until they were both dizzy.

"You got all dressed up," Jamie said.

"Not really." Kate smiled. "I was afraid I'd be underdressed. My mother wouldn't even sit beside me if I wore this to our church."

"It's not what you wear on your body but what you have in your heart." Amanda appeared from the kitchen with a casserole dish in her hands. "Remember, Hattie said if we were staying for the potluck, we should bring something. I made a fruit salad this morning."

"Are you staying?" Kate asked.

"Of course." Amanda nodded. "I never turn down a big dinner like that. Since we all live in one house, this covered dish will take care of as many of us as want to stay."

Gracie clapped her hands and did a wiggling dance in the middle of the floor. "Can we stay, Mama? Lisa says they always stay and now I can play with her more, and Mama, can she go swimming with me someday and maybe even have a picnic on the dock?" She stopped for breath and then went on. "And we could even play Barbies on the deck and . . ."

Jamie laid a finger over Gracie's lips. "Right now you need to settle down, little girl."

"Yes, ma'am," Gracie said. "Did you know that Lisa already lost a tooth and the tooth fairy gave her a whole dollar?"

"Well, her tooth fairy may be richer than the one who visits our house, but it will be a while before you lose a tooth," Jamie said as they left the house and stepped out into the warm morning breeze. "Why don't we all go in my van? Seems kind of crazy to take three vehicles."

Amanda headed straight toward the van, her baby bump well defined in a sleeveless bright-blue tunic worn over capri-length leggings. She'd changed her regular flip-flops for a pair of electric-blue ones with multicolored stones. With her red hair twisted up in a messy bun, she looked downright adorable that morning.

Kate hesitated but only for a moment before she fell in behind Amanda, opening the door for her so she didn't drop the fruit salad. She'd never been to a potluck. Oh, well, it was only half a mile from the church to the cabin, so if things got too awkward, she could excuse herself and walk home. She really did feel like a duck out of water.

"Do you realize what we are doing?" Kate asked.

"Riding together to church and staying afterward to eat every kind of potato salad and chicken casserole imaginable?" Amanda asked right back.

"No, she's talking about the three of us all arriving at the little country church together." Jamie giggled. "Well, if Bootleg is anything like most small towns, it will provide fodder for the gossip mill for a whole week. Hey, Amanda, did you and Conrad ever attend this church?"

"No, we were on our honeymoon the one Sunday we were here," she answered.

"Us neither, not on the honeymoon or any of the weeks we spent here in the summertime." Jamie glanced across the console and met Kate's eyes.

"I thought that's where you and Gracie met Victor and Hattie," Kate said.

"No," Gracie piped up from the backseat beside Amanda. "We met them down at the lake. They were walking and we were fishing and they stopped and talked to us. And then we saw them at the festival."

"That's the first time she remembers them. She and I actually met them first when she was in a stroller and we went to the festival while Conrad did some business from the cabin," Jamie explained. "And you? Did you go to church with him?"

Kate lifted one shoulder in a slight shrug. "I was only here for the honeymoon week. By the time the second summer rolled around after that, I wouldn't have gone anywhere with him. So I guess this is a first time for all of us."

"Except me!" Gracie piped up. "But don't y'all worry. I will show you around and tell everyone who you are. Lisa is going to be so surprised that you came with me."

☙

According to her grandmother Mama Rita, Jamie was ninety percent bluff and ten percent mean, but the mean was so bad that no one had better call her bluff. That particular Sunday morning, mean was taking a backseat to bluff. It wasn't that she was afraid to go inside the church, but it would be insanely awkward.

She was lucky to find a parking space not far from the front, where people were still going inside. "Best I can do," she muttered.

Amanda pushed the button to open the wide back door. "Good enough. I'll take this to the fellowship hall. Save plenty of room on whatever pew you find."

"I'm going to find the restroom before I come in, so save me a seat, too," Kate said.

Gracie put her hand in Kate's as soon as they were out of the van. "I'll show Kate where it is. I gotta go, too."

Jamie intended to slip in the door and sit on the back pew, but evidently every mama, daddy, grandpa, and granny in the whole county had come out to see the Bible school program that morning. She searched both sides of the church for empty seats as she made her way from the back to the front and found absolutely no space except for the front pew. She sure wasn't going to turn around and take a second look, so she slid into the corner of the long oak pew and picked up the songbook right beside her. Her hands trembled as she turned the pages without seeing the words at all. She could feel the people behind her staring and hear the buzz of whispers. It didn't take a lot of imagination to figure out what they were saying.

She'd never thought of quietness having a color, but it felt stone-cold gray that morning when everything went silent. She glanced over her shoulder to see Amanda, head high and belly forward, eyes straight ahead and then flashing a smile when she finally located Jamie on the front row.

At the funeral, she'd wanted to slap the shit out of that whining redhead, but right then Jamie was so glad to have someone beside her that she could have hugged Amanda.

"Looks like we should have left twenty minutes earlier," Amanda whispered as she settled down, leaving enough room for Gracie between them. "No way we'll sneak on over to the fellowship hall and hide in the shadows like we could have if we'd gotten a backseat."

The buzz of conversation started as soft as the flutter of butterfly wings, but then it got louder and louder until it sounded more like a swarm of bees. Jamie chanced another glance, and there was tall, beautiful, blonde-haired Kate coming up the aisle holding Gracie's hand. Now everyone in church would be speculating about which one of them that the little girl belonged to. She looked like the dark-haired woman, but the tall blonde brought her into the church.

"God, Jamie! Is this the best you could do?" Kate sat down beside Amanda.

"Short of sitting in someone's lap. You are welcome to see if you can find someone willing for that if you want to," Jamie smarted off.

Amanda giggled.

"What's so funny?" Kate asked.

"God, Jamie."

"I'd rather be Queen Jamie," Jamie whispered.

"Shh." Gracie put her finger over her lips. "It's about to start and I need to think about my verse that I memorized."

"And what is that?" Jamie asked.

"'Blessed are those who mourn, for they shall be comforted,'" she said. "What does *mourn* mean, Mama?"

"It means being sad, like you were at your daddy's funeral, and getting happy again," Jamie said.

"Kind of like when we were sad at our house and now we are happy in Bootleg? I'm glad God blessed us," Gracie whispered.

The preacher rose and went to the old oak lectern. Other than a few sounds of folks shifting around to get comfortable, the noise stopped again.

"Today we are having our annual Bible school program instead of a sermon. If all the children and their teachers will come forward and take their seats in the choir chairs behind me, we will begin."

Gracie stood and went straight to the chair without any supervision or even looking back at her mother. Jamie was amazed. In their huge church in Dallas, Gracie wouldn't let go of Jamie's hand from the time they walked inside until they were back in the van on the way home.

Beginning with each child reciting one of the beatitude verses, the service was adorable. The whole group sang two different hymns and did a skit in which Gracie played a little girl from the days when Jesus was on the earth. She said her two lines loud and clear. After Hattie asked the congregation to bow their heads for the benediction, everyone stood and kids scattered every which way to find their parents in the sea of faces.

Kate touched Jamie on the shoulder and smiled. "She did so well up there. Has she been in lots of these little plays? At her age I would have been terrified."

"This is her first one," Jamie answered. "I'm shocked. At home she's very shy and won't get two feet from my side when we are away from the house."

"It's because it's not a big, overwhelming place," Amanda said. "This is the kind of church that Aunt Ellie took me to my whole life. I can't imagine going to one that holds five hundred people."

Kate laughed. "Try three times that."

Jamie nodded. "Or four."

"No wonder she's intimidated. Anyone would be. You should move to a small town to raise her, Jamie."

"What about you? Wichita Falls isn't a rural community," Jamie said.

Hattie pushed her way through the children to join them before Amanda could answer. "You should all stay here at the end of summer and raise your kids in Bootleg. Follow me and I'll take you to the fellowship hall so you can meet everyone. We're so glad you all came this morning. Wasn't that program just the sweetest thing? And Gracie did so good with her parts. She's fitting in right well with the children, too."

At that moment Jamie knew how Moses must've felt when the Red Sea parted—the whole crowd separated to let Hattie lead the way to the fellowship hall. Gracie's hand was tucked in Hattie's. Jamie filed in behind them with Amanda and then Kate behind her.

When they reached the fellowship hall, Jamie felt as out of place as a chicken at a coyote convention, but she kept her head up and followed Amanda's lead. Amanda introduced herself to the two women who were already working at taking lids off the dishes and getting them organized. Jamie took her cue and stepped right in behind her to do the same. "I have never been to a potluck, but I'm willing to help any way I can."

"I'm Kate, and I'll help, too." Kate's tone said that she was every bit as nervous as Jamie.

"Pleased to meet all of you. I'm Ruth, and this is my sister, Hilda. With Hattie we pretty much take care of the kitchen part of the duties, but we're always glad when you young people step up to help. Oh, there's Paul and his daughter. I understand y'all gave him a nice bed this past week."

"Right glad to have you ladies in church. Shame what happened, but then, some men are just born rascals. It ain't y'all's fault, though. God will take care of it all." Hilda nodded toward the tables. "We set out the meat dishes first, then the potatoes and vegetables, salads after that, and then desserts at the far end."

Hattie bustled into the kitchen and started to work. "And the tables are already set with plastic cutlery. I had to stop and give all my kids a special hug for doing so good, so I'm a little behind."

Gracie tugged on Jamie's skirt tail. "Mama, can I go over there and talk to Lisa?"

"Just don't leave this room." Jamie caught sight of Paul talking to Lisa and, from his body language, he was telling her the same thing. The little girls met in the middle of the room and hurried over to a corner, where they plopped down on the floor and put their heads together.

Paul zeroed in on Jamie and came toward the tables where she and Amanda were busy arranging desserts.

"I wanted to come over and tell you that I've slept better the past couple of nights than I have in ages. Thank you again for giving me the bed." His brilliant smile lit up the whole fellowship hall.

"You are very welcome. Gracie sure talks a lot about Lisa," Amanda said.

"Well"—he turned his full attention toward Jamie—"Lisa seems happier than she has in a long time since y'all arrived in Bootleg. She was just getting a little closure with her mom's passing, and then the fire took everything from us. If Hattie hadn't shared some pictures of her mother taken at church functions, we wouldn't even have that."

Guilt pricked Jamie's heart. She'd thrown every picture of Conrad into the trash except the one in Gracie's room. Maybe she should have saved a few more. In later years that one could get torn or misplaced, and then Gracie would have nothing.

Hattie pushed her way in between Amanda and Jamie and set two pies on the table. "I was glad to share what I had with you. And it makes me happy to see Lisa and Gracie helping each other get through these tough times."

"Where's Kate?" Amanda glanced around the room.

"Hilda has her marking lids so they know which dishes to put them back on when this is over," Hattie answered.

"Well, thanks again," Paul said. "And Jamie, anytime that Gracie wants to come to our house for a playdate, she's sure welcome. Lisa really likes her, as you can see." Paul nodded toward the other side of the room, where the girls were whispering to each other.

"I wonder what they're talking about," Amanda said.

"Probably what dessert they'll snag first." Paul laughed as he walked away.

Jamie fought the urge to fan her warm face with the back of her hand. Dammit! She wasn't a teenager with a crush on a new boy on the block.

"And there's that blush again," Amanda teased.

"Hush!" Jamie hissed. "I get flushed when I'm hungry. Right now I'm thinking about moving to a little church when I go home. I cannot believe how these folks are treating us."

"He makes you nervous," Amanda singsonged and then lowered her voice to a whisper. "And in church and so soon after widowhood."

"I've been a widow for months. Ever since you came into the picture," Jamie said.

"You mean—" Amanda asked.

"Only a few times, and only because I insisted," Jamie said.

"Well, damn!" Amanda rolled her eyes to the ceiling. "Forgive me, Lord! I didn't mean to cuss in church."

"Did you think you were the only one he was sleeping with?"

"No, but"—Amanda's pert nose wrinkled—"don't it bother you that he . . . well, you know?"

"Not anymore," Jamie said.

"Let's think about food and put off this conversation until later. I'm too big to dodge lightning bolts," Amanda said.

"Why are these people being so nice?" Kate whispered as she carried more desserts out to the tables.

Amanda shrugged. "It's simply the way things are done. Now, if there had been no Iris, things might be different."

"Then thank you, Jesus, for Iris," Kate said. "This food all looks scrumptious."

"And I get to eat for two." Amanda grinned.

"Lucky girl," Jamie and Kate said at the same time.

❧

Kate felt privileged to sit beside Gracie, who kept a running conversation going with Lisa on the other side of her. Across the table, Victor had finagled it so that Jamie and Paul were side by side. Of course, Hattie, Victor, and Amanda were all at the same table with them and close enough they could talk about summer, the upcoming festival, and the food.

No one said a word about Conrad, and Kate was glad for that. She had enough to think about with those letters in her suitcase and still no decision about whom to give them to or whether or not to share them with Amanda and Jamie or tell Waylon about them. She had sent the will by registered mail down to the legal department at the oil firm, and she'd gotten word that they had received it. Hopefully by the middle of the week, they'd know how to handle it, since Darcy was deceased.

"So how long have you been at the Bootleg school?" Jamie asked Paul.

"Twelve years. Came here right out of college and stayed. My grandmother lives in Seymour and owns rental property up here and down there, too, so I have family close by. I was raised out around

Amarillo, and I got to admit it took a while, but I learned to like the rural way of life pretty quick," Paul answered.

"And I was raised in this area and wound up in Dallas. Strange how we go looking for something different." Waylon sat down beside Paul. Kate's pulse quickened when he glanced her way. "Hello, Kate and everyone else."

"Glad to see you here," Paul said.

"How'd your students do at the spring livestock show this spring? Got any showing during the summer?" Waylon asked Paul.

"They did real well at the show. Several of the cattle and sheep got ribbons and trophies," Paul said. "No one is doing anything this summer. I'm kind of glad. What with the fire and all, I'm pretty busy."

"Got any guys that'd be willing to do some hay hauling, send them out to my place. Looks like I've got a bumper crop coming in," Waylon said.

"Maybe. I'll ask around, and if I find any, I'll tell them to call you. You going to be in town all week or down in Dallas chasing bad guys?" Paul glanced at Jamie.

"Back and forth. Got hay to get into the barns, but we're still looking into leads in the case," he answered.

Well, la-di-da, Kate thought. *That's more than you've told us. We don't get even that much when we ask. Until you start telling us something, I won't share the letters, and believe me, what's in those could help.*

Chapter Ten

"I love potlucks, but I will be so glad to get home and get out of my Sunday clothes," Amanda said on the way home.

Potlucks all the time would be a disaster on the waistline. There was no way Kate could eat like that every week and not be the size of a small elephant by the time summer was over.

"I'm taking tamales next week." Jamie parked in front of the cabin.

"When it's my turn, I'll get fried chicken from the deli at the convenience store," Kate offered.

"Then we get to stay every time?" Gracie asked. "I love it here, Mama. Let's not ever go home."

"Who's that on the porch with your aunt Ellie?" Kate pointed toward the porch. She was looking forward to a nap or maybe an afternoon with a book down under her willow tree. Hopefully, after a couple of *nice to see yous*, she could slip away.

"Our friend Wanda. This is a nice surprise." Amanda hurried out of the car, kicked off her shoes when she got to the porch, and sat down in a rocking chair beside them.

A surge of jealousy shot through Kate. Her mother would never just show up unannounced and wait on the porch for her. No more than Kate would do that. That's what phones were for and why appointments were made.

But the way that Amanda greeted the two women . . . her hands started moving around as she described the potluck and her day . . . well, Kate envied her that moment.

"Look, Mama," Gracie said as she bounded out of the van. "There's Lisa's truck! I wish we could really stay here forever."

Paul drove up beside Jamie's van and crawled out of his truck. He threw his cowboy hat into the passenger seat and helped Lisa get free of her seat belt. Gracie grabbed her hand, and together they skipped across the yard and into the house.

"I'll be back to get her in an hour. If you need me, here's my number." He handed Jamie a piece of paper. "And thanks for letting her come over and play awhile."

"Anytime." Jamie smiled.

It was evident that Paul did affect Jamie, just like Amanda teased her about. But Kate wasn't Jamie's keeper, and she had more pressing things to think about that day than whether or not Paul and Jamie had chemistry.

"Hello, I'm Kate." She introduced herself when she reached the porch. She stayed long enough to be polite and then went inside, changed into shorts and a comfortable shirt, and left by the back door. She went a little farther down the shoreline, because she spotted a big weeping willow tree that offered shade. She pushed back the limbs and spread out her quilt, settled in with her Kindle, and chose a book by Heather Burch titled *One Lavender Ribbon* that had been on her to-be-read pile for a couple of years. The blurb on the back mentioned letters, and of course, that appealed to her right then.

She read a few pages, yawned, and laid the Kindle aside. She only planned to shut her eyes for a minute, but when she awoke the sun was low on the horizon and Waylon was sitting beside her, his boots off to one side and his knees drawn up with those big arms wrapped around them. She shut her eyes tightly and then snapped them open—no, it wasn't a dream. He really was sitting there, staring out at the lovely sunset with all the colors in a painter's palette.

"Good morning," she said.

"More like good evening."

She propped up on an elbow. "How long have you been here?"

"An hour or so. I've been protecting you from spiders and snakes." He smiled.

"And how many did you shoot? Spiders and snakes, I mean?"

"Not any. I ran them off with my evil stare," he answered.

"Well, thank you for that."

He turned to face her. "I saw that dirty look you shot my way at dinner. If I had something I could tell you, I would. We really are following leads, but they keep taking us into dead ends. Look at the way the water is reflecting the sunset. Isn't that beautiful?"

Kate didn't give a flying flip about the colors in the water right then. "So is this going to be the case that you don't solve and everyone will have doubts about me and those other two the rest of our lives?"

He shook his head, sadness in his eyes. "I hope to hell not. It wouldn't be fair to my folks to do that."

"But your parents have passed away." She frowned.

"Yes, but they did not want me to be a policeman. They scrimped and saved my whole life to put me through college and help me become who I am, even though they wanted me to stay on the ranch and run it. I owe it to them to finish on top of the mountain," he said. "I'm freezing my retirement and quitting the police business at the end of summer."

"Why?"

"I'm tired of the city, of the commute back and forth to the ranch, and this past year I'm liking ranchin' better than chasin' bad guys," he said.

"I know exactly what you are talking about. My mother is retiring in December. I step up at that time and take over the firm. My dad was a professor and died when I was twenty-nine." She bit the inside of her lip in frustration at herself for volunteering anything at all.

"I'm sorry. What happened?" Waylon asked.

"Heart attack—it was sudden."

"I was older, but I don't expect it hurt any less," he said. "They're both gone, and now all I think about is leaving the force and coming home to be a rancher. I waited too long for them to ever see it. Were you close to your dad?"

"I adored him. He was a gentle soul, a history professor with a specialty in the Civil War." She'd opened the can of worms and it was impossible to put the lid back on the subject now.

"So you were vulnerable when Conrad came into your life?" Waylon asked.

Until that moment, Kate had not realized just what a big part the timing had played in her life. "I guess I was."

"Explains a hell of a lot," Waylon said. "I couldn't figure out how anyone could con a woman like you."

The sun had dropped below the trees, and that magical part of the evening had arrived. Called twilight, it wasn't yet dark and yet wasn't still light. Part of Waylon's face was in shadows, part still clear—his chiseled features defined and sexier than ever.

She turned to stare at the lake instead of Waylon. "So you think I got conned because I was at a low place in my life?"

"I imagine that Conrad could spot a woman with a soft spot a mile away. I wouldn't even be surprised if he stalked you to learn your habits before he introduced himself."

☙

Waylon wanted to hug Kate close to him. Yet with this murder case hanging over her head, she was vulnerable again, and he would not be like Conrad, in any sense of the word.

"Why would he single me out?" Kate asked after a few minutes.

"You are rich. You are beautiful, and he thought he could make you submit to his will, like Iris. If you'd had children, he would have threatened to take them if you didn't do what he wanted. I'm surprised he didn't threaten your mother," Waylon said. "And besides, you have gorgeous eyes."

"My eyes?" She frowned.

"Oh, yeah! The eyes are the windows to the soul, so he stepped in and—"

"And he conned me," Kate finished for him. "How do I know you aren't doing the same thing just to get more information from me?"

His eyes locked with hers. "Because I'm not like that."

Finally, she blinked and looked out across the lake. She wanted to believe him. She really did. "Well, I'd sure like it if you solved this case. I don't want the suspicion of murder hanging over my head the rest of my life."

"I'll still be on it until my paperwork is finished," Waylon said. "And for your sake, I hope I do get it all tied up with a pretty bow."

They sat in silence for a few minutes. Twilight had deepened into full dark, the moon providing the only light under the weeping willow tree branches.

"Did you ever have any regrets about going right into the family business?" he asked.

To his surprise she nodded. "I was groomed to take over the oil business from the time I was a little girl. Disappointing Mother was not an option. I don't know what I would have done differently, but it would have been nice to have a choice," she said.

"Well, if you'd like to—" He stopped midsentence and pulled his phone from his shirt pocket.

"Well, shit!" he muttered after he'd listened a few seconds. "Maybe Paul will find some guys willing to help." Another moment and he rolled his eyes. "Then we'll be working until midnight and using spotlights to get it all in."

He inhaled and let it all out in a whoosh as he shoved the phone back into his pocket. "That's the foreman of my ranch. He says that three of my summer hired hands have come down with the flu, so I'm really going to be shorthanded for the rest of the week." He rolled up on his knees and then stood. "If you'd like to see if you'd like the ranching business, I could sure use a hay truck driver. I wouldn't ask you to throw bales, but anytime you want to come out to the place and drive, I'll pay you minimum wage."

"I might take you up on that." She smiled.

He offered her his hand, but she shook her head. "I think I'll stay here a little longer. I want to think some more before I go back to the cabin."

"Thanks for the visit, Kate."

"Right back at you." She smiled.

❧

Driving a hay truck might be just exactly what Kate needed for a few days to convince her that her job in the city was ideal. She picked up her Kindle and the quilt and was on her way to the cabin when the buzz of conversation on the deck above caught her attention.

It had been several days since she'd found the letters and sent the will down to her lawyers. She'd hoped to have that part of the thing settled when she told Jamie and Amanda about the letters and let them read them, but there were still no answers to what would or could happen to the cabin. Still, tonight might be the right time to go ahead and tell them.

"What's going on here?" Kate asked.

"We don't need you to settle our argument," Jamie said.

"You don't even want this cabin, so just butt out," Amanda said.

"Life is not fair and we don't know yet who will wind up with this place. Why do you even want it, anyway?" Kate asked.

"I like it here, and Victor said there's an opening at the school for an elementary teacher." Jamie tipped up her chin a notch. "You'd only sell the place if you inherited it, and like I've said, it'll be Gracie's since she is his oldest living child."

"What if we all inherit equally? I get a third. You each get a third. What then?" Kate asked.

"God, what a nightmare that would be." Jamie groaned.

"You have money and a fancy job in Dallas. Why would you even want this place?" Amanda asked.

Kate laid the quilt and her Kindle on a table and sat down in a lawn chair. "Arguing about it now isn't going to solve anything. The property could be tied up in court for years. We should all go home and wait until something is decided."

Jamie hiked a hip on the railing. "No, Gracie likes it here. She's coming out of her shyness more and more. Amanda has a business in Wichita Falls that she's not going to leave. You have one in Dallas. You do the math."

"I'm not leaving," Amanda said. "I've got time and I don't want to be cooped up in an apartment. I like this fresh air and sunshine, and I'm staying right here until I have to leave."

Kate glanced at Jamie.

Jamie pushed away from the railing. "Like I said, it is amazing how much Gracie has come out of her shell this past week. I want her to have the rest of the summer here."

"So we'll all have to agree to disagree about who's going to wind up with this property," Kate said.

Tonight was definitely not the time to bring out those letters. Everyone needed to have a level head when they found out what was in that will. Hopefully, in the next few days, something would be decided about Darcy's involvement.

And maybe the argument is an omen that it's not the right time, that niggling little voice in her head said.

I don't believe in omens or fate. Choices that we make determine our future, not fate or karma, she argued.

Amanda almost snorted. "Miss Fancy Pants With Money speaks and we're supposed to bow down and worship her wisdom."

The smart-ass statement brought Kate back to reality. "Don't take it out on me because you are angry at Conrad."

"Besides, that's downright mean," Jamie said.

"So now the two smart wives are going to gang up against the one that barely made it through high school," Amanda smarted off.

"And now you are getting malicious." Jamie's tone said her claws were about to come out. "I'm not looking down on anyone." She glanced toward Kate. "Or up to anyone, either."

"Yeah, right," Amanda said.

"Mama Rita says that familiarity breeds contempt. I'll take care of part of that tomorrow. Gracie and I will be gone all day. Victor offered me a job at the school just for the summer. The secretary quit without notice, so Gracie and I will be spending our days there."

"Well, thank you, Jesus." Amanda raised both arms toward heaven.

Kate looked from one to the other. Jamie was right. They did need some time apart, and there was no way she was staying in the cabin with Amanda every day. That hay truck job was looking better and better.

Chapter Eleven

Jamie inhaled the familiar scent of what could only be described as school when Victor took her inside Bootleg Elementary that morning—pure vitamins to her heart and soul. He led her down the hallway to the office and pointed at the desk. "Basically, you will answer the phone all morning. Office closes at noon during July and August, and the principal will drop by later today to visit with you. There's a stack of filing over there, if you don't mind doing it. The secretary that quit left the files in a mess."

"So you haven't hired a secretary yet, either?" Jamie asked.

"Haven't had a single bite on the job. Got someone in mind?"

Jamie immediately thought of Amanda but shook her head. She damn sure didn't want to work with that woman after the argument from last night.

"Don't y'all keep all this on the computer?" she asked.

"We do, but these files are a nightmare. She's put stuff in them that hasn't been entered, and they need to be organized and then checked with what has already been put in the computer. You want to tackle it?" Victor asked.

Jamie didn't even flinch when she looked at the stack of paperwork. "I don't like to be bored, so yes, sir."

Gracie tugged on her arm. "I can help, Mama."

"Yes, you can." Jamie smiled. "You'll be a big help."

Victor winked broadly. "Man, this is the school's lucky day. We're getting two secretaries for the price of one." He lowered his voice to a whisper. "Hattie says if Gracie gets bored to call and she'll be glad to keep her for you at no charge."

"Thank you," Jamie said.

"And now I will leave you to it." Victor waved as he left the room.

First things first—Jamie found the teachers' lounge across a small hallway and made a fresh pot of coffee. The cabinets were empty except for one lonesome little package of cheese crackers, and she earmarked those for Gracie's midmorning snack. When the coffee was ready, she chose the biggest mug in the dish drainer and filled it. She made a mental note to bring her own tomorrow and to pick up a package of crackers or cookies on the way to work.

"Hey, Mama, look at that." Gracie pointed toward a television and a basket of DVDs. "I see *Little Mermaid* and *The Chipmunks* and . . ." She went on to name a dozen of her favorite children's movies and then turned around and crossed her arms over her chest. "And why were you and Amanda and Kate fightin' last night?"

"That was big-people stuff," Jamie answered.

"Well, I don't like it," Gracie said. "I like Kate and I like Amanda and I love you and big people aren't supposed to act like that."

"I will remember that." Jamie bit back a giggle. "So what's it going to be? Movie? Barbies? Or looking at books?"

"*Little Mermaid* first," Gracie said.

Jamie got the movie started, left the door open so she could hear and see Gracie, and went to work. She opened the first of twelve file drawers and shook her head. Lord love a duck! How did these poor people find anything in that mess? Before she could start on the stack of to-be-filed papers, she needed to straighten up what was already filed. Starting at the back of the first drawer, she removed the dark-green folder and carried it to the desk.

After she'd organized the whole thing by date, she couldn't decide whether to file to the front or the back. She dug her cell phone from her purse and called her grandmother, who did volunteer work at the health clinic. "Mama Rita, I've got a summer job and I need help." She went on to tell her everything.

"Put the newest forms to the front. That way they'll be able to open the file and see exactly what happened recently. And I'm glad you are working at something where Gracie can go with you, but don't get too comfortable up there," Mama Rita said.

"They do have an opening for a third-grade teacher," Jamie said.

"Promise you will think before you jump," Mama Rita said. "You tend to let your heart rule your mind."

"I promise," Jamie said.

She slipped the paperwork back into the folder, now all neat and organized so that the newest documents were on top. At midmorning she was on her third cup of coffee and was chewing up the last of her half of the orange crackers when a middle-aged woman entered the office.

She swallowed quickly and covered her mouth with her hand. "May I help you?"

"I'm Paula Greeley, the principal here at Bootleg Elementary." She stuck out her hand.

Jamie shook it, hoping the whole time that she didn't leave orange stains on Paula's hand. "I'm pleased to meet you. It's been quiet here this morning, so I've gotten half this drawer organized. This needs to be done before I can work on that pile of papers or start doing anything on the computer."

"Thank you!" Paula dropped into a chair and fanned herself with the back of her hand. "It's going to be another scorcher out there, and us chubby people take a while to cool down. Victor says that he's been talking to you about teaching here this fall."

"Do you know who I am?" Jamie eased down into the chair behind the desk and ran her tongue around her teeth.

"I know exactly who you are. The whole town of Bootleg knows about you three women, and we commiserate. What a nightmare! But nothing that man did surprises us, not after Iris. No one here is going to hold that over your heads." Paula grabbed a tissue from a box on the desk and wiped sweat from her forehead, then pushed her salt-and-pepper hair back behind her ears. "Are you even interested in the position?"

"I'm not sure," Jamie answered.

"Moving here would sure enough be a cultural shock from inner-city Dallas," Paula said, "so I imagine you'd have to give it a lot of thought."

Jamie smiled. "Yes, it would, but I'm amazed at how much my daughter is thriving here. You are right, though, it's something I need to think about."

"So far we don't have any applicants, so you've got time. But about the first of August, they'll come out of the woodwork. All the plum jobs will be filled and people will be looking for anything, even if it means teaching at a little backwoods school like we have, so let me know if you decide to apply." Paula stood up. "Until then, thank you for taking on this part-time job for us."

"Thank you for the consideration and for giving me a summer job."

Paula smiled. "From the looks of that drawer up there, we both got a good deal."

⁓

Kate expected Jamie and Gracie to have gone to school that Monday morning when she awoke, but she was surprised to see that Amanda's vehicle was also missing. That meant for the first time she had the place to herself. She stuffed a biscuit with leftover bacon and grape jam and carried it to the porch.

After she'd eaten it and finished a second cup of coffee, she began to pace from one end of the porch to the other and back again. Still nothing from the lawyers, and the idea of not sharing the letters was weighing on her heart. The other two had every right to know what was going on. There might even be something in them to help Waylon.

She picked up her phone and called the lawyer. While it rang, she crossed her fingers like she'd done as a child when she really, really wanted something. The angels who granted wishes must've been on strike that day, because the news was that they hadn't found anything out yet.

She could go home and let the dust from all the drama settle. She'd go to court and get her maiden name back, and since she'd be the new president of Truman Oil, no one would dare voice out loud anything about the Conrad scandal. She'd about talked herself into packing her bags and leaving when her phone rang.

"We're about ready to go to the hay field," Waylon said.

"Were you serious?" she asked.

"Pays minimum. Work until we can't see anymore. No dress code. You can work barefoot if you want in the truck," he said.

"Where's your place?"

"The ranch is easy to find. Take the county road out of Bootleg toward Wichita Falls. The ranch is about three miles down that road on the right. You'll see a big metal sign above the cattle guard that says 'Double Back Ranch.' Turn there and follow the path. I'll meet you in the front yard. How long until you can get here?"

"Twenty minutes."

"You'll drive an old work truck with no air-conditioning, so you might want to pull that pretty blonde hair up in a ponytail," Waylon said.

"See you soon," she said before she changed her mind.

She picked up a cooler from the kitchen and stopped by the convenience store in Bootleg to buy bottles of water and a six-pack of cold Coke. The thermometer in her Caddy said that it was 101 degrees, and driving a truck with no air-conditioning would make for thirsty work. She had to stand in line to pay and noticed a rack of baseball hats for sale. She picked out a pink camouflage one, removed the price tag, stuck it on her head, and pulled her ponytail out the hole in the back. Then she saw the sunblock and picked up an extra bottle of that.

She paid for her items, followed his instructions, and drove up in the front yard twenty-two minutes later. He was leaning against a flatbed truck, a bottle of water in his hands and sweat glistening on his arms and face.

"Sorry I'm late, I had to make a stop, and there were five people ahead of me," she said.

"I don't count two minutes as late, darlin'," he drawled. "I like the hat. You ever driven a stick shift?"

Her mouth went dry at the endearment, and all she could do was nod.

"Well, this truck is your Caddy for the afternoon, and I'll gladly give you all the work you want to do," he said. "We'll be in the hay several days a week for the rest of this month, so anytime you want to come out here and take a look at country life, you are welcome."

"I learned to drive stick in my dad's reconditioned '55 Chevrolet." She set her little cooler in the back of the truck. "Here's some water and Coke so no one dies of thirst."

"Beautiful and smart. A woman after my own heart." He grinned. "Your dad really was a trusting soul to let you drive his vintage car."

"Oh, he never did let me drive the '63 Corvette that Mother bought for their twentieth anniversary, even though he did leave it to me." She grinned.

"You own a 'Vette?" he asked.

"And the '55 Chevy and his pride and joy, a '32 Ford Deuce." She grabbed the cooler and carried it to the truck.

"Like Abby's on *NCIS*?" Waylon asked.

"Her car is red. Mine is black. Daddy said that it might have been a moonshiner's car at one time. You driving out to wherever you are hauling hay, or do I need to give you a demonstration of my skills?"

"Where are those cars?" Waylon asked.

"In a special climate-controlled room at the oil company. I drive them every so often just to keep the cobwebs blown out. You want to see them sometime?" she asked.

"Can I drive that Deuce?"

"That depends on lots of things. For now who's driving this rig, me or you?"

"Why did you decide to drive for me today anyway?"

"Trouble in paradise. Inheritance does bring out the claws." She settled into her seat and reached for the seat belt, but there wasn't one.

"Fightin' over the cabin?"

"Looks that way."

"And since you are the one with the biggest bank account, they are taking sides against you?" he asked.

"Nope, I'd say we're all pretty much standing on our own rocky soil."

He started the engine and put the truck in gear. "I'm kind of glad to hear that. If y'all were getting along like sisters, I'd continue to think you were putting on a show to cover something up."

"We might argue and even come to blows someday, but I'll stake my oil company on the fact that not a one of us had anything to do with Conrad's death," she said.

"That's pretty positive. How can you believe in those other two that strongly?"

"Jamie might have been thinking about divorcing the son of a bitch, but she would never kill Gracie's father. Amanda, bless her heart, will bitch and moan, but she wouldn't have the nerve to pull the trigger, and besides she was still living in that first year of bliss," Kate answered.

"And you?" Waylon stopped the truck at the edge of a field.

"I didn't give a damn. To kill someone, you have to care. I would like to have my maiden name back and have it cleared from all doubt. Other than that, I was over Conrad a decade ago. Are those guys going to work with me?" She pointed to four teenage boys waiting under a shade tree.

"That's your crew. What you do is drive this truck at about five miles an hour. Two will be on the ground throwing bales up to the catcher, who will toss them back to the stacker. When the truck is full, you'll go back to the barn, where they will unload it and then start all over again," Waylon said.

"Where is this barn?" she asked.

"The guys will give you directions. There's a bathroom in the tack room if you need it. You'll have a few minutes while they unload and stack in the barn."

"I think I can remember all that," she said as she slid across the bench seat. "Now give me the wheel. Does the radio work?"

"Like a charm. It'll probably still be working when this thing finally bites the dust, but the air-conditioning went out years ago." Waylon opened the door and hopped to the ground. "And thanks, Kate. This is a big help. It frees up a man to throw or stack."

"Hey, I'm doing this for money, not thanks."

He chuckled as he slammed the door shut. "And what are you going to do with your huge paycheck?"

"Buy tickets to Six Flags if Gracie doesn't win them at the festival," she said. "If I work all week, she and I might even send out for pizza from down at the convenience store one night. And if Jamie and Amanda are still bitchy with each other, we won't share with them."

"Beautiful, smart, and funny." He shook his head as he walked away.

Waylon would never know what those three words did for her ego that day. She smiled as she shifted into low gear, let out on the clutch, and eased forward with a single lurch. A young cowboy hopped up on the back and two others started throwing bales up to him as she inched the truck along.

She turned the knob on the radio, and a country music station came in loud and clear. Maybe those cowboys liked her kind of music; maybe they liked rock or rap. But she was the driver, and as such she had control of the dial.

"Hot enough for you folks?" the DJ asked when the first song ended. "Well, turn up the air conditioner and enjoy the Monday madness. We'll play ten of the most popular songs from last year in a row. At the end of the ten songs, the thirteenth caller who can tell me what month these were on the list will win two tickets to Six Flags Over Texas. First one is Carrie Underwood's 'Heartbeat.'"

"Was it February or March?" Kate asked as she kept her foot steady on the gas pedal. She'd listened to country music every day on the way to work at the oil company, on the way home, while she took her shower, and sometimes while she did extra work at night so she wouldn't be behind the next morning.

When they made trips to the barn to unload the hay, she got out and helped stack the bales, but she kept the engine running so they could hear the music. By the time Waylon sent a text calling it a day, she'd put away four of the Cokes and six waters and was still thirsty. Never before in her life, not even at the gym, had she sweated so much or felt so grimy. Lord, she'd have to have her Caddy detailed and fumigated by the weekend if she rode home in it every day smelling like hay, sweat, and dirt.

She drove the loaded truck to the barn and parked it, bailed out, and headed for the bathroom. Using brown paper towels from a dispenser, she cleaned up as best she could with cold water. By the time she returned, Waylon was helping the guys unload the last of the hay.

"Good job. The guys say that you can drive for them anytime and that they like your music," Waylon said. "Would you like to stay for supper? I've got a couple of steaks laid out to throw on the grill."

"I'm filthy dirty," she said.

"So am I." He smiled.

Her stomach growled—a steak did sound really good. "So you can cook?"

"You bet I can. It's not far to the house, so we'll walk. Do you cook?"

"I can make soup from a can and a mean ham and cheese sandwich," she answered.

"You any good at putting together a salad?"

"I can manage in a pinch." Her long legs matched his stride with no problem.

He opened the gate for her and stood to one side. The yard sported a big pecan tree on each end and a nice wide screened-in porch.

"Kick off them shoes. We don't stand much on ceremony. We're pretty laid-back out here in the hinterlands." Waylon sat down on the back porch steps, yanked off his boots, and padded barefoot over to a garden hose curled up in the yard. He turned on the water and sprayed the dust from his feet and then leaned over and wet down his dark hair. "Damn, that feels good. Come join me."

When in Rome, Kate thought as she removed her sandals and set them on the porch. The polish on her toenails was badly chipped, and her feet looked like she'd walked a mile in a sandstorm. Thank goodness she'd washed her face in the barn bathroom or it would probably look the same. But then she was on a ranch, not going to a fund-raiser.

If everyone jumped off the cliff, would you follow them? I told you to get a mani-pedi two weeks ago. I can't believe you are wearing sandals when your toenails look like that. Her mother's voice in her head faded quickly when Waylon squirted her feet and all the way to her knees with cool water.

She could practically feel the cold stare of disgust if Conrad had seen her washing up with a garden hose. He'd expected her to maintain the image that he wanted. She banished him from her thoughts and concentrated on getting as clean as possible.

"Hey, did you find anything out about that girl you asked us about. Stella?"

"Estrella," Waylon said. "We checked on her after I called and leaned on the florist again. Conrad sent flowers to her address once, but they were for her sister. Both the sister and Estrella had a rock-solid alibi, so that didn't pan out and that's more than I should be saying. Want your hair done?" He changed the subject.

"I'll pass on that, but my hands and arms won't." She held them out.

He squirted the water up to her elbows and then turned off the hose. "There are paper towels on the porch." He motioned for Kate to follow him. "Want a cold beer while we get supper going?"

"I'd love one." She dried her hands and arms with paper towels and tossed them into a trash can.

Cool air greeted them as he opened the door into the house. He went straight to the refrigerator, took out two cans of icy-cold beer, and handed one to Kate. "Bottoms up."

She pulled the ring at the top and drank deeply. "Tastes great after a long hot day."

"Nothing like it." Waylon nodded. "Have a seat and catch your breath. I made a little hash brown casserole, and it'll take five minutes to heat it in the microwave."

"I need to make the salad," she told him. "I've been sitting all day, remember?"

"Then we'll get to it." He nodded. "I got to admit that I was surprised when you showed up. I expected you to be some hoity-toity city gal who didn't know the gear shift on a hay truck from the back end of a cow."

"Or from the underside of a bull?" Kate asked.

Waylon spewed beer all over the tabletop. He grabbed a towel and wiped up the mess. "I was damn sure wrong about you, Kate." He whistled as he lit a gas grill in the middle of the stove burners.

"As a person or as a killer?" she asked.

"As a person for sure. The jury is still out on the killer issue, but my gut says that I might have been wrong there, too. Time will tell," he answered.

"Well, we got that hoity-toity business out of the way and maybe a step away from me being one of the bad guys you chase. Now, where do I find the makings for a salad?"

"Left bottom drawer in the refrigerator," he said.

When she opened the fridge, he reached around her to get the steaks, and his hand brushed her side. Sparks flew, but she attributed them to hunger, not attraction.

"How do you like your steak, Kate?" he asked. "Oh, and while we are cooking, we'll have jalapeño poppers for an appetizer."

"Medium rare. I love poppers," she answered.

The small pan of cooking oil heated quickly, and he dropped four poppers in, waited until they floated, and dipped them out. He added four more and nodded toward her. "They are best when they're hot. Help yourself."

She picked up one of the poppers and bit off the end. Just the right amount of cream cheese and bacon mixed with a spice that she didn't recognize. Was that chili powder?

"These are amazing, Waylon. It's so smart to have that grill right on the stove," she said.

"Mama insisted on it. She loved having it inside the house where she could fix the rest of the meal at the same time." He bit into a popper and smiled. "Got plenty of chili pepper in this batch, didn't I?"

"Just the right amount." She reached for a second one.

"So are you coming back tomorrow?"

"Maybe." She glanced through the archway to the dark living room. It reminded her of the little place she'd had before Conrad—cozy and comfortable.

"It's not a big house, but we didn't need anything else."

She tore lettuce into small pieces and then added a diced tomato and cheese cubes to the bowl. He leaned against the counter and watched. Strangely enough, it didn't make her the least bit uncomfortable.

"Mama never wanted a big house until sale time. Then she would have liked a big dining room so we could have the top bidders in the house for a private supper."

"Sale time?" she asked.

"We have a cattle sale in the fall. We cull the herd. There's a sale barn on the north side of the property. I'll show it to you sometime. It has stalls for the cattle we want to sell, a balcony for the buyers, and a ring for the auctioneer to bring in the merchandise. It usually starts on Friday, and Saturday night when it's over, we have a huge party for everyone in the community."

"I'd love to see it, and a cattle sale—it sounds like fun," she said. "Do folks get to attend whether they buy anything or not?" She finished making the salad and set it on the table.

He slapped the steaks on the grill. "That's right. Everyone looks forward to the Kramer party every year. We've got a couple of hands who smoke a beef, and the women all bring side dishes."

"Like a huge potluck?"

"Something like that." He circled her waist with his hands and moved her away from the bar into the kitchen nook.

She was sure that later when she examined her skin, his handprint would have left a mark from the sheer heat that radiated through her entire body.

"I'm glad they didn't build anything bigger. I like the coziness of a small house."

She heard every word, but she was more interested in the feelings his hand evoked. She hadn't felt so alive in years, maybe in her entire life.

She could see two buttery-soft brown leather recliners placed at either end of a long matching sofa facing a huge stone fireplace with bookcases on either side. The room reminded her so much of her father's study that she got weepy eyed.

"Do you have an office?"

He shook his head. "I pay a CPA to take care of all the financial stuff. Once a month I take her the receipts, and every three months I pick up the paperwork for taxes. This isn't a huge operation, Kate. Nothing like your oil company. By Texas standards, it's a hobby farm. I run about two hundred head of cattle. We grow our own hay, and I have one full-time employee who lives in a trailer here—Johnny was born on the ranch."

"And the rest of your employees?"

"Live in the area and drive to work. I hire a lot of high school and college kids for summer work and for the cattle sale in the fall, which is a small affair when you consider what some sales involve," he said.

He hit a button on the microwave, and the aroma of cheesy potatoes mixed with that of the grilled steak filled the room. Conrad had not cooked, so this scenario was a first time for her, and she liked it.

When the steaks and potatoes were on the table, Waylon bowed his head and said a quick grace. "Mama insisted on us giving thanks. It was ingrained so deeply into my being that I still do it without thinking."

"That's nice." She smiled.

Maybe she should give him the letters after all. It appeared that he genuinely wanted the case settled, and what was in those letters from Iris to Darcy could help him do that, but she wanted to see what was going to happen with that will before she made up her mind.

"I have ice cream for dessert. Would you like to take it and coffee to the living room?" he said when they'd finished their supper.

"Thanks for the offer, but it's getting late, Waylon. If we're going to have a repeat of this day, then maybe I'd better go on home. Besides, I'm too full for dessert. I'll help you get things cleaned up, though," she said.

"Not necessary. It'll all go into the dishwasher. I'll walk you out to your car. Then I can look for you tomorrow, for sure?"

"Yes, you can," she answered. "What time?"

"Ten o'clock is fine. We have to wait for the dew to dry so the hay doesn't mold when it's stacked in the barns."

He escorted her through the kitchen and the screened porch with his hand on the small of her back. It was such a simple gentlemanly gesture, but it sent her on a roller coaster of emotions, from worry that this was all staged to draw more information about Conrad out of her to plain old hot desire.

Has he talked about Conrad one time tonight? the voice in her head asked. *Has he asked you to confess to anything?*

Don't confuse me, Kate argued. *I've been conned before.*

Kate bent to pick up her sandals and tripped over her own two feet. She reached out for something, anything at all, to break her fall, but all she got was an armful of air. Instantly, Waylon's strong arms were around her, steadying her and drawing her to his chest. She looked up to thank him, but before she could say a word, he had tucked his rough knuckles under her chin. She barely had time to moisten her lips before his mouth closed on hers in a fiery kiss that glued her feet firmly to the soft carpet under them.

"Wow!" she said when the kiss ended.

"Yes," he drawled. "I've wanted to do that since I met you."

Common sense said that she should go to the car. Her heart wanted to stick around and see if the next kiss could possibly be as good as the first.

"I have to go," she whispered as she took a step back.

"You aren't angry, are you?"

She shook her head. Why would she be upset about a kiss like that?

"No, I'll see you tomorrow."

Will you pay me in kisses? I don't need the money.

He walked her the rest of the way to her vehicle and brushed a sweeter kiss across her lips after he'd opened the door. "Text me when you get home so I know you made it all right."

"Will do," she said, not trusting herself to say more.

She drove all the way home and had parked in front of the cabin before she realized that she'd left her sandals lying in his yard. She was still barefoot.

Chapter Twelve

Amanda climbed the three flights of outside steps to her apartment, opened the door, and flipped the light switch. It was only six o'clock, but dark clouds covered the sky, making her little home as dark as midnight. The doctor's visit had gone well, and she didn't have to come back for two weeks. *Time for a quick shower.*

She'd had lunch in the back room with Aunt Ellie and Wanda after the appointment. They'd talked about the baby, about the weather, but she didn't mention the argument from the night before. There was no need to upset Aunt Ellie. God was going to answer her prayers and give her the cabin.

So why did she feel like eating railroad spikes and spitting out thumbtacks? Everything was fine.

She picked up pictures scattered around the living room one by one. Conrad smiled back at her from every one of them. She gathered them up and laid them on the coffee table. With one hand on her back and using the arm of the sofa as a brace, she lowered her body to a sitting position. Then she started to study the pictures. Her eyes sparkled in every one of them, but Conrad's looked bored in all the ones after the wedding.

"I was so happy," she whispered, "and such a fool. Why did you marry me, anyway? You had Gracie, and she's a beautiful soul."

No answers fell from heaven to land in her lap, but a loud clap of thunder did startle her.

"I haven't even changed the sheets on the bed since he was here." She stood and paced in a circle through the tiny space. "You came to my bed after you'd been with other women. Not Kate and maybe not even Jamie in the past few weeks, but who knows what other hussy slept with you? I can't stay here with your pictures staring at me."

She'd planned to take a shower to get rid of that lotion the ob-gyn had used, and quite possibly to spend the night in her apartment, but the thought turned her stomach. She could throw the pictures in the trash, but the trash man didn't come until the end of the week.

Trudging back through the living room, she picked up her purse and turned off the light. When the door was locked, she headed back south to the cabin. Even with the arguments, she felt more at home there than she did in Wichita Falls.

The heavy summer rain on the road obliterated everything from her sight except a vision of Conrad in those pictures in her mind. In the next half hour's slow progress, she finally admitted to herself that there were probably no divorces. She was nothing more than the third wife of a polygamist who'd married her because she was gullible.

At Dundee the rain slowed to a drizzle, and by the time she got to Mabelle, the skies were clear, but the sun had set and it was dark. Stars twinkled around a three-quarter moon. Conrad had loved looking at the moon with her out on the minuscule balcony at her apartment. Had it all been a farce, or were some of those tender moments the real deal? Now she'd never know. She wasn't sure she even wanted the answer.

She had hoped that she could slip into the cabin and go right to her room. She didn't want to argue or to even see those other two that night. She wanted to lie in her bed, stare through the darkness at the ceiling, and beg God to help her find closure. Kate's Cadillac pulled up in front of the cabin at the same time Amanda did, canceling that idea.

Jamie was sitting in a rocker on the porch with her bare feet propped on the railing.

"This is not closure. This is another argument," Amanda muttered as she got out of her truck and started across the yard with Kate on her heels.

"Where in the hell have y'all been?" Jamie asked. "Better yet, what have you been doing, Kate? You are barefoot."

"I worked for Waylon driving a hay truck all afternoon, and then I had supper with him. Amazing steak! You should have tasted the pepper poppers. And I get paid for driving the hay truck anytime I want to work," Kate answered, her tone so happy that it shocked Amanda.

"Why would you do that kind of work?" Amanda gasped. "And where are your shoes?"

"I remembered them when I was halfway home and didn't want to go back and get them because I didn't want Waylon to know his kiss affected me like that," she answered. Words spilled out of her almost as if she were Gracie.

"Sweet angels in heaven." Jamie rolled her eyes. "You better start at the beginning."

"Before I even get a shower?" Kate grinned.

"Before you do anything. You can't be sleeping with the enemy." Amanda slapped the arm of the rocking chair. "Or maybe you are doing this to throw suspicion on us and get it off you. You sure that you didn't kill Conrad?"

"For the last time, I did not kill him or have him murdered, either one. I've never had a sister, but I imagine this is the way siblings argue!" Kate grinned.

"We are not sisters in any sense of the word," Amanda said coldly. *God Almighty!* There was no stretch of the definition that would ever make her own kinship with either of those two women. What had Kate been drinking or smoking? Or maybe she'd done a lot more than just kiss Waylon.

"That's what Gracie said the first day we were here. She said we were like *Sister Wives* on television," Kate said.

"Well, I don't share well with others, and I would never have married Conrad if I'd known he already had two wives," Amanda said. "I think sister wives have a screw loose in their heads."

Jamie slapped a hand on her forehead. "Gracie's babysitter watched that!"

"You need to be more careful about who you leave her with," Amanda said.

Jamie shook a finger at her. "Don't tell me how to raise my kid."

"Don't you two get your underbritches in a wad. You are definitely not my sisters in any sense of the word, and I'm damn sure glad—even if we are fighting like siblings. Here's what happened." Kate started at the beginning and told the tale with every detail, including how Waylon's kiss made her feel. "So what should I do? Give up my job because I liked his kiss?"

Jamie pulled her dark hair up into a ponytail and secured it with a rubber band she took from the pocket of her denim shorts. "I expect that real sisters would act like we do sometimes."

"But real sisters would love each other sometimes, too," Amanda said. "And I don't intend to ever love either one of you. However, if a parent died with no will and only one piece of property, they might all get a little greedy. As for you and your summer job, Kate, go for it."

"I disagree. He's just softening you up for information," Jamie said.

"No, he is not," Amanda argued. "He needs help on the ranch."

Jamie held up a hand. "We'll have to agree to disagree. Now, on to another subject. I got offered a job today, too."

Well, crap! Amanda thought. *That means she'll probably stay here.*

Kate sat up straighter. "Go on."

"The principal and Victor want me to apply for a position that's open, but I only have a week or two to think about it." Jamie paused. "I could sell my house, and I wouldn't have that mortgage hanging over my head. I could rent something here a lot cheaper, or maybe even live in the cabin until the probate court decides what's happening to it."

"Which, like Kate said, could take months, maybe years." Amanda sat down in a rocking chair and frowned. Did living in the cabin mean the same as possession being ninety percent of the law?

Kate nodded and headed inside. "The cabin is better off if it's occupied. What about Gracie? You should ask her what she thinks."

Jamie and Amanda followed her. Amanda opened the cookie jar in the middle of the table and took out a fistful. Jamie went to the refrigerator and brought out a pitcher of freshly squeezed lemonade.

"Of course I'll talk to her before I make a decision. But I know what she'll say. She's always, always loved this place, and she'll float on clouds if she thinks we can stay here forever," Jamie said.

"Well, she's definitely like a breath of spring, spreading laughter and smiles everywhere." Kate filled three glasses with ice cubes and set them on the table. "That lemonade looks wonderful. I haven't had the real thing in years."

"Looks good to me, too," Amanda said. "About last night and all this arguing?"

Kate poured three glasses full of lemonade. "No one can live in the same house twenty-four hours a day, seven days a week and not disagree. It's not possible. Doesn't matter if it's a married couple, a parent-sibling situation, or an insane one like we have. We are only here for the summer. At the end of it, we'll split and go our separate ways. You two might stay in touch since you'll be raising half siblings, but I'll have no connection with you."

"Not even for a Christmas card?" Jamie asked.

"Well, maybe that much, and maybe you'll invite me for Gracie's birthdays or graduation," Kate said.

Jamie threw up a hand. "Don't have her growing up so fast. She's the only baby I ever get. I want to savor every moment."

"You should," Kate said.

"And my baby? Are you coming to his birthday parties and graduation?" Amanda asked.

"If you invite me," Kate answered.

"You will be invited." Amanda sipped at her lemonade. "This is a big jump from what we are talking about, but I went to my apartment and I looked at Conrad's pictures. It was in his eyes."

"What?" Jamie asked.

"I thought it was a twinkle, but when I really studied him, it was something else, like you see on those big game hunters on television when they bag a tiger or a huge white-tailed deer. I can't describe it."

"How did it make you feel?" Kate asked.

"Used," Amanda said without hesitation. "Do you feel Conrad in this house? I don't. I came here hoping to feel him, but I never have. At first all I had was anger at y'all and then at him." She sighed. "This is going to sound corny, but I think Iris is smiling that we are here and we're finding out about him."

Kate would probably have something to say about that, but Amanda didn't care. She wasn't going to let either of them intimidate her.

"I believe she is," Jamie said.

Amanda glanced at her and then back at Kate, expecting some kind of superintelligent remark about the dead being dead—forever, amen.

Kate shrugged. "I agree, Amanda. I have no idea about what happens to good folks in eternity, but it would be nice if Iris and Darcy could see that things didn't go Conrad's way."

Amanda could hardly believe her ears. "Well, thank you for that."

"It's just my opinion." Kate yawned.

☙

Kate took a long shower and was on her way to her bedroom when she noticed that someone had left the kitchen light on, so she went to turn it off. Jamie was sitting at the table with a cup of hot tea in front of her.

"Still pondering the idea of a drastic move?" Kate asked. "Did you talk to your grandmother about it?"

"Yes, I did, and she told me to think about me and Gracie before I leap. Sometimes I turn a blind eye to common sense and don't check to see if I'm leaping into fire or water," Jamie answered.

"You have to do what your heart tells you," Kate said. "Things happen in our lives to turn us around. I've never believed in fate or karma or any of that stuff, but I do believe in our choices directing our future."

Amanda had gone into the bathroom right behind Kate and now joined them with a big white towel wrapped around her head and a terry robe belted above her pregnant tummy. "And that means?"

"Think back to the most horrible moments in your life and the happiest ones. Didn't they both have a bearing on who you are right now?" Kate asked.

Jamie pushed the cup of tea back. "I saw a lawyer right after Christmas last year. He told me how much it would take for me to get a divorce—I was saving my money."

"What has that got to with what Kate said?" Amanda asked.

"Just going there made me happy, even though I was terrified. It gave me back some of my power. I understand what she is saying," Jamie answered.

"When were you going to divorce him?" Amanda asked.

"I'm not sure I would have gone through with it. Gracie loved her dad, and even having a part-time father was more than I had as a kid."

"Sometimes anything isn't a bit better than nothing," Kate said.

"Hindsight." Jamie chuckled.

"My two cents—you should apply for the job," Kate said. "If they hire you, then it was meant to be. If they don't, you won't have regrets later. And you need to get in touch with Social Security. I think Gracie is entitled to some benefits. You could put it in a trust fund for her college if you are too proud to use the money to make her life easier."

"I never even thought of that," Jamie said. "And I'm not crazy. Moving here would be an adjustment, going from the big city to Bootleg, from being a team of teachers for any given grade to being the single third-grade teacher in the whole elementary school."

"It'll be a tough decision, but only you can make it," Kate agreed.

Jamie smiled. "It would be great if we were little kids and our parents still made our decisions, right, Kate?"

"Hell, no!" Amanda yelped. "I wouldn't want my mother to make a single decision for me."

"For me, this is only a summer thing, not a lifetime change. At the end of my vacation time, I'll put on my high heels and go back to work," Kate said. "And Amanda's right. I don't want my mother making decisions for me, either."

"What do your shoes have to do with anything?" Jamie asked.

Kate pointed to her toes. "Think about it."

"Symbolism," Amanda said with a big grin. "Even if we fight and even if we hate the one who gets the cabin, maybe we will see this as being the summer we shed our fears as well as our shoes?"

Kate yawned again. "And on that philosophical note, this tired woman is going to bed."

Chapter Thirteen

When Amanda was bored she baked—cookies and yeast breads were her two specialties. That Wednesday morning she was almost to the point of being so tired of doing nothing that she was ready to go back to Wichita Falls and go to work again. She opened the pantry doors to find all the makings for chocolate chip cookies, peanut butter cookies, and snickerdoodles. In thirty minutes the house smelled like the cinnamon and sugar topping on snickerdoodles and she was stirring up the dough for a double batch of peanut butter.

At noon when Jamie and Gracie got home, the little girl did a happy jig in the middle of the floor when she saw several containers filled with various kinds of cookies. She wrapped her little arms around Amanda's big belly. "I really do love you. I like made cookies better than them you get at the store."

"Homemade," Jamie whispered.

"So do I." Amanda hugged her back. "After you have lunch, we'll have some with milk for dessert."

"Yay." Gracie clapped her hands.

"Jamie, I would be glad to babysit her some mornings. That way you wouldn't have to wake her so early and I'd have some company," Amanda offered.

"Man, you must be lonely." Jamie laughed.

"Since I was thirteen, I've had a job of some kind. I'm not used to time on my hands," Amanda said.

"Please, Mama! Amanda could teach me how to make made cookies." Gracie wiggled in anticipation.

"We'll talk about it later," Jamie answered. "Right now, we're going to have sandwiches and tomato soup. But thank you for the offer, Amanda."

"And then we'll eat cookies." Gracie pumped her fist in the air.

"I promise"—Amanda grinned—"that I won't let her watch a single episode of *Sister Wives*."

⁂

By midafternoon, dark clouds had begun to gather in the southwest. The weatherman had predicted rain by four, and it looked like he might be right on the nose. Waylon shielded his eyes with his hand and hoped his crew could get what hay was down and baled into the barns before the storm hit. The wind picked up right after three, when Kate drove her last truckload into the barn. The boys unloaded and stacked it while she went to the bathroom.

"Hey, looks like we might have an early supper tonight," Waylon yelled over the sounds of the first big drops hitting the tin roof.

"I'm going to drive that truck right there as close to my car as I can get it and I'm going home tonight," she said.

"What'd I do to make you mad?" Waylon teased.

"Not one thing, but I haven't seen Gracie since Sunday. She leaves before I get up and she's in bed when I get home. I miss her," Kate answered.

"And her mother and the other wife?"

"They could leave and never come back. But Gracie is a different matter. I'd give Jamie a million dollars for her if she'd sell her to me."

Waylon made a big show of sticking his fingers in his ears. "I can't hear this. That's human trafficking and against the law."

Of all the things that Waylon admired about Kate, her compassion topped the list. Well, maybe right after the way she felt in his arms when he kissed her. He'd thought that kind of emotion was only for those crazy love stories that women read.

"Then don't hear it," she said as she crawled back into the truck when it was unloaded.

He quickly rounded the front end and got into the passenger's seat. "I'll ride back to the house with you. The wind coming off the rain could have some hail behind it. I don't want to have to run between the hailstones."

"What happens tomorrow?" she asked.

"With us? With the investigation? With what?"

"The hay fields? There is no us, and you can't discuss the investigation."

"This is the second cutting. We'll wait a few weeks and hope for a third one. You ever driven a tractor?" Waylon asked. "Or walked a fence line?"

"No, but I can learn," she answered.

"Then if it's not raining in the morning, show up about eight o'clock and we'll figure out another job for you," he said.

"I'll be here." She parked the truck next to her car.

Waylon's gaze caught hers across the seat. "I like working with you."

"I like working at something that doesn't require me to think about numbers of barrels, the price of crude, and whether to have enough faith in my geologists to drill in virgin territory." She smiled.

"Wait right there." Waylon jumped out of his side, raced around the truck, opened her door, and scooped her up like a bride. He liked the way she felt in his arms, with her head next to his chest and giggles bubbling up from her body at the bouncing as he ran to the driver's door and settled her into the seat.

"Wouldn't want you to get your feet all muddy," he said.

"You could have laid your coat across the puddles," she teased.

"Ain't wearin' one." He kissed her on the forehead. "Enjoy your evening with Gracie."

"You know I will," Kate said.

Waylon slammed the door and waved until he couldn't see the taillights of her car anymore. Then he two-stepped with an imaginary Kate all the way to the house, rain pouring down on him the whole time.

 relax

Kate drove slowly so she could savor what had just happened. She hadn't had so much fun since—she couldn't remember when she'd been so carefree or said what she thought. She liked working at the ranch and flirting with Waylon. She loved the way his kisses sent tingles all the way to her toes and how he was so impulsive. Who else would pick her up and run through mud puddles with her? She was still living in that aura when she got to the cabin and slung open the door.

Gracie wrapped her arms around Kate and hugged tightly. "You're home! I missed you. Amanda made cookies and they are so good. Do you want one?"

"You know I do, but I could sure use a big juicy hamburger first. Let's all go to the Dairy Queen for supper. My treat."

The little girl backed off a step and looked up into Kate's eyes. "I love you, Kate. I've been wanting a hamburger all day long."

Kate wasn't sure at that very second whether Waylon's attention or Gracie's meant more to her. That sweetheart of a child could sure put a smile on a person's face.

"I thought you loved *me* and wanted cookies," Amanda said.

"I got enough love for everyone and I can want hamburgers and cookies," Gracie said.

"Well, then, if you'll give me fifteen minutes to get cleaned up and it's all right with your mama, we'll go to Seymour for burgers." Kate walked on air the whole way to the bathroom.

"Can we take Mama and Amanda with us?" Gracie asked.

"Of course," Kate answered.

"I'm in," Amanda said quickly.

"You don't have to ask me twice," Jamie said.

The rain was still coming on strong when they left Bootleg, but by the time they reached the Dairy Queen in Seymour, it had slacked off to a drizzle. Gracie was the first out of the car and ran right through puddles to the door, which she held open for the women.

"I miss that," Amanda said as gingerly made her way to the café.

"What? Running through puddles?" Kate asked.

"Skipping. Giggling. Puddles. All of it. I want that for my baby when he gets here. But right now I'm so hungry for a double-meat bacon burger and a double order of fries that I'll just think about that."

"Amen!" Jamie said.

Gracie went ahead of them to the order counter, stared up at the menu, and pointed at the pictures. Amanda was right behind her, so she answered Gracie's questions about hamburgers versus tacos or chicken strips.

"Gracie!" Lisa yelled from across the store.

"Lisa! Look, Mama, Lisa is here. Can we sit together?"

"She's with her dad, and this is Kate's party," Jamie said.

"Will you ask if she can sit with us, Kate?" Gracie's big brown eyes begged.

"Sure, I will. Give me that burger buster basket, a medium drink, and a chocolate malt," she ordered before she steered Gracie toward Paul and his daughter.

Paul pushed back his chair and stood up. "Hey, you're Kate, aren't you?"

"Yes, I am. We weren't formally introduced when you came to get the bed." She held out her hand.

He shook it firmly and then let it go. Nothing in his touch made her blush like Jamie did when he was close by.

"Gracie wants to know if Lisa can sit with us. We'll be at that table right there." Kate pointed to a nearby one.

"No problem. As soon as her food arrives I'll bring it right over."

"Thank you. Want to go with me now, Lisa?" Kate asked.

"Is it all right, Daddy?" Lisa asked.

"Sure, sweetheart. I'll wait for you right here. We're in no big rush." Paul smiled.

Lisa put her hand in Kate's, and her short little legs did double time to keep up with Kate's long strides.

"Lisa, who are your friends?" the lady behind the counter asked.

"This is Gracie and that is her mama." Lisa pointed to Jamie. "And the tall one is Kate and the fat one is Amanda."

"I'm sorry." Jamie blushed.

"No need. She's just saying out loud what I feel like." Amanda waved off the apology. "Have you decided what you want, Gracie?"

"What did you get?" Gracie asked Lisa.

"A hamburger and fries and the coupon for a free ice cream cone," Lisa answered.

"We get ice cream, too?" Gracie's brown eyes popped wide open.

"Yes, you do. It's on the side of your kid's meal bag. Is that what you want, Miz Gracie?" the lady asked.

"Yes, ma'am. Mama, I want to come here every payday if we get free ice cream," Gracie said.

"Sounds like a plan to me." Jamie smiled. "I'll have a cheeseburger basket with a side of onion rings and a large drink."

"And for you?" the woman asked Amanda.

"The left side of the menu to start with, and then we'll go from there," she answered. "I'll have the double-meat bacon burger, double fries, a large drink, and a large chocolate malt with double malt and no whipped cream."

"Y'all sit anywhere you want and I'll bring your food out soon as it's ready." She set five cups on the counter. "Help yourself to the soda fountain, and you girls don't forget your ice cream."

"Never." Lisa grinned. "Miz Jamie, can me and Gracie sit in a booth all by ourselves?"

"As long as your dad and I can see you," Jamie agreed. "What do you girls want to drink?"

"Orange," Lisa said.

"Me, too," Gracie chimed in.

Kate remembered the days when orange or grape were her choice of soda. That was when her father took her for a burger on Sunday evenings—not every week, but when he did, it was a big treat.

"Can we please take that table over there rather than a booth?" Amanda picked up her cup and headed for the soda fountain. "Booths don't offer much wiggle room."

"I remember those days very well," Jamie said. "I felt like an elephant."

"Was Conrad there with you?" Amanda filled her cup and headed for the nearest table. "This one okay with y'all?"

"Fine with me," Kate answered, more than a little jealous that they'd both have a child, even if it was by Conrad.

Jamie set her cup to the side and carried drinks to the little girls. Then she went back and took care of her own drink and sat down at the table with Kate and Amanda. "To answer your question, out of the nine months, I saw him eight weeks. He just happened to be home on the night she was born and was there the next day when we took her home. But on the following day, he left for a week. Of course, he was sad, but he had to work and his import-export business was just getting off the ground in those days," Jamie said sarcastically.

"So you were basically a single mom, too," Amanda said.

"Oh, yeah! Kate, just how long was he in this business, anyway?" Jamie asked.

"I'd guess about eight years, so he might have even told the truth when he said the business was just getting off the ground. Before that, he sold cars, put in his own little used car lot for a while, and did a couple of other things. By then I didn't care and refused to finance his schemes." The only thing that she had cared about then and right up to that very moment was the fact that her child had not lived. And that evening, watching those two little girls whisper and giggle, made the ache in her heart even more painful.

The lady took the little girls' food to them first. Then she went back to the kitchen and returned with a tray laden with their food. "Enjoy! Tonight the peanut parfait sundae is on sale for half price."

"Thank you." Kate smiled.

"And if y'all need anything, just holler."

"So." Amanda picked up her burger and folded the paper back. "What is happening tomorrow? Does this weather make a difference in either of your jobs?"

"Not mine," Jamie said. "If you were serious about watching Gracie, I'm going to take you up on it one day a week just to give her a break."

"And you?" Amanda glanced at Kate.

"I'm going to the Double Back Ranch to learn how to drive a tractor or walk a fence line if it's not raining," Kate answered. "I've never worked outside before, and I kind of like it."

"So if you wind up with the cabin, maybe Waylon will hire you every summer," Jamie said.

This would be a good time to tell them about the letters, the voice in her head said. *Not when things are going so smooth. It's going to cause another argument, and I want this evening to be nice—for Gracie. She doesn't need to ride home in a tense car with three angry women.*

"That's still being checked on," Kate said quickly. "How about you, Amanda? You got any desire to make a move to Bootleg?"

"Well, I called the bank here in town and talked to the president. He says there could possibly be an opening about Thanksgiving. One of his tellers is retiring. Baby is due the first of September, six weeks to recover after that, so it would work out fairly well."

"What about your store?" Jamie asked.

"Wanda would buy out my half in a heartbeat. I can put in my application and still have lots of time to think about it," Amanda said without hesitation.

"I can't believe we're talking about moving here. Do you realize that Conrad's been gone only a couple of weeks?" Jamie squirted ketchup from a dispenser onto her fries. "Kate, you look as if you are seeing angels floating down from heaven. What on earth is out that window that's mesmerizing you?"

"I'm not looking out the window. I was watching Gracie and Lisa. They are adorable. And about Conrad—maybe he's only been dead two weeks by the clock, but if we're all honest, he's been dead a lot longer than that, right?" Kate said.

"Would you ever think of leaving your big, fancy job and moving to a place like Bootleg?" Amanda asked.

"I'd never leave my business behind, but if I had a daughter like you have, I might reconsider everything."

"Never say never," Jamie quipped.

Chapter Fourteen

Amanda was so antsy that she decided to bake again all morning on Thursday. She rationalized making more by saying that she would take two large platters of cookies to the church for the potluck. Gracie was delighted to sit at the table and help stir, mix, and sample the broken ones as they came out of the oven.

"I like cookin'," Gracie said. "Because I get to eat the mistakes."

"I like it because it helps keep my hands busy. We'll have to think of something for lunch for your mama, though, other than cookies."

"Why?" Gracie giggled.

"How about toasted cheese sandwiches and some noodle soup?"

"Yes!" Gracie pumped her fist in the air. "And cookies and milk for dessert like yesterday."

"You got it, kiddo! Well, I'll be . . . danged." Amanda caught the cussword before it left her mouth.

"What? Another broken one?" Gracie asked.

"No, I think I'm nesting. I cleaned my room this morning and put away all the little boy things that Aunt Ellie brought when she delivered the bed and bassinet."

"Amanda, why is it a bad thing that my daddy married all of you?"

She fumbled for an answer. "Because it's against the law."

"You know what my Mama Rita says? She says that I have to obey her when she tells me something, but what my mama says is the law. Is it like that?"

"A whole lot." Amanda put the last of the cookies in the oven and checked the clock. It was time to open two cans of soup and get things ready for dinner.

"Then if my mama had told my daddy not to marry you, he wouldn't have done it?" Gracie asked.

"This is a different kind of law."

Gracie frowned. "Like the detective that likes Kate a lot. Mama says he's the law. If he'd told my daddy not to marry you and Kate, then he wouldn't, right?"

"I don't know about that, but what makes you think that Waylon likes Kate?" Amanda asked.

"I'm a little kid, but I'm not stupid." Gracie folded her arms over her chest and huffed. "I can see the way he looks at her. Like Mama looks at chocolate."

That was the straw that broke the proverbial camel's back. Amanda burst out laughing, and Gracie joined right in.

"Why is that funny?" Gracie asked when they'd both gotten control.

Amanda hugged the child. "I hope my baby grows up to be as smart as you."

"Mama says it's my half brother. What's the other half?"

"Half brother means you have the same daddy but not the same mama," Amanda explained.

"Does that mean I'm a big sister for real?"

Amanda sure wished that Jamie was there to have this conversation. "It does mean that. Do you want to be a big sister even though you don't have the same mama as my baby?"

"Heck, yeah, I do." Gracie grinned with a chocolate chip stuck to her teeth. "I don't care who the mama or the daddy is as long as it can be my brother."

"Hello, what's this about a brother?" Jamie asked as she made her way into the house.

"Amanda's baby will have my daddy, but Amanda will be the mama. And we've got cookies, Mama. Lots and lots of cookies!" Gracie ran to give Jamie a hug.

Jamie grinned. "The simplicity of innocence."

"We are making noodle soup for dinner, Mama. Tell me about your day," Gracie said.

Jamie picked up a still-warm cookie. "I want to hear about your day and then I'll tell you about mine."

"I wish Kate was here to tell us about hers. I miss her when she's gone all day." Gracie sighed.

❧

Driving a tractor, even with the radio blaring loudly, left a lot of time for thinking, and that's what Kate had been doing all morning. The fact that she'd been selfish with the knowledge in Iris's letters and will kept circling back to haunt her even when other things took top priority.

She liked this mindless work of plowing a field. She liked being outside in the sunshine and wearing sandals or going barefoot. But what she liked most of all was the freedom in her soul when she smelled the fresh-plowed dirt or looked at a barn full of hay that she'd helped harvest.

Kenny Chesney was belting out "She Thinks My Tractor's Sexy" when she made the final loop around the field.

"Oh, yes, I do." She grinned. "And my mother would have me committed for saying that."

She picked up her phone from the console beside her and poked in the speed-dial number for the lawyer as she drove the tractor back to the barn. They'd located Darcy's will only to learn she'd left all her earthly possessions to her mother's church—Hattie's church. Now it was a matter of getting things legalized and seeing what the church wanted to do with the cabin and the money they'd found in the bank box.

She turned off the engine and slung open the door. It was time—past time, really—to let everyone know about the will and the letters.

Today!

That would take her one step closer to getting all this closed and out of her mind. Waylon reached up, put his arms on her waist, and brought her to the ground like she weighed no more than a bed pillow. "Ready to get some lunch?"

"The way I've been eating, I'll have to live at the gym when I get home." Her heart fluttered around like a butterfly in her chest. Yes, his touch had that effect on her, but she had to tell him about the will and the letters, and it had to be today, and that was as much to do with the jitters as his hands on her waist. The past few days she'd started to feel guilty for not telling him or the other two. Right now she just wanted it out in the open, even if it caused a fight with Waylon or with Amanda and Jamie.

He laced his fingers with hers, and they started toward the house. "Darlin', you will always be beautiful in my eyes."

"That's sweet of you to say." She took a deep breath and said, "I've been holding back on you. I have some information that could help."

He put a finger on her lips. "If you held something back, then I believe you had a reason. What is it and why are you going to tell me now?"

"I found letters that Iris wrote to her daughter, Darcy. There is a will—she left everything to Darcy, and in Darcy's will, she left everything to her mother's church," Kate said. "That means it could be tied up for a while if either Jamie or Amanda contest it, I guess."

"Let's go in and have some chili. I put a pot on this morning before we got started, and it should be about simmered down real good. You can tell me everything over lunch," he said. "But I don't know what a will has to do with his murder or a bunch of old letters, either one. Did you read them?"

"Of course. The will was sealed, so I didn't open it, but the rest of them were in unsealed envelopes. Can I be arrested for that?" She opened the cabinet doors and took out two bowls while he stirred the chili and then put silverware on the table.

"I wouldn't think so." He grinned. "They didn't go through the US mail. Besides, if Iris wrote them, she left them for someone to find, and since Darcy is dead . . ." He dipped up the chili.

She started talking, too fast, but she had to get the load off her chest. "The first letter told Darcy about Iris's last will, so I knew what was in it. She left everything to her daughter and nothing to Conrad. She had hired a private investigator to look into him after they were married, but she was so ashamed of herself. Besides, he was threatening her in some way if she didn't give him control of her money and assets. She was not his first wife, Waylon. He was married twice under a different name—Swanson. One of those women died in a suspicious car wreck. The other one divorced him, and I'd bet dollars to cow chips that he got a lot of money at that time," Kate said.

"You sure do remember details well."

"You can see the letters if you want to cross-check my information," she said.

"That would be good, but go on." He set the bowls on the table.

"Okay, then," she went on. "His birth certificate name is Cain Smith and he was born in New Orleans, Louisiana. Mother is Linda Smith. Father unknown. He was raised in foster homes because his mother was or maybe still is an alcoholic. The detective could not find the mother."

"This is just the lead I needed." He grinned. "I can trace back now and maybe figure out what happened."

"Slow down," she said. "Where does that leave us?"

"Us?" He looked up with questions in his eyes.

For God's sake, did he think that, just because they'd exchanged a few kisses and she was finally telling him what she'd known for days, they were in anything other than a working relationship? Or maybe a friendly one if she stretched out the matter?

"Us as in me and Jamie and Amanda? Were we really married to him? Is my marriage even legal? What happens to the cabin now or his van and his bank account? I have no idea what he had, but it's sure not mine."

She'd unloaded the burden, and now she wanted answers—right now!

"I'd say you'll have to get in touch with your lawyers on that one, but I suppose that all his belongings will probably be divided among his children—depending on the story with Darcy. Do you know what's involved in his assets?"

Kate shook her head. "I'm not sure. His accountant took care of his business, both personal and professional. I despise his accountant. She's probably as crooked as Conrad was. You might start there. When I called him about the utilities on the cabin, he said that since Conrad wasn't there to authorize the payments, no more would be made. They were probably in cahoots in all kinds of scams."

"And that is another good lead. I'm going to Dallas after we get done eating. Want to go with me?" he asked as he picked up his phone. "Give me a minute here to call Johnny."

The back door opened before he finished hitting a speed-dial number. "Hey, Waylon," a man called out.

"Come on in, Johnny. I was about to call you."

A tall, well-built guy with close-cut hair and a square jaw came into the kitchen. "Is that chili?"

"Help yourself. Meet Kate, our new hired hand. This is Johnny, my right-hand man." Waylon made introductions and then turned back to Johnny. "I'm going to Dallas this afternoon. Hopefully, I'll be home tomorrow."

"Okay." Johnny filled a bowl with chili and carried it to the table. "It's nice to meet you, Kate. You'd be one of those women that Conrad married, right?"

"Yes, I am, and it's nice to meet you, Johnny," she said.

Would that always be the way she'd be seen in the community? At least in a city the size of Fort Worth, very few people knew her or that a robbery had gone bad in Dallas.

"My pleasure," Johnny said with a smile. "Guess what, Waylon? We've got a set of twin calves. Born too late for this fall's sale, but in my opinion they'll be good breeders. Both bulls, and they've got some fine lines. That's what I came to the house to tell you, though I do love a good bowl of chili," Johnny said.

Johnny's biceps bulged the seams of his knit shirt, and his dark hair had a ring where his cowboy hat had set all morning. That he'd been in the military was evident by his body language. The way his eyes didn't miss a thing told Kate that he might have even been in the Special Forces.

"So what branch were you in?" she asked him.

"What?" Johnny brow furrowed. "Oh, you mean the military, not the creek at the back of the ranch. Navy SEALs."

"Overseas duty?" she asked.

"Spent some time in Kuwait. Texas is a paradise compared to that. Good chili, Waylon. I'll keep an eye on the calves until you get home and then you can see them for yourself." Johnny didn't talk much more as he set about eating. When he finished, he carried his bowl to the sink, rinsed it, and put it in the dishwasher. "Don't worry about a thing. I'll keep it runnin' smooth until you get back home and pin a couple of medals on those two who killed that bastard. I remember Iris and how she always made special treats for us at Bible school."

Waylon chuckled. "I sure would like to get this settled."

Not as much as I would, Kate thought as she finished the chili.

"Get it done and get back here for good." Johnny waved as he left by the back door.

"You sure you don't want to go with me?" Waylon turned back to Kate.

"No, I do not. If I get that close to home, Mother might pull me right back into the business, and I really want to get all this finished before I go back," she answered. "I'm just sorry that Darcy died not knowing that her mother had figured out what a horrible mistake she had made. She talked about a bank deposit box, too. A key was in one of the letters. If that's in your purview, go by my office and Mother will give it to you."

"Whatever is in there will be Darcy's, and since she is dead, it will go to whomever she listed as the beneficiary. But I would imagine you and those other two are free to live in the cabin until it's all settled," he answered.

"I'm going to tell Amanda and Jamie about this. They have a right to know," she said.

"You should. Please tell them to keep it under their hats. I want to put my best folks on researching every alias that he used. He did stay pretty true to what con men usually do." Waylon got to his feet. "Funny how things work out, isn't it?"

"His choices brought him to a fatal end for sure. But what did you mean by staying true?"

"They nearly always use the same initials. Would you send me an e-mail this afternoon with all that information? That way I'll have it when I get to the precinct and we might be able to get something accomplished today."

"I will as soon as I get to the cabin," she said. "How will this help you find his killer?"

"If we know the past and the way he lived then, it helps us figure out what was going on just before he died."

"I'll bet that it has to do with another wife or at least another woman," she said. "That was his game. Find a woman. Charm her. Fleece her. And move on."

Waylon laid his hand on hers. "You are the exception."

"How's that?"

"He didn't fleece you."

"That was the only way to hold on to a little bit of my dignity," she whispered.

Chapter Fifteen

Kate got inside her Caddy, started the engine, turned up the air-conditioning, and hit the button to roll down the window. "If you clear my name, I'll let you drive my vintage cars as a reward," she teased.

"Darlin', that could be considered a bribe," Waylon said.

"Oh, really? Are you tempted?" She wished the same cool air that pushed the heat out the window could do the same for her body. But as long as Waylon braced a forearm on the window and leaned down so that their faces were only inches apart, the AC wasn't going to cool anything down but the car.

"We could ride down there together and it wouldn't seem like such a long trip," he said.

On one hand she wished she could change her mind. But common sense said she needed breathing space away from him. "I really need to go home. I promised to bring some things from the convenience store, and they'll be waiting for them. Call me when you get back."

"I'll be home on Sunday at the latest. If I make it in Saturday night, will you go to dinner with me on Sunday?"

Kate laid a hand on his arm. "We have a potluck, remember?"

"But I want to take you to Wichita Falls to my favorite burger shop. Once you eat there, you won't want to get too far away from this area. Who knows? Someday you'll leave the big city behind like I'm doing." He straightened up and headed toward the house as he waved over his shoulder.

"Some things are simply impossible," she whispered as she rolled up the window and headed back toward Bootleg.

Never work. Too much change. Those words played through her mind as she drove home.

Home. Was it really where the heart was? If so, where was her heart?

Your heart should be focused on our business. And what makes you think that cop can clear your name? All that information you gave him might be a load of crap. The voice in her head was definitely her mother's. *I told you not to marry Conrad. Why can't you ever pay attention to me? Don't get involved with that man. You have no sense when it comes to men.*

She shook her head so hard her ponytail whipped around and slapped her in the face. "Heavens, Mother! You can't even refrain from saying you told me so in my thoughts."

And what do you expect to accomplish by letting that cop drive your cars? Do you think that will make him fall in love with you? I've told you over and over to focus on your job and the company.

"Hush," she said loudly and turned on the radio to the country music station that she liked.

She missed the turn to go into town for beer and soda and was trying to keep her mother out of her mind when she parked in front of the cabin. She slapped the steering wheel with both palms and turned around to go back to the store.

The heart is a fickle thing. It trusted Conrad. I cannot let it guide my decisions, she thought as she pushed open the glass door to the store. She picked up the beer and diet soda pop and added a couple of bags of chips.

"Anything else?" the lady behind the counter asked.

Your heart did not trust Conrad. If you'll remember, you did have doubts even on your wedding day, but there'd already been the big splash of a shower and the wedding plans. Teresa was back in full force.

"Are you all right?" the lady asked.

Kate came back to reality with a jerk. "I'm so sorry. I was off in la-la land."

"Happens to all of us. Anything else?"

"Yes, please add half a dozen burritos and maybe a dozen cheese sticks from the deli." Kate pulled out her credit card.

She toted her bags out to the car and put them in the backseat, got inside, and in a few minutes realized she was on her way back to the ranch instead of the cabin. She braked hard, leaving a trail of dust behind her from the dirt road.

"Get your head on straight, Kate!" Her voice bounced around in the car like marbles in a tin can, echoing from every surface to remind her that she should think about what she was doing.

Amanda waved from the front door when she finally pulled up in front of the cabin for the second time that evening. "Hey, we're all fishing from the dock. We're having a picnic supper down there in a little while. Come join us. Did you bring beer and soda pop?"

"Yes, I did. I'll just haul it all down there instead of unloading in the house," Kate said.

"Need some help? I came up to go to the bathroom. Whoever built this place should have put a toilet in the boat shed."

"Got a couple of bags of chips and burritos that you can carry. I'll take the heavy stuff," Kate answered. "I probably should wash up."

"You look like hell, but so do the rest of us." Amanda smiled. "We'll all smell like fish before dark anyway."

"Kate, come and see the fishes that I caught. One is big enough to eat for dinner tomorrow," Gracie hollered as Amanda and Kate made their way down the steps to the boat dock.

Just seeing her put a smile on Kate's face. "You are quite a fisherman, Miss Gracie!"

"And I got four," Hattie called. "We'll have enough for a fish fry before the sun sets."

"Hey, Hattie and Victor. We haven't seen you two in a while." Kate set her bags beside the picnic basket over toward one side and sat down in the only empty chair left.

"Been busy with the festival planning board," Victor said.

"We hit a snag and had to make arrangements for a different kind of carnival, so we've both been up to our eyeballs in finding another one. Long as we have a Ferris wheel, I'm happy." Hattie watched the red-and-white fishing bobble dance out there in the water. "I hear you've taken on a job with Waylon. How's that going?"

"I drove a hay wagon on Tuesday, took Wednesday off because of the rain, and then went in today. It's quite a change from what I'm used to doing," Kate answered. "Waylon has police things to do tomorrow in Dallas instead."

"Here." Victor handed her a fishing rod and reel. "I baited the hook for you. Reel it in easy if your cork goes under."

Kate had never been fishing in her entire life, but she held the rod and watched the red-and-white ball at the end of the line. "How many fish would it take for us to have a fish fry?"

"Ten if they are good size," Hattie answered. "When we get enough, I'll make hush puppies and baked beans. Victor, you can bring your famous coleslaw."

"Hattie makes the best fried catfish in the whole universe," Victor said. "I'd marry her just to get the recipe."

"You old coot." Hattie giggled. "No woman in her right mind would marry you. I don't know how Lorraine put up with you all those years."

"Love, darlin'." His grin erased a few of the wrinkles lining his face. "She loved me, and truth be told, I'd never remarry, not even for your damned old recipe."

"Then don't tease me about it. I had my heart set on a big white dress and wedding cake." Hattie sighed.

"You are full of horse crap." Victor chuckled and stared straight at Kate. "But wedding cake does sound good. We haven't had a wedding in Bootleg in years."

"Get thee behind me, Satan!" Kate made the sign of the cross over her chest. "I'm only here until my vacation time runs out, then I've got a company to run."

"Well, rats!" Victor huffed. "I just knew from the way Waylon was stealing them long looks at you in church that something might be going on."

"It's only been two weeks since Conrad died," Amanda said.

"Oh, honey, that scoundrel died years ago for Kate. Now *you* might need to wear widow's weeds a year, but not her," Hattie said. "Look, I've got another fish, and this is a big one. Help me bring him in, Victor. My arthritis has been acting up all day."

"Well, so has mine, woman, and I've got a bite on my line. You are on your own," Victor said.

Jamie handed her rod and reel off to Amanda and hurried over to Hattie's side. She deftly slid the grip from the older woman's hands and worked the reel until she had a nice three-pound catfish lying on the dock. "Now that's going to taste really good."

"Would it be a winner in the contest?" Gracie asked.

"It could be, depending on the age category. For yours, Gracie, it would be big enough to get you those tickets to Six Flags you want for sure," Victor answered as he brought in a smaller bass. "I'll get what we've got cleaned and filleted and put in the ice chest while y'all go on and catch some more."

"When you get that done, we'll spread out our picnic and take a break." Hattie glanced over her shoulder.

"Who are you looking for?" Kate asked.

"Oh, I just mentioned a picnic on the lake and kind of invited Paul and Lisa to join us. He said if he could get away early enough, he just might," Hattie answered.

"Nothing like sandwiches and beer on a hot summer night," Victor said.

"Or fried chicken," Jamie said from the other end of the dock.

"If you fry up a good chicken, I'll throw Hattie in the lake and marry you instead," Victor teased.

"Not me." Jamie shook her head slowly. "I'm never getting involved with another man."

"Me, either, so don't ask," Amanda said with a grimace.

"Guess that leaves me with no one, since we all know Waylon will sweet-talk Kate into becoming a rancher before the end of the summer." Victor removed a long, thin-bladed knife from a leather sheath on his belt and began cleaning fish.

"Oh, hush," Kate fussed at him. "We can buy a wedding cake at Walmart and you can eat the whole thing, Victor, but I'm going back to Fort Worth when summer ends."

Were these people insane? Trying to fix Jamie up with Paul was one thing. She planned to stay in Bootleg if she got a teaching job, and they were both teachers, they had kids the same age, and it was plain that there was chemistry. Kate and Waylon had little if anything in common, and a few hot kisses and a little flirting would not turn her from an oil heiress into a rancher's wife.

She shuddered at the idea of being anyone's wife again. Lover, maybe. Wife never.

"You drank of the Bootleg water, my dear," Victor said.

"And that means?" she asked.

"Anyone who drinks the water in Bootleg ain't satisfied to live anywhere else," Hattie answered.

Kate rolled her eyes toward the blue sky. "That's a crock of horse pucky if I've ever heard one. I'm changing the subject. Was there something that any of you wanted to be other than what you are right now?"

"You mean like when we were kids?" Amanda asked.

"Anytime in the past," Kate answered.

"Well, when I was a little kid, I wanted to be Cinderella, but now that I'm a big girl," Gracie said, "I want to be a schoolteacher like my mama."

And if she needed money, an apartment, or anything else to realize her dream, by golly, Kate would take care of it.

Hattie patted Gracie's shoulder. "You'll make a wonderful teacher. You were so good at keeping things organized and put back into their proper place in Bible school. I wanted to be in the air force and fly fighter jets. But in my day, women weren't allowed to do that. I ran the convenience store in Bootleg for fifty years before my husband took sick and we sold it."

Kate could see someone as sassy as Hattie sitting in the pilot's seat of a fighter jet. Too bad she'd been born generations too early to get to do what she wanted.

"And you, Victor?" Kate asked.

"My daddy was the bank president, and I was trained up to follow in his footsteps. But once when I was about ten years old, the carnival came to town for the festival and I had the wildest hankering to run away with it and be one of the crew. Those girls in those cute little costumes were pretty amazing to a ten-year-old." He blushed.

Kate could see him mooning around after the ladies in their skimpy, shiny costumes and wishing that he could be a part of the carnival.

"And what would you be?" she asked.

"At the time a tightrope walker." He grinned.

"Lord help my soul!" Hattie gasped. "When you were ten, you were like a long-legged newborn colt."

"But it sure looked exciting," Victor said.

Was the excitement surrounding everything in Bootleg what had gotten a firm hold on Kate's heart and soul? If so, it would end and be nothing but a memory after she got back home in a few weeks—much like Victor's excited idea of joining the carnival. Kate was an oil woman, born, bred, and raised to work in that field. Could she ever be anything else?

Jamie reeled in a fish about the size of the one Victor had caught. "I wanted to be a teacher from the time I was a little girl."

Kate had no trouble believing that. Jamie was one of those people who had tunnel vision. It's a good thing that she didn't find out about Conrad before he was dead, or that one-track mind-set might have landed her smack in jail for life.

"I've worked in lots of places since high school." Amanda reeled in her line and laid her rod and reel on the dock. "Convenience store, auto supply business, lumber yard, retail clothing, banking, and now my little discount-clothing place. But as a child, I only wanted to be a mother. I guess I'm finally getting my wish. What about you, Kate?"

Kate kept her eye on the bobble dancing out there on the gentle lake waves. "I'm like Victor. I was raised to take over for my mother in the family business, and I suppose it's too late now to think about anything else."

"It's never too late to change," Hattie said. "When we sold the store, I didn't think I would ever get used to staying at home every day, but I did, and before long, it was the best job I ever had. I get to be more involved with the church and the festival, and I get to go fishing when I want. So don't ever think that you can't change your mind."

Even at forty-four years old?

"So if I want to run away with the carnival in a couple of weeks, no one will shoot me?" Kate teased.

"I wouldn't shoot you, but I'd rather you stayed here in Bootleg," Victor said.

"My mother would drop graveyard dead if I even mentioned such a thing," Kate said softly.

"Naw, she wouldn't." Victor chuckled. "She might rant and rave for a while, though if she came to visit you here, she'd understand. And she might even taste the water here and be willing to join us."

"Well, I think the water tastes terrible, but I like it here," Gracie said. "I talked to Snugglies last night and he said he wouldn't mind if we lived here forever."

"Who is Snugglies?" Victor asked.

"He's my teddy bear, and I tell him everything," Gracie said.

"Well, then, I guess he's very important," Hattie said.

"Oh, yes. He's almost as important as my mama," Gracie told her and then started singing. "Come on, little fishies, eat the worm on my hook."

Before she could sing the line the fourth time, something took the cork under the surface. "Come help me, Mama," she squealed.

"I can't," Jamie shouted. "I've got a bite, too."

Kate laid her fishing pole to the side and hurried over to Gracie's side. Putting her arms around the little girl's shoulders, she gently held the rod steady and helped her turn the handle on the reel. Victor looked like he was about to dance a jig right there on the rough wood platform when they brought in another nice-size catfish. With those moves, maybe he could have mastered the tightrope.

"Would you look at this, Hattie? We're going to have a feast," he yelled.

"I'm not hard of hearing!" She tapped her ears. "But take a look at Jamie's fish. It's almost as big as Gracie's! Your singing worked, child. You really might snag the biggest fish at the festival."

"I'll get these two cleaned up while y'all get out the picnic," Victor said.

"Kate, do you really think my song helped?" Gracie eyed her seriously. "Or are they just tellin' me that to get my hopes up about them tickets?"

Kate hugged the child to her. Would her daughter have looked like Gracie? Or would she have had blonde hair and blue eyes?

Gracie wiggled out of her embrace. "You smell like a hay barn."

"And how would you know what a hay barn smells like?" Kate asked.

"My friend in Dallas, her grandpa lives on a ranch and we went there for rodeo day. It made me sneeze. Mama said it was raggy weed."

"Ragweed." Jamie smiled.

"Then if you ever went to Waylon's ranch, do you think the hay will make you sneeze?" Kate asked, thinking that she might take her out there some Sunday afternoon just to see the animals and play for a while. Surely Waylon wouldn't mind.

Kate picked up her sacks of food and carried them to the quilt that Hattie was busy smoothing out on the grass.

"No, ma'am," Gracie said quickly. "I'm not sneezing right now and I smelled hay on you. And if I go to Waylon's, I'm going to ride a horse."

"And who told you that?" Jamie asked.

"Waylon is a cowboy even if he is a cop. And I bet he's got a horse and I'm going to ask him if I can ride it." Gracie plopped down on the quilt.

"Hey, fishermen and ladies." Paul waved as he started down the grassy slope with his daughter.

"Lisa!" Gracie squealed and took off up the hill to meet her little friend.

Hattie waved. "Come on down and join us. There's plenty of food. The kids can even fish some more if they can be still. They might rather run up and down the shoreline and play."

"Kate!" Gracie ran back holding Lisa's hand. "We are starving. Can we have a burrito while we wait?"

"Of course you can. There's fried cheese sticks, too." Kate removed two from the sack and handed them to the girls.

"Thank you, Miss Kate," Lisa said.

"You're welcome." Kate wanted to smother both of them with hugs.

"Thank you." Gracie said with a big smile. "Let's go sit by the water and eat them."

Kate loved the sight of them sitting on the grass, talking with food in their mouths, because they were so excited to see each other. She'd had acquaintances in her life, but she could never remember a time when she was that carefree, even as a child.

༄

Paul sat down on the edge of the quilt. "Jamie, how's your first week going? I've been meanin' to stop by the office and welcome you proper, but I couldn't get away from the ag barn."

"Busy," Jamie answered. "I'm cleaning the file cabinets and reorganizing, getting things ready for school to start."

"I heard that you might be interested in the elementary opening," he said.

"Haven't made up my mind, but I'm thinkin' about it," she said.

"Well, Lisa will be over the moon if you decide to stay in Bootleg."

"So will Gracie." Jamie smiled, her pulse kicking in a little extra beat when the summer breeze wafted the scent of his shaving lotion her way.

"I'm confused," Amanda said. "Here we are, three women who were all married to the same man, and Bootleg is taking us in and acting like we are sisters. Is there something wrong with all you people or with us? Aren't small towns supposed to be all cliquish and gossipy?"

"Oh, we are both of those things." Hattie set out a platter of chicken salad sandwiches and a relish plate. "But Iris wouldn't want us to treat y'all badly. But I got to admit we are all glad that one particular man got what he deserved."

Victor opened his mouth to say something before he snapped it shut and whispered out the side, "He is Gracie's daddy, so we need to be nice, Hattie."

And therein would probably be a big problem with any kind of relationship between her and Paul. He, like the rest of Bootleg, despised Conrad, and Gracie was Conrad's daughter. Not that Jamie was entertaining notions of the chemistry between them leading to anything. No, sir! It was far too early in this thing for her to—she felt crimson flooding her cheeks . . . again.

Hattie sighed. "She's such a lovely child that I forget that she's his."

"It's easy to do," Kate said.

"Well, let's get on with our picnic. We don't need to talk about rubbish. What's been going on at the ag barn?" Victor asked.

"Not much, but I hear that the office is getting a thorough straightening." He winked at Jamie and turned to face Victor.

Her heart tossed in an extra beat and she couldn't have wiped the smile off her face—not even by sucking on a lemon.

∽

Not many days turned out to be almost perfect, but for Kate that one had. Even with the threat of nothing at all good coming from the information that she'd given Waylon, she still felt good about the day. She'd gotten part of the load off her chest, and now all she had to do was tell Amanda and Jamie. Down deep inside, she hoped neither of them asked exactly how long she'd known about all this. Maybe they'd be so excited or bummed out about the will business that they wouldn't even think about the timing.

Jamie had started reading *Pipsie, Nature Detective* to Gracie on the deck that evening, but she'd fallen asleep in her mother's lap before the second page was finished. It was another of those moments when

Kate wished she'd had a daughter but then realized if she had, the child would be thirteen now and in those "I know everything" years and certainly wouldn't want Kate to read a children's book to her.

Jamie carried her into the house, returned with a bottle of beer, and got comfortable by sitting in one chair and propping her legs up in another. She set the bottle on the table between her and Kate. "You still smell like hay."

"Well, I haven't had a bath yet. That's next on my agenda. You still smell faintly of fish," Kate said.

"So." Amanda laid a hand on her stomach. "I hope I can be as good a mother with this baby as you are with Gracie and as Paul is with Lisa."

"You will be as good as both of them, but I've got something serious to talk to y'all about now," Kate said.

"More serious than kissing the detective who's trying to hang us out to dry?" Jamie asked.

"Yes, it is more serious. And I hadn't kissed a man in thirteen years," Kate said.

"Good God almighty!" Amanda's voice got higher with each syllable until it completely squeaked out at the end. "You mean you were faithful to Conrad?"

"Not by choice, more by workload. I lost the baby and found out what a horrible person he was all the same week. After that I buried myself in my job. Now back to this other thing. I found a whole pack of letters hidden in my bedroom. They were up under the dresser, addressed to Iris's daughter, Darcy. I read them, and believe me, they will open your eyes. I've given all the information to Waylon. He's asked us not to tell anyone, not your aunt, Amanda, or your grandmother, Jamie, or my mother, either. It has to be a secret so that it doesn't interfere with the investigation," Kate said.

"Oh, I love secrets," Amanda said. "Will it help us to figure out who gets this cabin?"

"Probably not, but we won't have to move out anytime soon. It's likely that the church will own it when everything is settled," she answered as she headed down the hallway and returned with her suitcase.

"Good Lord, how many are there?" Jamie asked.

"There are a few—you need to read the letters for yourselves. Did you know the room I'm staying in is Darcy's? Iris's daughter grew up in this house. When she was a little girl, she used to hide things under the bottom drawer of the dresser. One morning that drawer got stuck." Kate went on to tell the rest of the story, leaving out none of the details of the letters that were still fresh in her mind.

"Oh. My. God!" Amanda threw her hand over her eyes when Kate finished the story. "I'm changing my name back to Hilton as soon as I can get it done."

"And I'll be changing mine and Gracie's to Mendoza when we go home. I wonder how much it will cost," Jamie said.

"A little over two hundred dollars," Kate answered.

"How do you know that?" Amanda checked the potatoes.

Kate stirred the small pot of beans. "Because I looked into it one time, and I'll gladly pay for all of us to get it done."

"You'd do that for me?" Amanda asked.

"He cheated us all, and I have the money," Kate answered.

"I can pay for the name change," Jamie said. "I'm not in the habit of taking charity."

"Me, neither, but I'm pretty much broke unless I want to get into my small savings account. I'll take you up on the offer," Amanda said.

"I'll get the legal staff on the name-change papers sent to us tomorrow morning. They'll send down whatever we need to do, and when it's time to go before the judge, we can make a day of it."

"Only two weeks ago he was alive, and now we are talking about changing our names. It's surreal," Amanda whispered.

"Not as much to me as to you," Kate said. "But I wish I'd hired someone to dig into his past like Iris did. I knew he was a con, yet it never dawned on me that he wasn't even Conrad Steele."

"I had no idea, either," Jamie said.

Amanda laid her hand on her stomach. "It all hit me with so much force that I might be reeling for a month or maybe a year."

Kate was sorry that she'd lost her chance at motherhood, but she was glad she'd never have to worry about raising a child with Conrad's—or Cain's—blood. She couldn't imagine Gracie being anything but a sweet child, but a boy? Amanda would have a heavy load raising a son if he was like Conrad.

Chapter Sixteen

Jamie awoke on Sunday morning and propped up on an elbow to stare at her daughter. How on earth she and Conrad had created such a delightful little girl was totally amazing. After reading through those letters, Jamie might even go so far as to say that her daughter was a miracle. With Conrad for a father, she could have been a conniving little girl, but she wasn't. She was as open as a book and as sweet natured as Mama Rita.

She glanced at the clock and rubbed her eyes, then looked at it again. She had exactly forty-five minutes to get up, eat breakfast, and get ready for church.

She slung her legs out over the side of the bed and headed straight for the bathroom, knocking on Amanda's door and Kate's on the way.

"Rise and shine, ladies. We have overslept," she called out and purposely slammed the bathroom door shut.

Amanda was standing at the bathroom door when she opened it again. "Pregnancy shrinks the bladder down to thimble size," she grumbled.

"We've got to hurry, and it's my turn to make the covered dish for the potluck." Jamie moved to one side to let Amanda inside the bathroom.

"It can be my turn, Mama." Gracie rubbed the sleep from her eyes. "We can take the cookies me and Amanda made."

"Coffee is making," Kate said when Jamie and Gracie made it to the kitchen. "I'm not going to church, but I'm in as big a rush as y'all. Waylon and I are skipping services this morning."

Amanda arranged cookies on a plate. "Oh, really! Have you got a room reserved?"

"No, we do not!" Kate poured three cups of coffee and set them on the table. "Did either of you do any interesting reading last night?"

"I did," Jamie answered. "That's probably why I overslept. Talk about tangled webs and twists and turns. Now what? This place should go to a dead woman?"

"But since she's already passed on, then we're back to square one, right?" Amanda asked.

"Not necessarily," Kate said. "She left a will, and whatever she wanted done with her possessions will probably be taken into consideration."

"Well, crap! This is turning into a never-ending cycle."

"Cereal, toast, and orange juice." Jamie talked as she set things on the table. "Gracie, don't diddle-daddle around now."

"I won't, Mama. I don't want to miss church. Do I still get to go home with Lisa after church is over?"

"Oh, shoot!" Jamie sighed. "I forgot about that, but yes, you can go home with her. However, if you want to take your backpack with toys in it, you might have to let me bring them over later."

"I got it ready. And I got my play clothes in there and my old shoes." Gracie poured cereal into a bowl, added a teaspoon of sugar and milk, and started to eat.

"Miss Organization there." Amanda buttered two pieces of toast when they popped up.

Kate patted Gracie on the shoulder. "That's a good thing."

"So are you going to sit with Waylon this morning, Kate?" the little girl asked.

"No, remember what I said while ago. I'm going to skip out on church. Waylon and I have some business to take care of," Kate said.

"You can miss church one time, Kate, but if you miss two times it makes God cry, right, Mama?" Gracie said.

"That's what Mama Rita says." Jamie nodded.

It took some serious hustle, but Amanda, Gracie, and Jamie walked through the church doors with three minutes to spare. Folks were still meandering in from Sunday school and taking their seats. Hattie rushed over to Jamie and hugged her tightly.

"I'm so glad to see y'all. I was afraid Gracie was sick. Where is Kate?" she asked.

"We just overslept." Jamie patted Hattie on the back. "Kate and Waylon are off to Wichita Falls this morning. I hope it's something to help close the case. Why don't you and Victor sit with us today?"

"We'd love to, and there's plenty of room for Paul and Lisa, too, on that empty pew right there." She motioned to Victor.

Amanda giggled and whispered, "They are playing matchmakers, but don't say a word. And at least he is an intelligent man with a credible background."

Jamie won the fight with the blush. "Yes, he is. I've already figured Victor and Hattie out, and we've got a lot to get settled before any of us can take steps even into friendships, don't we?"

"You might preach that sermon to Kate." Amanda giggled.

%

Kate wore one of the sundresses she'd brought along to Bootleg, topped off with a cute little turquoise and silver necklace and her sandals. Using a curling iron, she managed to give her hair some extra volume. Makeup consisted of a brush of light-brown eye shadow, mascara, and a little lipstick. And then the time was gone.

She picked up her purse and carried it to her favorite rocking chair on the front porch, but Waylon drove up in his big black crew-cab truck before she could sit down. She waved and started in that direction. He shook the legs of his starched and creased jeans down over the tops of his boots when he got out of the truck and rushed around to open the passenger door for her.

"You look like a fresh breath of spring after a long winter," he said.

"Thank you. I hope that is a good thing," she answered.

He pulled the seat belt across her body and snapped it shut, and then brushed a soft kiss on her lips before shutting the door. She watched him in the side mirror until he disappeared. Good Lord, but he did fill out those jeans well. She would far rather be looking at him than singing hymns.

"So how was your weekend in Dallas? Was what I gave you any help at all? I let Amanda and Kate read the letters," she said.

"And?"

"And they said they wanted to finish every one and then we'd talk about them tonight. Your turn, even though I know you can't discuss the case," she said.

"The information was a tremendous help to my partner and his new partner, whom he's bitchin' about." Waylon chuckled. "Anyway, between the three of us, we've got some solid suspects on the list and aren't out there chasing our tails. It's lookin' good, so thank you."

"The letters?"

"I'd like copies of them for the evidence files just so we have something tangible with all those names he's used. We'll run our own investigation, but if we had a copy of the old report, it would be good," he answered.

"I'll get that done this week."

She had to clasp her hands in her lap to keep from clapping and doing a wiggle dance right there in the truck. To keep from acting like she felt, she turned on the radio and flipped through several stations with preaching before she found one that played only country music.

She could tell by the way he had fidgeted that he was nervous that morning, not wanting to tell her something and yet needing to do so. The closer they got to Wichita Falls, the more he relaxed. Was she losing her famous ability to read people, or had the music calmed him down?

If she'd been in her office trying to broker a deal to buy a smaller oil company that was failing, right then would have been the moment when she made her big move. The buyer would have arrived all tense, and with a little small talk, he would relax and then she would ease into the business aspect of the deal.

Suddenly, she realized that she didn't miss the business. It was her turn to tense. Maybe Hattie was right and she was ready for a big change. Her hands went clammy and her chest felt like it had stones in it.

"You okay?" Waylon asked.

"Yes, why do you ask?" She'd admitted that she liked working on the ranch. She'd owned up to the fact that she loved Gracie. Jamie and Amanda could pick up and move, but she shouldn't entertain such a foolish notion.

"You went all stiff and the air in the truck got heavy," he answered. "So what were you picturing in your mind that made it hard for you to breathe?"

"I was thinking about work, and it hit me that I didn't miss it. I'm a workaholic like my mother. I love my job. I hate change. I should miss being there at the office, right?"

"You are preaching to the choir. At least up to six months ago, when I sat down on a bar stool with a beer in front of me and my precinct friends around me and suddenly I didn't want to be there. I wanted to be on the ranch full-time. I love my job, too, and I sure hate change, so I know where you are coming from."

"So what is your goal?" she asked.

"To finish this case, get my paperwork all signed and sealed, freeze my retirement, and come home to the Double Back Ranch for good. The closer the time gets, the more I want that now that I've made up my mind," he said.

"What about your partner? Is he quitting the force, too?" she asked.

"No, he's still got ten more years before he gets to decide whether to stay or go. And besides, I know he secretly likes the woman who's his new partner. She's smart and has all the newest ways of doing things that get the job done," he said. "And she's a helluva lot better looking than his last partner."

"That would depend on who was doing the judging," she said.

"So you think I'm a little bit good-looking?" He smiled.

"Waylon Kramer, that's the low end of the scale. You measure way on up past that." She flirted.

"Well, now that chases away even more dark clouds." He grinned.

"Speaking of dark clouds, look over there." She pointed toward the southwest. "Think that might be bringing in some rain?"

"I hope so. The hay is all in, and the next crop could sure use some watering. Maybe we'll get caught in it and have to spend the night up here in Wichita Falls," he said.

"And now we have Luke Bryan with one of his top tunes from last year, 'Strip It Down,'" the radio DJ said.

"Have you seen this video?" Kate asked.

"Yes, I have. The city boy knows he's lost it with the country girl, and the country boy can't forget the city girl," Waylon said. "Which one am I? And which one are you?"

"At heart, you are a country boy, but you've been in the city too long. At heart, I'm a city girl, but I'm learning to love the country life. Where does that take us?"

"To a happy medium, I hope," he answered. "What do you get from the video?"

She ran what she could remember from the video through her mind. "I see a young farmer who needs to take his woman to a nice place and let her get all dressed up. And then I see a corporate bigwig who used to be a cowboy and fell for a woman in cowboy boots. Now they're both miserable and wanting another shot at love. Which one are you?" Kate asked.

"Both. I've worn the suit and the cowboy boots. Which one would impress you the most?" he asked.

"Neither," she answered.

"Oh, come on," he said, grinning. "Surely you know if you like a cowboy or a detective better."

"Right now I'd like for all this crap to be cleared up, and I don't care if a cowboy, a detective, or a big old tomcat does the job," she said.

The grin faded. "A tomcat?"

"Like in those cozy mystery books," she said.

"The cat really solves the case?"

"Sometimes. Maybe you'd better get a cat."

He shook his head. "Okay then. With all the information you gave us, we do have some good leads, but you were in that cabin with Conrad after Iris died, and so were Amanda and Jamie. A good prosecutor would argue that one or all of you found those letters months ago and, individually or collectively, you all murdered him. Y'all are still at the top of the suspect list." He grimaced. "Maybe even more than before. That's what I wanted to tell you and didn't want to tell you at the same time."

"Well, shit!" she said. So that's the reason he'd been so antsy that morning when he picked her up. Nothing was decided and everything was even worse than before. In all the scenarios she'd thought about, that one never entered her mind.

"Exactly." He frowned. "I can turn this truck around and take you home if you want."

"Hell, no. I want that big hamburger you promised me," she said.

"Okay, then, but I'll understand if you turn me down on the next news."

"You mean that's not all of the bad news?"

"This has nothing to do with the case, but knowing that the bunch of you aren't in the clear by any means might mean that none of you want to cooperate. You've heard about the festival?"

She nodded. What in the hell could a fishing festival have to do with the case or anything else for that matter?

"Well, several years ago my mother bought an old stagecoach at an auction and the parade committee, plus the Bootleg citizen of the year, rides in it during the parade. I get it out of the barn where we store it and shine it all up for that day," he said.

"And you're going to chase down Conrad's real killer in an antique stagecoach?" she asked.

He laughed. Dammit! Why did he have to be so sexy when he brought out the charm?

"No, but while all the spiders are chased out of it and it's still clean, Victor and Hattie want to have a picnic at the ranch so the girls can have a ride in it," he said.

"As in more than just Gracie? As in Lisa?" she asked.

"Yes, ma'am."

"When is all this supposed to happen?" she asked.

"Festival is next Saturday. The stagecoach would still be clean on Monday evening," he answered. "Hattie says that she'll bring a picnic lunch for us to have beside the creek on the back side of the ranch and the kids can play in the water."

"Why are you asking instead of Hattie?"

"She and Victor thought if it was my idea, it might not look so much like they were pushing Paul and Jamie together," he answered.

"So if you aren't too mad at me for being the messenger of bad news about the case, then I'd ask you not to tell Jamie who really thought up the whole plan."

"Well, I expect I can keep that secret." She smiled. "Truth is, I've wanted to ask you if I could bring Gracie to the ranch for an afternoon or morning."

"Anytime." He grinned.

ⁱⁱⁱ

Waylon had let emotions get in the way of his job for the first time in his career. He liked Amanda and Jamie, and he'd hate to see them prosecuted. But Kate was a different story. He believed her, and he damn sure did not want to see her behind bars. He shouldn't even be taking her out for a hamburger or hiring her to work on his ranch, but dammit, there was something there between them that he couldn't ignore.

He'd sworn off women after his second divorce and he'd stayed pretty faithful to his vow of bachelorhood until he met Kate. God or fate or karma damn sure had a wicked sense of humor.

"Gracie told me she wanted to come to your ranch and ride a horse someday so I know she'll be delighted, but I feel like I should ask Jamie first," Kate said. "Now, let's put all that on the back burner and you can tell me about this burger joint. Is it a chain? Do we have them in Dallas and Fort Worth?"

"It's not a chain. It's one of a kind and it's called Bobby Jo's. They only make burgers and hot dogs. None of this diversifying business. And they peel their own potatoes for their fries and make their own chili for the burgers and hot dogs."

"Chili for burgers?" She frowned.

"Don't knock it until you've tried it," he said. "A chili burger is two pieces of meat, two pieces of cheese, and a scoop of hot chili that melts the cheese. You usually have to eat it with a spoon, but it's pretty damned good."

"Sounds like it. Do they do chili cheese fries?"

"Yep, and they are amazing," he said.

"How'd you find out about this place?" she asked.

"My daddy was a big fan of hamburgers and hot dogs, so when we drove up here for a load of feed or to go to the stockyards, we always went to Bobby Joe's. The original owner died some years ago and they changed up the sign a little bit to be Bobby Jo's, as in a girl's name. She's his granddaughter."

Kate's stomach growled.

"That's a good sign," Waylon said. "You want to go in there hungry."

He drove past a mall and several other places to eat, made a few turns that had her completely lost as to how she'd ever find her way back out of the maze without him, and then parked in a lot crowded with trucks and cars.

"We're lucky," he said. "We got here before the church crowd. Welcome to the best-kept secret in North Texas."

She stepped out to the smell of grilled onions and burgers. "It smells heavenly."

"Tastes even better."

With his hand on the small of her back, he ushered her inside, and a cute little red-haired woman left her place from behind the hostess counter and hugged him tightly. "Waylon Kramer, where have you been keeping yourself? This gorgeous woman is too good for the likes of an old cop like you."

"Kate, meet Bobby Jo. Bobby Jo, this is Kate Steele, and I agree with what you said, which makes me the luckiest man in the place today."

Kate blushed scarlet but did remember to hold out her hand. "I'm pleased to meet you, Bobby Jo. I hear you make an awesome burger."

Her handshake was firm, and her blue eyes twinkled. She had kinky red hair that she'd pulled up in a messy bun, and she wore a T-shirt that advertised the business. "My cooks do, and I'll fire their asses the day they don't. Y'all come on back here. You can have the VIP table today." She dropped Kate's hand and motioned for them to follow her, leading them through a maze of tables filled with people who had already been served.

"First class," Waylon said as he seated Kate. "Thanks, Bobby Jo."

"Anytime, darlin'." She went up on tiptoe to kiss him on the cheek. "I loved this man's daddy. He always left me a dollar tip just for bringing him the menu. That's all Grandpa let me do in those days. Your server will be with you in a minute." As she left she pulled a set of sliding doors shut, leaving them in a small enclosure with a window facing a tiny little garden.

"This is great, Waylon," Kate whispered.

"I've been in here dozens of times, and I didn't even know there was a VIP table." He grinned. "She must like you."

The doors opened, and a waitress appeared with two glasses of water and a couple of one-page menus. "What can I get for y'all today?"

"I want the double bacon cheeseburger, chili cheese fries, and a Coors in the bottle. Longneck if you have it," Kate said.

"Well, that was quick. How about you, sir?"

"The same, and add a foot-long hot dog with cheese and chili, no onions on anything for me," he said.

Kate handed her the menu. "Hold the onions on mine, too."

Waylon's hand closed over hers. "You know this means we have to sit here and talk for an hour so the beer will be out of our system before we leave."

"As long as we don't talk about the murder, I don't suppose that will be a hardship," she said. "I have a question to get us started. Have you ever thought of drilling for oil on the ranch?"

The waitress brought their beers and set them down. He took a long sip of his before he answered. "No, thank you. We make a fine living with our Angus cattle. I might look into the equipment to make big round bales of hay in the next couple of years, though. It would mean not having to go out to feed cattle twice a day. But I'd rather talk about something other than ranching."

"Such as?"

"You. The future. What happens when your vacation ends? How much I like the color of your eyes. Those could be starters," he said.

"Maybe we'd best see if I'm indicted for murder before we think about us or the future," she said. That could have a huge bearing on whether he'd ever see the color of her eyes again.

He covered her hand with his. "I do not believe you killed Conrad. I just have to find who did so that you are cleared."

"Thank you for that. Now let's talk about today and whether the chili in this place is as good as what you make. Or we can talk about how much I adore Gracie and really would steal her if I could figure out a way to do it legally."

"Whatever you want to talk about is fine with me. Hell, woman, you could read that menu backward to me," he said.

"Now that's a pickup line if I ever heard one." She laughed. "When we finish eating, would you mind if I did some shopping?"

"Darlin', I'll sit outside the dressing room door and enjoy the show as you try on clothing. Think you could model one pair of jeans for me?"

"It could be arranged." She nodded. Jeans? She hadn't bought jeans in years. She worked in power suits, and when she was at home, she wore sweatpants and T-shirts. It might be fun to try on a pair and maybe some boots. If she was going to work on a ranch in the wintertime, she would need boots.

Where in the hell did that thought come from? She almost gasped.

Chapter Seventeen

Is my mama going to die?" Gracie asked Amanda over breakfast the next morning.

"Of course not! Why would you ask that?" Amanda frowned.

"My daddy just up and died. He didn't tell me he was going to die, and if my mama is going to die, will my Mama Rita take care of me? Will I have to go back to Dallas and leave the cabin?"

"Your mama would have told us if that was happening, don't you think?"

"My daddy didn't tell me anything. I wish I could stay here forever." Gracie propped her elbows on the table and rested her chin in her hands. "I didn't like that funeral. Everyone was so sad and then after the preacher finished, everyone was mad. Mama was really mad until we came here and now she is happy. I don't ever want to live in our old house again, because she might be mad like that again."

"We were all mad. So was Kate and so was I," Amanda said.

Gracie went back to eating. "You'd tell me the truth if my mama was going to die, wouldn't you?"

"Yes, I would," Amanda said.

"Would you tell me if Kate was going to die?" Gracie asked.

"I promise that no one is going to die," Amanda said. "And if I know they are going to pass away, I'll tell you. Now let's finish our breakfast."

"Okay, but did my daddy die because I didn't tell him good-bye the last time he came to see me and Mama? Lisa said she wouldn't tell her mama good-bye when she was sick and she died. Is it our fault?"

Why couldn't Gracie have gotten up with her mother that day instead of sleeping until almost nine o'clock? That way Jamie would be answering these questions. Amanda wasn't a mother, not yet. A little voice in her head reminded her that she would someday have to answer more questions than these. Her child would want to know why the other kids had a father and she didn't. What had happened to him and could she see pictures.

"No, darlin', your daddy did not die because you didn't tell him good-bye. Some really bad men killed him."

"Why?" Gracie's eyes widened. "I heard all y'all talking about it, but why? I want to know why bad men killed my daddy, but everyone talks in whispers or in big-people talk when I'm there."

Amanda hauled her heavy body up from the chair and hugged Gracie, then took her by the hand and led her to the sofa. "You didn't have anything at all to do with your daddy's death."

"Promise?" Gracie snuggled in close to Amanda.

"Cross my heart."

Gracie held up her hand. "Pinky swear and I will believe you."

Amanda laced her smallest finger with Gracie's. "I do hereby pinky swear."

Gracie giggled. "That sounds funny."

Sighing with relief, Amanda nodded.

❧

Kate and Waylon were on the way from plowing fields all morning to the ranch house when Waylon hung back to answer the phone. She went on into the house and washed up in the bathroom. When she came out, he was still talking, and from all the gesturing, it was not a good conversation. She knew anger when she saw it.

He was probably mad about something with the investigation or with his paperwork concerning when he could leave the precinct permanently. It had nothing to do with her, she hoped. She kept walking right out the front door without looking back over her shoulder.

When she parked in front of the cabin, her phone pinged with a text from Waylon: Can we talk?

She turned off the engine and typed: For what and why?

The return message said: Meet me at the dock?

She sent back: One hour in the church parking lot.

Black clouds gathered in the southwest again that afternoon. The rain that they thought might be coming the day before had gone around Bootleg and Mabelle and hit around Archer City with severe wind and even marble-size hail.

If the rain materialized, she didn't want to be on the dock when it hit. And if this was going to be a big black moment with Waylon, she sure didn't want Gracie to hear it. Before she could get out of her car, Jamie pulled in right beside her.

Kate stepped out and pointed at the sky. "Looks like a storm coming our way."

"Let's go get a glass of sweet tea and a cinnamon roll and sit on the porch. I love the smell of rain in the air," Jamie said.

Kate jogged from her car to the porch. "You haven't eaten yet? It's almost one thirty."

Jamie hit the first porch step by the time Kate got to the door. "I wanted to finish a file drawer, so I worked an extra hour. I sent Amanda a text, and she sent one back to say that she and Gracie were making yeast bread and cinnamon rolls."

Kate shook her head. "I smell cinnamon all the way out here."

With hands on her hips, Gracie waited for them in the middle of the living room floor. Her hair had been french braided and her little faded shorts and shirt had the remnants of flour stuck to them.

"You scared me," Gracie scolded her mother.

"I'm only an hour late. Didn't Amanda tell you?" Jamie said. "Where is my welcome hug?"

Gracie squared her shoulders. "You can have it later. I'm mad at you and Kate both."

"What did I do? Are you mad at Amanda?" Kate asked.

"Bad men killed my daddy. He didn't die because I didn't tell him good-bye. You should have told me, Mama, or you should've, Kate."

"Oh!" All the wind left Kate's lungs in a whoosh.

Amanda came out of the kitchen and shrugged. "I didn't know what to do."

Jamie sank down on the sofa and patted the spot beside her. "Come and sit beside me and we'll talk about it."

Gracie crawled up into her lap and laid her head on Jamie's shoulder. "I been afraid for you to go anywhere if I didn't tell you good-bye. I thought you'd die, too."

"That isn't why your daddy died. Some bad men came in the flower shop where he was buying roses and they shot him," Jamie said. "This is really not your fault, sweetheart."

Kate had been almost thirty when her father died, and she had not told him good-bye. They'd had a horrible argument the night before his heart attack, and she'd stormed out of the house in anger. Poor little Gracie was only six, and she'd been carrying this burden around the better part of a month.

"Amanda said it's not my fault that he's dead. And that it's not Lisa's fault that her mama is dead," Gracie said.

Kate sat down on the other end of the sofa and held Gracie's hand in hers. "Amanda is right. Sometimes bad things happen and it's nobody's fault."

"It's those bad men's fault and I hope Waylon shoots them." Gracie tilted her chin up a notch. "Now, let's go have some cinnamon rolls. Me and Amanda worked hard all morning. She's nesting, you know."

"Oh, she is?" Kate smiled.

"I don't know what it means, but I hope it lasts a long time, because I like cookies and cinnamon rolls," Gracie said.

❧

The first raindrops hit the windshield of his truck as Waylon pulled into a space in the church parking lot. He sat there for five minutes, hoping that Kate hadn't changed her mind. When she finally pulled up beside him and motioned for him to come over to her vehicle, he wasted no time getting out of the truck. He started to open the passenger door of the Cadillac but noticed her long legs going over the seat.

He hurriedly got into the backseat and scooted over into her embrace, pulling her so close that their hearts beat in unison. "Bad news. All that information checked out, but the one suspect we thought it might lead us to didn't pan out. I was so angry. I hope you didn't think it was at you."

"I didn't, but I did know that you needed some cool-down time. That means I'll get top billing on the list of suspects, because I have the money to pay someone to kill him, right?"

He nodded. "I'm sorry. We'll keep digging."

"Thank you for that much. Gracie had a meltdown today, and Amanda had to take care of it. I'm going to talk to the girls tonight about all this. In my opinion, Gracie needs a day at the ranch next week. Meeting with you this afternoon is good. I can tell them that's what we were talking about," Kate said.

He wanted to kiss her again, but with the newest turn of events, maybe that was a bad idea. It wouldn't be good for her case or his record if he was romantically involved with the lead suspect in his final case.

"I should be going," he said.

"Me, too. I've got a lot to tell the girls, and hopefully, the festival and the day at the ranch will help Gracie. I didn't realize that a little kid went through the stages of grief just like an adult."

"Me, either." He scooted across the seat and out the door. "Thank you, Kate, for everything."

"It is what it is." She shrugged.

But why can't it be different just this one time, Waylon thought as he started up his truck engine and drove away. *Why couldn't we have met under different circumstances—like at a party or even on a couple of bar stools?*

❧

Kate watched the rain splat against the windshield and the side windows for five minutes. What-ifs played through her mind the whole time. What if they came and took her away in handcuffs? What would Gracie do if the policemen took her mother? Did Mama Rita have enough money to take care of her properly? And Amanda? What if her baby was born in prison and they gave it up for adoption?

Finally, with no answers to any of the questions, she crawled over the seat and headed home. Home. Was that what the cabin had become?

She stopped by the convenience store and picked up two bottles of wine and a couple of two-liter bottles of Diet Coke for Amanda and tossed in a bag of Gracie's favorite gummy candies. Other than Conrad's monthly overnight visits, her life had been in a nice comfortable rut for the past thirteen years, and now it was one big mess after another. Paying him the million-dollar settlement would have been so much easier than all this, but then she would have never met Gracie—or Jamie and Amanda. The latter two were beginning to get under her skin, but not as much as that little dark-haired girl.

There was no way she could get from car to cabin without getting wet, so she embraced the rain, enjoying the feel of its warmth as it soaked her from head to toe. When she reached the door, she kicked it with her sandal and yelled, "Hey, Jamie or anyone in there, would you open the door, please?"

Her phone rang at the same time Gracie slung open the door. She recognized the ringtone as the one she had assigned to her mother, but it stopped before she could answer it.

"What's in the bags?" Gracie asked.

"Wine for me and your mother. Diet Coke for Amanda and a bag of those sour candies that you like," Kate said.

"Thank you, thank you." Gracie wrapped her arms around Kate's long legs. "I love you, Kate."

"Not as much as I love you, Gracie."

"I love you to the moon and back." Gracie grinned.

"Well, I love you a bushel and a peck and a hug around the neck," Kate said.

Gracie drew her dark brows down over deep-brown eyes and asked, "Is that a lot?"

"More than to the moon and back," Kate said.

"Okay, then you love me more today, but tomorrow I will love you more. Mama, guess what Kate brought me?" She fished the candy from the bag and went down the hall in her famous run-everywhere mode.

Kate went to her bedroom and changed into dry clothing, then sat down in the rocking chair and hit the speed dial for her mother.

"I told you this was going to turn into a nightmare before it was over. That's the reason I wanted you to be out of town for a while," Teresa said without so much as a *hello* or *hey*.

"And here I thought you wanted me to be rested in December when I took over your office," Kate said.

"Don't you get sassy with me! Have you seen the Dallas newspaper?"

"No, I have not. Here in the hinterlands we use smoke signals—they tell me we might get the Pony Express to deliver newspapers to us pretty soon," Kate answered.

"This is not a laughing matter." Teresa's voice hit a brand-new high.

"Okay, Mother, what does it say?" Kate sighed.

"Third page. Upper half. A columnist is talking about the murder and he's gotten all kinds of information from somewhere, like all of Conrad's aliases, his real name, and that he was a polygamist, and he lists his three wives at the time of his death. And your name and the fact that you are an oil heiress is right there in black and white."

"Did it say anything about Gracie?" Kate gasped.

"Who the hell is Gracie? Another wife?"

"No, she's Jamie's . . . Conrad's . . . daughter. I've told you about her," Kate whispered.

"Nothing about a Gracie, but there is something about an Iris, and he says that you three should be behind bars. Do you have any idea what that is doing to your reputation?"

"Maybe we should sell the whole company before that happens," Kate said.

Total silence. For a minute she thought maybe she'd caused her mother to go into acute cardiac arrest at even suggesting such a thing. She held the phone out from her ear to be sure she hadn't lost the connection and then yelled, "Mother!" into it.

"Have you lost your mind?" Teresa finally said.

"Maybe I have, but if there's a dark cloud hanging over me, then it wouldn't take long for the company to go down the tank. People don't trust multi-million-dollar business deals to women who may or may not have murdered their husbands."

"Are you drunk?"

"Haven't had a drink yet, but I'm planning on having half a bottle of wine before I go to bed, so I might be willing to give the company away about midnight," Kate answered. "You know that several bigger companies have been sniffing around us for years. Talk to them and get a backup plan before this gets any bigger."

"God almighty," Teresa fumed. "I can't believe you'd even suggest such a thing."

"If anyone had told me six weeks ago that I would think about selling out, I would have thought they'd lost their marbles, but . . ." Kate let the sentence hang.

"But that was before you got labeled a murderess in the Dallas newspaper," Teresa said.

"That's right. Think about what I said. We'll talk later. Right now I need to have an important conversation with Jamie."

"More important than your future? Maybe what I should do is stay in my office, weather the storm, and send you to a country where they won't extradite you back here to stand trial," Teresa said.

"Buy four tickets if you do. Good night, Mother," Kate said, hit the "End" button, and headed for the kitchen.

"Hey, Gracie said there was wine, and it's even cold." Jamie already had the glasses on the table.

Amanda came from the hallway into the kitchen. "And I hear you bought Diet Coke for me. Thank you."

"You are both welcome."

"And you are spoiling Gracie, but we both love it," Jamie said.

"I'm enjoying every minute of it. To Gracie." Kate poured the wine and then held up her glass to clink it with Jamie's.

"Wait. I want to toast, too, if it's to Gracie. She and I have so much fun when Jamie lets me keep her." Amanda hurriedly filled a glass with ice and Diet Coke. She touched it with the other two, and they all sipped at the same time.

"We made the Dallas newspaper," Kate said and went on to tell them what her mother had said.

"Well, shit!" Jamie said. "I wonder what that will do for my teaching job there."

"Probably put you on the fired list there and might get you an award here." Kate giggled.

"It's not funny," Jamie fumed.

"Did they mention names?" Amanda went pale.

"Oh, yes, and probably even where we are all from. I didn't ask, but we could pull up today's paper on the Internet and read the column," Kate answered.

"I looked into that banking job. They couldn't hire a suspected murderess," Amanda said.

"There's a job at the school that you could do," Jamie said. "They haven't hired a secretary yet. And if they aren't going to throw my application in the trash, then they'd probably consider you for that job. Thank God, Victor is on the school board."

"Wow!" Amanda slumped down into a chair. "That would be an amazing job. I'd be off when my child was out of school and during the summer. Thank you, Jamie."

"You are welcome." Jamie poured more wine into the glasses. "Was your mother angry, Kate? I remember her from the funeral, and she looked pretty fierce to me."

"Oh, yeah, she furious, but not at the paper or the columnist."

"At you? We're innocent. Why can't people believe that?" Amanda wailed.

"It's not the guilt or lack of it that is the problem. It's the taint it leaves behind. Who is going to trust me if they even think I might have had a hand in this? Trust is what our business is built on. It's our image. We do multimillion-dollar deals."

And right now I wish that I was a plain old dirt farmer.

"Crazy, ain't it, but the only place we might be welcome is right here in Bootleg," Jamie said. "This settles it. I'm putting in my application for the job tomorrow. Want me to get the paperwork for you to apply for the office job, Amanda?"

"Yes," she answered without hesitation.

"Reckon I could be a janitor? I've learned how to run a tractor. I bet I could master a floor buffer in no time," Kate teased. "On another note, listen to Gracie giggling back there as she talks to her dolls. That is the sweetest sound in the world."

Jamie smiled. "This is going to sound hinky, but like Amanda said earlier, I think Iris likes us being here. It's like her spirit needed to find rest. You found the letters, Kate. Gracie is bringing a little girl's laughter back into the cabin."

"I believe that spirits linger until things are settled," Amanda said. "It's taken a long time, but maybe us being here is bringing Iris and Darcy closure, and if it sounds crazy then so be it. I read those letters today and they are so sad that they made me cry."

"I've got a couple more things to tell you while Gracie is out of earshot." Kate told them they were still on the suspect list and then asked what they thought about the ranch day for the kids. "If they don't win the fishing contest, it wouldn't be such a big blow to their little egos."

"Yes," Amanda and Jamie said at the same time.

"Then that's settled," Kate said. "I'll tell Waylon that it's a date."

"There's nothing we can do but pray that the real killers do something stupid and get caught," Amanda said. "I know I didn't kill him. I also know that neither of you did. The cops just have to figure out the rest, and we'll sit right here in Bootleg until they do. We're protected here. I can feel it."

Jamie stretched up her hand, and Amanda gave her a high five.

"I'm going up to Wichita Falls tomorrow, so I'll be gone all day. Aunt Ellie and I are having supper together after she gets off work. I'll try to be home by dark so I'll be back in my safe place." Amanda giggled.

"And I promised Gracie that we'd go back to Dallas after we get finished at the school and get some more of her clothing and toys, so we'll be gone most of the day. Paul has given Lisa permission to go with us, and we're planning on McDonald's for supper. We'll slip in and out and hopefully the police won't slap the cuffs on us." Jamie grinned and poured more wine in her glass.

"This is pretty serious stuff for y'all to be teasing about," Kate said.

"Lighten up. We're innocent." Jamie held up her glass. "To never spending a day in jail."

Kate poured more wine into her glass. "When I get this down, I'll be mellow enough to call my mother back and talk to her some more about all this mess."

Jamie chuckled. "I'd never get that mellow. Now my grandmother is a different story altogether. She raised me."

"Why?" Amanda asked.

"Mama doesn't have much sense when it comes to men, and most of her boyfriends didn't like me. When I was four, she dropped me at Mama Rita's place and never came back," Jamie said.

"You mother didn't fight for you?" Kate asked.

"No, ma'am. She signed the papers giving Mama Rita the right to adopt me."

Amanda set her empty glass on the side table. "Sounds kind of like my situation, only my mama was sixteen when I was born and she lived with Aunt Ellie, who was her older sister. When she was nineteen, she married a man and she said she was coming back to get me in a few months. But then she had a couple of kids and she embraced his traditions that didn't have room for a little red-haired stepdaughter," Amanda said. "Aunt Ellie filed desertion papers when I was six and adopted me. I have no complaints. She raised me in a good home."

"Where did your mom go?" Jamie asked.

"Iran. She met a man at a restaurant where she was working, and they fell in love. When he went back to his country, she went with him," Amanda answered.

"Why would she leave you behind?" Kate asked.

Amanda shrugged. "Aunt Ellie said that she was pregnant again and the new husband wasn't too keen on a stepdaughter."

"Have you seen her since then?" Amanda asked.

Amanda shook her head. "No, she never came back to Texas. I get a Christmas card from her sometimes, but she never remembers my birthday. I have two half brothers I've never met. But you know what? It's all good. Aunt Ellie was and is a good mother to me."

"My father was a loving, sweet, gentle man," Kate said. "My mother is the bulldog. I got a lot of my father's trusting nature. Conrad never would have snowed Mother like he did me."

"Or my Mama Rita, either, but I bet that he preyed on women who were vulnerable," Jamie said.

"Probably so, but I've learned my lesson," Kate said.

"Oh, yeah." Jamie's head bobbed up and down.

Amanda swiped at a lonely tear making its way down her cheek. "Damned hormones. Lately everything makes me weepy. I even cried over a television commercial about toilet paper, but those little bears were so cute."

Kate picked up what was left of her wine and touched their glasses. "To the future."

"To the future," Amanda and Jamie said.

"And now to bed." Kate stood up. "But first I'll need an apple and a handful of Amanda's sugar cookies."

"Apple?" Amanda asked.

"If you eat fruit, it nullifies all the calories in cookies and wine. Like if you drink diet soda pop after or with a candy bar." Kate grinned.

"She jokes." Amanda pretended shock.

"Hey, now!" Kate teased, and it felt really good.

CHAPTER EIGHTEEN

Waylon and Johnny had spent the whole afternoon on Friday getting the stagecoach ready to roll—cleaning it up and hitching the horses to it, taking it from the ranch to Bootleg, which took three hours, unhitching the horses and putting them in the vo-ag barn. Thank goodness for Paul's offer to keep them there overnight.

He wished that Kate could have ridden up in the driver's seat all the way to town with him that evening. But after that damned newspaper leak—which had to come from his office—there was no way their names could be linked as anything other than detective and suspect. At least not in public.

"If I had that damned columnist in my crosshairs, I would pull the trigger without blinking," Waylon declared to the air that evening as he ate alone in his kitchen.

He was flipping through channels on the television when his phone pinged.

The message was from Kate. `Princess Gracie has requested your presence at a living room movie showing.`

`Yes`, he wrote back.

The next message said: `Her Majesty would like pepperoni pizza, please and thank you.`

He grinned as he typed in: `Yes, be there in twenty minutes.`

As long as he could see Kate and spend time with her, he didn't care—on the lake, in the house, or out taking a drive in the rain.

He noticed that Jamie's van was gone when he parked and wondered where she was as he jogged from his truck to the porch, pizza in hand. Before he could knock, Gracie swung the door open.

"Kate says for me to let you in. She'll be here in a minute. She's talking to her mama on the phone. Come on in out of the rain and put the pizza on the table," Gracie said.

"Yes, ma'am. Where's your mama?" Waylon asked.

While he unloaded the food, Kate walked up behind him.

His well-honed sixth sense, developed on the force, told him that she was there even before she spoke. That wonderful scent that she wore blended with the sweet coconut smell of her hair and the aura that belonged to no other woman in the universe sent his senses reeling.

"Gracie is babysitting us," Kate said. "Amanda started having pains, so Jamie drove her to the hospital in Wichita Falls so they can monitor her for a few hours to be sure it's not labor. They figure it's Braxton-Hicks."

"Well, then, Gracie, since you are the babysitter, do you think we can have some pizza and bread sticks?" Waylon asked.

Gracie sighed. "I thought you'd never get here. Can we put a quilt on the floor and watch our movie while we eat?"

"We sure can," Kate answered.

"What are we watching?" Waylon carried the pizza boxes back to the living room. "Will the babysitter let us have a beer with our supper?"

"Of course." Gracie giggled. "And I'm not really the sitter. Y'all are. Big people can have a beer, but little kids have to drink milk or juice. Can I please have a soda pop?"

Kate nodded. "Pizza does not go with milk or juice. You can have a Coke, but let's make it one of the caffeine-free ones."

"I don't care if it's got calves in it or not." Gracie removed the quilt from the back of the sofa and spread it out on the floor. "We are watching *Homeward Bound*. Mama says it's a good movie."

"Isn't that like twenty years old?" Waylon whispered.

"Twenty-four, to be exact, but you take what you can get at the convenience store rental. We don't have cable television here at the cabin," Kate answered.

"Let's go to the movies, then." Waylon nodded.

Gracie plopped down in the middle of the quilt and nodded toward the sofa. "You old people can sit there."

"Ouch!" Waylon winced.

"Painful, isn't it?" Kate nudged him with her shoulder as she passed.

By the end of the movie, Waylon wanted to marry Kate and adopt Gracie. They were both adorable all through the movie, crying when the cat, Sassy, was nearly killed, giggling at the antics of the young dog, Chance, and worrying about the older big yellow one, Shadow.

Gracie declared that as soon as they moved all their stuff to the cabin, she wanted a cat just like Sassy. Kate had fallen in love with Shadow, and Waylon wondered if she'd ever considered having a big dog.

As the credits rolled, Gracie yawned and crawled up in Kate's lap. "I wish my mama was home. I'm sleepy and I don't like going to bed all by myself."

Kate wrapped both her arms around the little girl. She would have made an amazing mother. Gracie was the child that her husband produced with another woman, and she was humming to her. That took some kind of special person.

The strumming of a guitar playing the first chords of "Girls Like Us" came from the end table.

Waylon chuckled.

"What?" Kate asked. "It's either Jamie or Amanda."

He handed her the phone. "Fitting song choice."

Kate flashed a smile over the top of Gracie's head and put the phone on speaker. "Hello, Amanda, what's the news?"

"We are about five minutes from the cabin. I had false labor. Everything is still on schedule and fine. Sorry we're only calling now—the storm messed with the cell service. Jamie is driving and we just passed the convenience store. See you soon."

Kate hit the "End" button, and Gracie wiggled out of her embrace, yawned, and stretched. "So we don't get a baby tonight?"

"That's right, but your mama will be here real soon," Waylon said.

"I'm glad." Gracie yawned again.

"For which one? That the baby isn't here or that your mama is almost home?" Kate stood up and folded the quilt, picked up the paper plates from the coffee table, and carried them to the trash.

"Both," Gracie answered. "Amanda told Mama that if she had the baby now, she'd have to leave him in the hospital, and I want to bring my little brother home. And I really miss my mama."

Waylon helped by taking the empty beer bottle and the Coke can to the trash. "Is that my cue to leave?"

"No rush," she said.

"I've loved every minute of this evening." His phone rang.

"Mama's here!" Gracie shouted simultaneously.

The two women came through the door talking while he answered the call. He listened for a minute and then said, "I'm on my way." He crossed the room in a couple of long strides. "Glad everything is fine, Amanda. Victor has gotten his car stuck in the mud down at Hattie's. They saw my truck parked outside when they came home from getting ice cream and they need help."

"I'll walk you out." Kate sucked in the fresh air when they were on the porch. "You never get this in the city."

He wrapped his hand around hers. "What?"

"Stars this bright or this scent after a rain."

"It's the smell of wet dirt." He stopped when they reached his truck and pulled her close to his chest. "I wish we'd met sooner, like when we were in our twenties, and that we'd had a whole yard full of little kids like Gracie. You would have been an awesome mother, Kate."

"But we weren't these people back then. We might not have even liked each other at that age. Look who I ended up picking later."

"I would have liked you at any age."

"Really?" Kate cocked her head to one side.

"Absolutely. Though you are right. Right out of college, neither of us would have enjoyed tonight the way we did. I'll see you tomorrow, Kate."

Watching her stand on the porch and wave until he was out of sight kicked his pulse into high gear.

Chapter Nineteen

"It seems like we've been waiting for hours."

Amanda checked the time on her phone. "It's not even seven o'clock yet. We've only been here ten minutes, Jamie. They have to get settled and get the preliminary talkin' done. Don't be nervous. If not, then we'll go back to what we were doing, right? You have a teaching job in Dallas. I've got the shop. It's not like we are going to have to stand on the street corner and beg for quarters."

"You are so right," Jamie said, fidgeting with a speck of lint on her skirt. "But Gracie is so happy here. I wish they'd call one of us into the meeting and get it over with."

"Don't think about time. Think about us sitting outside in the hallway on metal folding chairs. To me, it feels like we're in trouble," Amanda said.

Jamie smiled. "I was so shy, I never had to sit in the hallway. My teachers are probably still in shock that I grew up to become a teacher myself."

"Humph! Don't try to put that bullshit on my plate. The way you bowed up to me at the funeral, and with your temper, I ain't believin' a word of that," Amanda said.

"I was shy in high school. I learned to stand up for myself in college. How about you?"

"I was not a model student, so I did spend my fair share of time sitting on a chair just like this or in detention hall. I liked the latter much better."

"Why?" Jamie asked.

"Most of the time they assigned a teacher who'd rather be doing anything else but watching a bunch of unruly kids, so they'd leave the room. We'd break out the cards and I won enough money playing poker to buy after-school Cokes."

"Really?" Jamie gasped. "I figured you for a shy little thing like Kate and I were."

"Not until later, after Aunt Ellie got me straightened out in the church."

"Amanda?" Victor poked his head out the door. "We're ready for you."

"Wish me luck," Amanda said.

"You don't even need it."

"Thank you."

Amanda had dressed in her best maternity slacks and shirt, styled her curly red hair in a twist, and applied makeup. The job might not bring in the money that she'd made at the bank or even the clothing store, but it would be perfect for a single mother with a child. And Bootleg was a better place to raise a baby than in an apartment right in the city.

"Please have a seat," a lady she recognized from the church said.

The wing-back chair that Amanda sank into was a whole lot more comfortable that the metal chair out in the hallway. She waited while they shuffled through her résumé and recommendation letters she'd gotten from the bank, Aunt Ellie, and Wanda.

"I am Andrea Drysdale, the president of the Board of Education," the woman said. She introduced three of the other five members, finishing, "You already know Victor, who has highly recommended you for this position."

Amanda nodded at each of them. "I'm pleased to meet you all. You all know how I came to be in Bootleg, right?"

"We do," Mrs. Drysdale said and then lowered her voice. "And off the record, we're glad to hear that the man who conned Iris is dead. We aren't going to let anything that he caused or did influence our decision. Do you have any questions about this job?"

"Could I stretch the yearly salary into twelve payments so that I would have a summer paycheck? Do I work in the summer months, and if so, could I bring my baby with me?"

"Yes, most secretaries do like to have their checks in the summer. Though you will still work during that time. You can choose either the month after school is out or the month before school starts for your break. If you choose to work all three months, you will be paid extra. And you can bring your child during those months," Andrea answered.

"If you stay organized through the year, there won't be much to do but answer phone calls in the summer," Victor said. "Anything else?"

Amanda nodded and asked, "You have taken into consideration that the earliest I could start to work would be mid-October? And that right now they still suspect me and Jamie and Kate of murder?"

"We have and have made arrangements with a retired teacher to take the job for the first six weeks," Paula, the elementary school principal, answered. "And all that other business will take care of itself, we have no doubt. So?"

"Yes, I'm interested." Amanda's heart kicked in an extra beat as she fought the urge to do a wiggle dance in her chair.

"Amanda, we are offering you the job. We have the contract drawn up. The salary comes with health insurance. You will have to add dental and vision, but that will all be decided later when you put your baby on the policy," Victor said.

"Oh! Then you are hiring me right now?"

"Yes." Victor grinned. "Are you accepting?"

"Yes, I am. Where do I sign?"

☙

Kate waited on the porch with Hattie and Gracie that evening. She was every bit as antsy as Gracie, and nothing helped. Not ice cream or playing games or counting stars or trying to figure out how far the moon was kept them from wondering what was going on at the school.

When Jamie parked her van, Hattie raised a hand into the air. "Well, praise the Lord, they are home. I called Victor twice and he won't tell me anything. All he'll say is that it's classified. The old coot. I'll get him back."

Kate tried to read Amanda and Jamie's body language, but they didn't give a single thing away until they reached the porch. Jamie opened up her arms to Gracie and said, "You ready to move, kiddo?"

Gracie torpedoed herself into Jamie's arms. "This is just what I wanted, Mama." She planted kisses all over her mother's face.

"So you got the job?" Kate exhaled loudly. "Amanda?"

"I will start work six weeks after school begins."

"And you will let me babysit, right?" Hattie asked. "I'll come right here to the cabin so you don't have to take the baby out in the weather."

"Hattie, you are an absolute godsend. I'm so lucky to have you. They said if I work through the summer, I get extra pay." Amanda beamed. "I'm hoping that when I wake up, this not a dream. I can even take the baby with me in the summer."

How could Conrad have treated these two women the way he did? Kate could understand why he was such a son of a bitch with her. He'd married her for money and when he didn't get it, he rebelled like a petulant child. But Jamie and Amanda hadn't been born with the proverbial silver spoon in their mouths, and they damn sure didn't deserve what he had put them through.

"Is it real? They won't change their minds?" Gracie whispered.

"We are really going to live here." Jamie hugged her again. "I promise. We should call Mama Rita. I think you should tell her."

Gracie squirmed out of her mother's arms and danced around the porch. "Can we tell her right now?"

Jamie handed her the phone. "Don't hang up when you get done. I want to talk to her, too."

Kate hugged both Amanda and Jamie. "Congratulations to both of you. To all three of you, really—Gracie wanted this as much as you did."

"I have been racking my brain trying to figure out what you could do at the school." Hattie glanced over at Kate.

Kate patted the elderly woman gently on the shoulder. "I have a job in Fort Worth."

"But I can see in your face that you'd like to stay here. My mama used to tell me to never close a door until you see what's on the other side of it," Hattie said.

Kate had heard that before, but it really sank in that warm summer evening. She didn't really have two doors before her like in that old television show. A beyond-comfortable lifestyle had been given to her, one that she knew and could do. She imagined an extra door in her office. If she chose to step through it into a very different office, would she have regrets? But if she didn't, wouldn't she always wonder?

"Don't ever look back and wonder if you might have been happier if you'd chosen another pathway to walk," Hattie whispered.

Before Kate could answer, her phone pinged. She glanced down at it to see a message from Waylon. Shall we send them flowers tomorrow?

She smiled and sent one back. Already done and balloons for Gracie.

The next one said, Pretty sure of yourself. Call me when things quiet down?

She sent him a smiley face symbol.

"That was Waylon, wasn't it? I can tell by the expression on your face," Hattie said.

"I'd make a poor poker player." Kate smiled.

"When it comes to Waylon, I can read you like a book, girl."

Kate was so jealous of Jamie and Amanda that evening that it was a wonder she wasn't the same shade of green as the Hulk. They knew what they wanted and went after it. Kate knew what she wanted, but a nagging fear kept her from being willing to make a change. Pure insanity. She'd been in Bootleg less than a month. Not long ago she and Conrad's other two wives were at his funeral. That was not enough time for her to even consider a drastic change.

Decision based on the heart. Hattie's words stuck in her mind. The only time that Kate had done that, she'd wound up married to Conrad.

Be honest, the voice in her head argued. *You weren't paying a bit of attention to your heart in those days. That was one time your mother was right.*

Kate pushed the voice away. "Hey, I've got a bottle of chilled wine waiting, and Hattie brought over a sinful chocolate cake."

"And I can have milk with my cake, right?" Gracie was still wiggling in excitement.

With an arm around Gracie's shoulders, Kate whispered, "Out of a stemmed wineglass, so you can pretend."

Dear Lord, what have I done? was the first thought in Jamie's mind that Saturday morning when she awoke. The thrill of getting the job had passed, and the reality of actually moving from the city to Bootleg set in. All through the process of making up her mind and then signing the contract, she'd thought she was making the right decision even if it did seem rushed. But that morning she doubted herself. She moaned and immediately checked to be sure that she had not wakened Gracie.

Her child was gone! For a split second she panicked, and then she heard her out in the house laughing with Kate. Jamie hopped out of bed, and something fluttered in her peripheral vision. She whipped around to find Gracie's balloons straining against the strings holding them down. Right beside them was her bouquet of daisies. The congratulatory card was unsigned, but there was no doubt in her mind that Kate and Waylon had sent them.

"Stop it!" she scolded herself, not the balloons. "You made this choice. Now plow ahead without regrets."

She sniffed the air and caught a whiff of warm maple syrup, bacon, and coffee mixed together. Pancakes and coffee sounded like a right fine way to start the day.

Neither Amanda nor Kate looked a bit better than she did.

"Did we do the right thing?" Amanda asked.

Jamie sucked in a lungful of air and said, "Of course we did. It's normal to second-guess such a drastic change."

"Not as radical as if Kate said she wasn't going back to Fort Worth," Amanda said.

Jamie poured coffee into her mug. Maybe not, but to her it was every bit as big a decision as any one Kate would make. And now with the cabin undecided, she might have to rent another place and move furniture.

Kate motioned toward the stove. "Amanda left pancakes for you, and the syrup is warm."

"Still nesting, are you?" Jamie glanced at Amanda, remembering her days in that mode just before Gracie was born.

"Yes, and weeping at commercials, too. We're discussing whether or not we'll ever get married again," Amanda said.

"Not me," Jamie said. "What I've been through is enough for me without having to adjust to married life all over again."

Although, if she was honest, she'd never really done much adjusting with Conrad. He'd popped in and out occasionally, only staying a week at a time. That wasn't much of a marriage.

Amanda sighed. "It seems like all that happened years ago, instead of just a month."

"Don't it, though?" Jamie set her mug on the table and went back to get the plate of pancakes. "Where's Gracie?"

"She's waiting on the porch for your Mama Rita. So, say the perfect man came along and you fell in love with him. Would you change your mind?" Amanda raised an eyebrow toward Jamie.

She poured syrup on the pancakes and thought about the question for a full minute. "I'd have to do double time on the trust issue. He'd not only have to be good to me but also to Gracie. And believe me, if it happens, I will have him investigated," Jamie said. "If he finds out and don't like it, he can hit the road."

"That's exactly what I said. I may even hire two separate investigators to make sure it's done right," Amanda said.

"Did you ever . . ." Kate hesitated long enough to take a sip of coffee.

"Ever what?" Jamie asked.

"Think there was something too good about the whole dating process with Conrad?"

"You mean like it was too perfect?" Amanda asked.

"Exactly. Did you ever have an argument or a fight with him over anything, especially that first year?" Kate asked.

Jamie shook her head. "That is strange, isn't it? He always got his way, but then he was only home a week out of a month, and I didn't want to make that time unpleasant."

That should have raised a warning flag. No arguments. Making things so perfect for him so he'd be happy. God, what had turned her into a submissive little wife like that?

"Me, either," Amanda said.

"He was a master of manipulation," Kate said.

Oh, yes, he was, and so damned good that I didn't even see it until now.

"And not all that great in bed," Amanda agreed with a nod. "It had to be all about him, since I only got to be with him a few days. I won't fall for that crap again."

The heat started on Jamie's neck and moved around to her cheeks, darkening her light-brown skin to scarlet. "You, too, huh?"

"Oh, yeah," Kate and Amanda said at the same time.

Kate held up a palm. "But only for about six months for me and the same for Amanda. Mine was by choice and hers by death. You had to put up with him longer than either of us."

"That just makes me the bigger fool." Jamie sighed.

"You don't get to carry that burden alone," Amanda told her. "We'll share that one three ways. At least you were thinking divorce. I was looking forward to a vacation with him right here in this cabin. God, I was so stupid."

Jamie nudged Amanda with her shoulder. "And you don't need to carry that burden alone, either."

Gracie's squeals vibrated through the house before anyone could say another word. "She's here! Mama Rita is here!"

Jamie left her coffee and food and headed for the door in a semijog with Kate and Amanda right behind her. Gracie had bailed off the porch and thrown herself in Rita's arms and was attempting to tell her everything she knew in the seconds before Jamie joined them in a three-way hug.

"Did you see the stagecoach? Me and Lisa get to ride in it at the ranch on Monday and we get to have a picnic and"—she lowered her voice—"I'm going to ride one of them horses or maybe a four-wheeler if the horses are tired from pulling the stagecoach."

"I didn't see a stagecoach, but I did see a Ferris wheel." Mama Rita winked at Jamie.

"And funnel cakes? Did you smell them?" Gracie put her hand in Mama Rita's and led her to the house. "Come and see my room. I got balloons yesterday. I know that Kate and Waylon sent them, because Kate was smiling real big when they came. Did you have breakfast? We've got extra pancakes and bacon on the stove."

"I'm waiting for funnel cakes," Mama Rita answered. "You can give me a tour of the house and the deck while everyone gets ready."

Gracie skipped along beside her great-grandmother, chattering the whole time about the cabin.

"She does love it here," Mama Rita said to Jamie from the side of her mouth. "You made the right decision."

"Want to move with us?" Jamie asked, half in jest.

Rita chuckled. "Not this year, but I can see this as a lovely place to retire."

Jamie laughed. "Mama Rita, you are seventy-five years old. You've been retired for years."

For her to even say that she might move to Bootleg someday was huge. Jamie hugged herself, and all the doubts from that morning disappeared. Mama Rita agreed with her choice and that made everything right again.

"In my family, we don't really quit until we are eighty, and then we keep at something until at least ninety," she said as an aside to Kate before she gave Gracie her full attention. "Now what is this about a fishing dock, Gracie? Will we have time to go see it before we go to the festival? I'm going to be your cheerleader in the contest and we are going to win."

"I've been practicing with Hattie and I think I might win." Gracie pulled her great-grandmother into the house.

Kate smiled. "I reckon we'd better get dressed in a hurry, or we'll all be in trouble and have to stay home while Gracie and Mama Rita go to the festival."

Jamie laughed. "You are starting to sound like a country girl."

"Well, thank you," Kate said. "And I don't mean that with a smidgen of sarcasm, either."

Chapter Twenty

Old folks brought their lawn chairs and staked out a place to watch the parade that Saturday morning. The temperature was inching up toward three digits when the sirens from the Bootleg Volunteer Fire Department's big red truck sounded off. A few umbrellas popped up, providing shade, and Kate glanced around to see if any vendors were selling them so she could purchase one for Gracie and Lisa to share. But there were none.

Could it be that was her sign? Jamie's words continued to echo in her head. She should resign from the oil business and buy a vendor's wagon to travel around the state with all kinds of umbrellas. Every town had a festival, and everyone wanted a little shade in the hot summer. She smiled at the silly thought.

The Bootleg High School band, all wearing street clothing and crazy fishing hats instead of their usual uniforms, marched behind the fire truck. Twice the band stopped and performed a fancy two-step routine that garnered catcalls and applause from the crowd.

She took a picture of the band with her phone and then took several up-close snapshots of Gracie. Maybe she'd scatter pictures of Gracie throughout her new home, wherever it turned out to be.

Maybe *that* was her sign. She could travel around to the festivals taking pictures like they did on cruise ships and selling them to the people. The possibilities were endless. Lovers, married folks, old people, little kids—she turned her camera up and shot another picture of Gracie and Lisa with their heads together as they watched the band. Then she took one of Paul and Jamie standing about a foot apart as they minded the children.

There was a float from the church with the preacher and his wife riding on the back and throwing candy out to the crowd. One from the elementary school with all the teachers on it. Next year Jamie would ride on that one, and Waylon was right—Kate would need to be there to watch Gracie.

No, you won't. Her Mama Rita will always be here to do that job, her conscience said above the loud band music.

Kate didn't even argue. She'd be there anyway to take pictures of Gracie through the years, recording her growth by the festival pictures.

People dressed in all kinds of fishing costumes dashed between the next several floats, making the onlookers laugh with their antics as they gave out rubber worms and inexpensive lures to the crowd on the sidelines.

The whole thing had a Mardi Gras feel to it. She'd been to New Orleans once on a business trip and watched a parade from her hotel balcony, but it hadn't been as much fun as this one.

Finally, the stagecoach appeared at the end with Victor driving and Hattie waving a lace hankie from inside with several other folks. Gracie and Lisa hopped up and down and blew kisses at her. When she yelled their names, they hugged each other and beamed.

And then it was over. People picked up their chairs and headed toward the school, where two blocks had been roped off for vendors and the carnival had been set up in the parking lot. Kate tagged along behind the rest of her group for a few minutes, but then she saw a vendor selling cute hair bows and stopped to buy a couple with tiny pictures of Cinderella on the ribbons.

A booth offering an array of brightly colored scarves and shawls caught her eye, too. The one that stood out was a splash of bright colors swirled around on a background of blue. It reminded her of a sunset over the lake, but she had absolutely nothing that it would match.

Amanda has a cute little maternity dress that it would go with, though.

She was about to buy it when someone touched her hand.

"What do you think of our festival?" Victor asked at her elbow. "Seen Hattie around? I had to get the horses unhitched and I lost her."

Kate hung the scarf back on the display. "I love it! The parade was amazing, and I loved seeing you up there driving that stagecoach. Are you going to be our driver on Monday?"

"Oh, no, honey! Waylon gets to drive that day and Paul will ride shotgun. I'll be in the stagecoach to protect all the girls." He winked.

"How many of these festivals have you attended?" Kate asked.

"I haven't missed a festival since I was born back in Prohibition. Did anyone ever tell you how Bootleg got its name?"

Kate glanced over his shoulder, scanning the crowd for Waylon. "No, sir, they didn't."

"Well, let's me and you go that way." He pointed toward the left. "I saw the funnel cake vendor over there. We can have a midmorning snack and talk," he said. "Hattie will find me a lot quicker if I'm sittin' down. She and I have got to ride the Ferris wheel together. It's been our tradition since we was six years old. I was scared to death to ride it, but I wanted to so bad she rode with me. Helped me out—I couldn't be afraid in front of a girl."

Kate followed him to the funnel cake wagon, where he marched right up to the window, laid his money on the shelf, and said, "Give me the biggest that you got. Me and that good-lookin' blonde are goin' to share it."

The smell of the hot grease and sweet frying bread brought back a memory that she hadn't thought of in years. Her father had taken her to a medieval fair somewhere close to Dallas, and they'd eaten funnel cakes. It had been a fun day, and she'd fallen asleep on the way home that evening. When she awoke the next morning, her fingers were still sticky. She'd licked the sweet sugar from them and hoped that they could go to the fair again that day. Her mother and father had both gone to work before she went down to the kitchen for breakfast and the nanny fussed about her sleeping in dirty clothing. The memory put a smile on her face and filled her with happiness.

Victor carried the paper plate carefully to the table where Kate had sat down. He placed the plate in the middle of the small table and pulled out a chair across from her.

"You can have the first bite," he said.

Kate quickly pinched off a bite, popped it into her mouth, and then pulled a couple of napkins from the metal holder in the middle of the table. "You were going to tell me about Bootleg?"

"The lake came about in 1924, back before I was even born. Until then it was just a part of the Wichita River. Down in this area, it was far enough from prying eyes that folks who had a notion to make moonshine could use the banks of the river to do so. Didn't want to put a still too close to the house. If you got caught, you could lose your property." Victor told the story between bites.

When they finished the last strip of cake, he pulled a roll of bills from his shirt pocket and peeled off a five. "Go get us another one, but don't tell Hattie. She's going to want to share one with me later, and I sure don't want her to know that I've already had two."

Kate didn't have to stand in line, so she was only gone a few minutes. "Tell me more about Bootleg and how it got its name."

Victor pulled off a chunk of cake. "My grandpa was one of those bootleggers. Times got tough those days, and he found a spot on the river and started up a business. It's what saved our home place here in Bootleg."

Hattie sat down beside Kate, picked off a piece of the cake, and took up the story. "History has it when the community sprang up near the lake, they tried to name it Lincoln, after the past president, and then Lakeside, but nothing stuck. Everyone had called the place Bootleg for so long they all finally gave up on naming it anything else.

"Hey." Hattie looked across the table at Victor. "You old fart. I bet you wasn't going to own up to eating one of these before you shared one with me, was you?"

Victor held up his hands and grinned. "Busted!"

"Don't tell me you rode the Ferris wheel without me, too." Hattie's hands went to her hips and her mouth set in a firm line.

"Don't get your underpants all twisted up. I wouldn't do that. We got to ride it together or you get scared," he teased.

"Not me. I love the Ferris wheel."

Waylon sat down in the fourth chair and reached for a bite of the cake. "Good mornin', all y'all. I hear the picnic for Monday has been approved. What do I need to do or cook, Hattie?"

"You have the stagecoach ready, and me and Victor will bring the rest of it," Hattie answered. "Right now, we're going to go ride that Ferris wheel, aren't we, Victor?"

"Yes, ma'am, we are." He grinned. "And I won't eat another bite of this cake, so I'll have plenty of room to share one with you when we get done."

Kate loved these two old folks and would gladly adopt them. She'd send presents on their birthdays, for Christmas, and even Grandparents Day if they'd let her call them her own.

She waited until they were out of hearing distance before she said, "We should turn the tables on those two and get them together in their golden years."

"They are together," Waylon said.

"I mean in one house and married."

"Whole town has been trying to do that since before my mother died. They are happy, but they will never get married. They're too set in their ways. Are you going to ride the Ferris wheel with me?"

"What does riding the Ferris wheel mean? That we are friends for life?" She was flirting and knew it, but right then she felt as free and as excited about the day as Gracie.

He picked up the last of the funnel cake, tore it in two pieces, and fed half to her. His fingertips grazing her lips ignited sparks that flitted around the air like fireflies. Turnabout was fair play. She quickly picked up what was left and fed it to him, deliberately brushing the back of her hand across his freshly shaven cheek.

His sudden intake of breath and the way his eyes went all dreamy gave testimony that she'd had the same effect on him that he'd had on her.

"So?" she asked.

"So what? More funnel cake?"

"No. If I ride the Ferris wheel with you, does that make us friends for life like Hattie and Victor?" She hoped he said no—suddenly she wanted to be more than friends. It wasn't possible, but then, it wasn't a sin to want something even if there wasn't a chance in hell of ever getting it.

"Of course. And before I forget, here's my part of that flower and balloon order." He slipped a bill into her shirt pocket. The touch of his fingertips brushing across her breast sent another shock wave through her body.

She quickly jerked the money out and handed it back to him. "I didn't sign either of our names, and it's already taken care of."

"But they know I was in on it." He dropped the money into her purse. "Gracie hugged me and thanked me a dozen times for her balloons. And I pay my bills, so don't argue with me about this, Kate."

"Don't tell me what to do, Detective Kramer." She dragged out his name.

Damn! Damn! Damn! Now he'd gone and spoiled the whole feeling.

He crossed his arms over his chest. "I'm not Conrad. I'm not going to take your money or stomp on your heart. Don't compare me to him."

She gritted her teeth until her jaws ached. "Don't accuse me of things I didn't do. And don't bring up his name to me. And another thing—if you put cuffs on me and drag me to jail for something I didn't do, that classifies as stomping on my heart. And the final thing—I'm not going to ride the Ferris wheel with you. What if a columnist or reporter or even blogger is roaming around among all these people and they see us snuggled up together on a Ferris wheel?"

He stood to his feet. "You are right about the ride, but when you come back to Bootleg next year to enjoy the festival with Gracie, this will all be done. Save me a spot next to you."

"Who says I'll come back?"

She picked up her purse and was about to leave when Gracie yelled from across the street, "There's the funnel cake wagon and there's Kate. Hey, Kate, wait for us!"

"You could ride with Gracie and I could ride with Lisa and we'd be together, but not side by side," Waylon drawled.

"And I bet if we were really good at matchmaking we could get Jamie and Paul to ride together," Kate said.

"Hattie would be so proud of you in this moment." Waylon chuckled and then grew serious. "Trust me, Kate. I'm doing everything I can possibly do to clear your name."

"Let's go ride the Ferris wheel, Kate." Gracie grabbed her hand and tugged. "Mama says each kid has to have an adult."

"Well, in that case, you think I could ride with Lisa?" Waylon asked.

"And I could ride with Gracie." Kate shot a dirty look over her shoulder at Waylon. Damn, that man could be so frustrating!

"I'm not getting on that thing. Sure as I did, I'd go into premature labor," Amanda said. "Besides, I see Aunt Ellie and Wanda over there. Hey!" she called out and waved. "I invited them, but I didn't know if they'd get to come or not. This is great."

Paul looked over the kids' heads at Jamie. "Guess that leaves the two of us to ride together."

"I guess it does." Jamie smiled.

"What about these three lovely ladies?" Waylon looked back at Aunt Ellie, Mama Rita, and Wanda.

He was smooth, Kate would give him that.

"Wanda and I are going to park right there at that table y'all vacated and eat funnel cakes," Aunt Ellie said. "And you must be Jamie's grandma Rita? Want to join us? I bet we can talk Amanda into pulling up a chair with us, since she's not going on the ride."

"I outgrew rides years ago. Y'all kids go have a good time and don't worry about us. We'll catch up to you later on," Rita answered.

"Where's Hattie and Victor?" Gracie tugged on Kate's hand.

"They are already in line," Kate answered. "Are we ready to go?"

Kate and Gracie had reached the front of the line when the old fellow running it opened the gates to fill up the wheel again. She grabbed the money that Waylon had given her and handed it to the man. "This is for the next four seats."

The man looked at the bill and grinned. "How many times you plannin' on ridin'?"

"Is there enough for two times?"

"Honey, with fifty dollars, you could ride all day. I'll make change." He laughed as he handed her several fives and a few ones.

"Have you ridden one of these before?" Waylon looked up over his shoulder as the music started and the wheel began to move.

"Never," she said.

When they reached the top, the wheel stopped and the seat swung slightly. Gracie grabbed her hand and squeezed. "Don't be afraid. I'm right here with you."

"I'm glad you are, Gracie. Oh, my goodness. Look out there across the town. You can see the edge of the lake."

Gracie let go of the bar and reached up with both hands. "I can almost touch the clouds."

Kate held her breath until Gracie's hands were back on the bar.

Just like your father. Her mother's voice was back in her head. *Fearful of everything, even a cruise ship.*

Don't bring that up. Don't ever put it in my head again.

Thinking it, even in a mean tone, did not erase the words. That was the very thing that had caused the argument between her and her father the night he'd died. She'd given her parents a seven-day cruise to celebrate their thirty-fifth wedding anniversary, and he'd told her to get her money back, that there was no way he'd get on a ship like that.

Just like Gracie did not cause her father's death, you did not cause yours, the voice said. This time it was much gentler, and she smiled as the wheel made another turn and her bucket started back up.

"Your arms are longer than mine," Gracie yelled. "Hold them up and see if your hands disappear in the clouds."

Kate let go of her death grip on the bar and reached for the clouds. She didn't touch them, but there was exhilaration in trying. When the ride stopped, she and Gracie were the last ones to join the group waiting on them.

"Can we go have funnel cakes now?" Gracie asked Jamie.

"Please, Daddy?" Lisa begged.

"I've had those already, so I'm going to meander through the other vendors," Kate said. "If I don't see you before then, I'll meet you at the dock for the fishing contest."

"I'm going to sit right here a little longer and do some people watching," Amanda announced. "My feet are already starting to swell."

"See y'all later, then." Kate took off in long-legged strides to see the rest of the vendors.

Waylon fell in beside her. "Are we through arguing?"

"You overpaid for your half of the flowers," Kate said.

Victor and Hattie appeared out of the crowd and joined them. Victor had powdered sugar in the corners of his mouth, and Hattie had a huge bear in her arms.

"What flowers? Did you two send those bouquets and balloons? That is so sweet," Hattie said.

"That is classified information," Waylon said.

"Too much money appeared in my purse for his half of the classified stuff, so I'm buying us all one of those Indian taco things for lunch," Kate said.

"Hot damn! I love them things." Victor patted her on the back. "But first Hattie wants to look through all the geegaws the vendors have on this side of the street."

"The taco wagon is at the end, so we can eat there and then take in the ones on the other side," Hattie said.

"Sounds like a good plan to me," Waylon said.

They'd made it halfway down the lineup when Hattie threw a hand across her forehead. "I'm getting too hot and I need something to drink. Victor, cross the street to that Coke place and get me something cold. I don't care what."

"I'll go," Kate said quickly. "Hattie, you sit right here on the curb in this little bit of shade. Victor, you better stay with her in case this is heatstroke coming on."

"I'll go with Kate and help tote the drinks back," Waylon said.

How did anyone stay mad at him? Or better yet, how did anyone keep information from him when he smiled? No wonder he had such a good record for closing cases. He could talk a priest into revealing what was said in confessional.

Kate positioned herself in the line so she could keep a watch on Hattie. She and Victor were talking. Maybe she was simply tired and thirsty. The sun was broiling hot, and Hattie had been on her feet for a while.

Waylon touched her on the arm. "Are we okay?"

"I hate fighting. It's all I did with Conrad after that first year."

She hated saying his name. Would Conrad always stand between her and another relationship or even friendship?

Only if you let him, the voice in her head said, and this time it was her father, not her mother.

"It's all I did with both of my wives. They hated my work schedule and my paycheck and the apartment we lived in," Waylon said. "I vowed I'd never go through that again."

"So did I," she said.

"I didn't grow up in a fighting family," he said. "I had to learn the art of arguing when I got to college."

She nodded. "I know exactly where you are coming from."

Her first fight with her roommate had been over keeping the bathroom clean, and they hadn't spoken to each other for a week afterward. She'd thought at the time that nothing could ever be that awkward and uncomfortable again—little did she know.

"Hey, there's the rest of your family over there with Hattie and Victor," Waylon said.

The rest of her family—those words played in a continuous loop through her mind. Not a one of those folks was blood kin, but she cared about them, about their futures, about the baby Amanda was going to have soon and about Gracie's happiness. Did that make a family?

The hot July breeze whipped her hair around as they moved them up to the window. Waylon pulled out a bill and laid it on the counter.

"Two big Cokes, one sweet tea, and . . ." He looked over at her.

"A root beer," she said.

"I wonder if the other folks would want something?" he asked.

"We only have two hands each." Kate smiled. "And look, they're starting this way."

They passed one another in the middle of the road. Girls skipping ahead with Jamie and Paul behind them. Aunt Ellie and Mama Rita were right behind them, with Amanda and Wanda bringing up the rear. They looked like a family, and Kate envied them even the pretense.

"These drink wagons are going to make a fortune today," Paul said. "Especially with the kids thinking they have to run everywhere. It's worse than trying to herd cats."

"And that makes them hot, and the heat makes them thirsty." Waylon grinned.

"But they are so happy with their little red faces. Think how well they are going to sleep tonight," Kate said, wishing for the thousandth time that she had a whole bunch of kids to herd like cats that day.

❧

Kate felt sorry for Gracie on Sunday morning. She was still disappointed that she hadn't won the fishing contest in her category. She came in third place, netting her a new tackle box and some fishing gear, which she declared would help her win the next year. Still, it wasn't easy to go to church knowing that Jeremiah—a boy, at that—had won the tickets to Six Flags.

"At least I get to go to the ranch tomorrow and ride in the stagecoach. Jeremiah don't get to do that," she declared as they entered the church and headed up the middle aisle to join Hattie.

"Gracie!" Jamie chided.

"Well, I do, and that's better than Six Flags tickets, ain't it, Kate?"

"Maybe you could ask for those tickets for your birthday," Kate said. "I went to Six Flags one time, and it reminded me of the festival. Vendors and rides. Not a lot of difference."

"Then I'd rather have a pony for my birthday." Gracie skipped along to the pew where they usually sat.

They were getting settled when Waylon slid in the end space beside Kate. He leaned over and whispered, "My partner at the precinct called. There's a new lead. Nothing much yet, but on Tuesday I'm going to Dallas."

"On Tuesday the girls and I will be in town for our name change business," she said.

The song leader took her place behind the lectern and gave out a number. Kate had never heard the song, but she found the place in the hymnal. When the piano player started a run that sounded a whole lot like Floyd Cramer's, everyone in church began to clap along with the music.

The tune was simple but fast and the words repetitive: "Glory, glory, hallelujah, since I laid my burden down." Every other line repeated the line about laying down the burden. What Amanda had said about them sharing the burden three ways for being a fool when it came to Conrad came to her mind.

Kate thought of the load that Waylon was carrying as he tried to solve Conrad's murder. And even closer to home was the burden she carried about the oil company. Had God or fate or destiny put it all on her at this time of her life because it was time to make a change?

The last piano note hung in the air for a moment before the preacher went back to the pulpit. He opened his Bible and looked out over the congregation. "That congregational hymn should have opened up all y'all's hearts for my sermon. I was thinking today of that verse where Jesus says that his yoke is easy and his burden is light."

"Amen!" Victor said loudly, and several more folks echoed the same.

Kate nodded and tried to listen to the sermon, but her mind wandered. The burden of deciding what to do with her life weighed a lot more than the preacher said, and she doubted seriously that trusting Jesus would lighten the load.

But trusting your own heart might, a little voice whispered in her mind.

Chapter Twenty-One

Jamie awoke at the crack of dawn to find Gracie sitting up in bed and staring at her. "Is it today?" Gracie whispered.

She threw a pillow over her head and groaned. "Today is the day, but first we have to go to work. Amanda is going to the doctor this morning, so you can't stay home with her."

Gracie flipped back the covers and pumped both fists in the air. "I've been waiting forever for today. It's going to be even better than the festival." She grabbed the pillow and tossed it to the foot of the bed. "Today we get to go to the ranch and see the animals and ride in a stagecoach and have a picnic and smell hay. I like it when Kate comes home smelling like that."

Jamie sat up and stretched to get the kinks out of her back and neck. "You like it here in Bootleg, don't you?" She needed reassurance one more time that she'd made the right choice.

Gracie nodded. "I don't like it, Mama. I love it! I been tellin' and tellin' you that. We got a lake and fishin' and swimmin' and Miz Hattie and Victor and Kate and Amanda and Lisa. It's the best place in the world."

"But will you get tired of this and want to go back to Dallas?" Jamie asked.

In two bounds Gracie was back on the bed, hugging her mother tightly. "I'm not going to get tired of it here, Mama. When can we go to our old house and get the rest of our stuff?"

"Won't you miss your friends at school and Mama Rita?"

"Yes, I would, but I would miss this place more if we went back. Can I have a kitten, since we won't live in town anymore?"

Jamie hugged her daughter tightly, soaking in the scent of a little girl who was still fresh and sweet. Later, she'd smell like hay and sweat. "We'll see about a kitten. Let's go make breakfast and eat on the deck."

"Yes, yes, yes," Gracie squealed as she pumped her fist in the air.

All of Jamie's doubts about moving were erased by that gesture. Gracie was happy even after the excitement was over. Mama Rita had told her she'd made the right decision and that she might even retire to Bootleg. She was not going to let the doubts and fears cloud her world anymore.

Gracie twirled around in the middle of the floor, arms out to her sides. When she finally stopped, she fell backward on the bed and giggled. "Everything is still spinning, Mama."

"Well, you silly goose, you've scrambled your brain and it has to settle back down." Jamie laughed.

"I'm not a goose," Gracie argued. "I'm a little girl and I knew them people at the school were going to give you a job."

"How did you know?" Jamie asked.

"Because I asked God when we said our quiet prayer in Sunday school. Hattie says that if we ask God in secret, he will say okay and he did," Gracie said seriously. "Can we have pancakes for breakfast?"

"We sure can. Sausage or bacon?" Tears filled Jamie's eyes, but she quickly wiped them away before Gracie saw.

"Both." Gracie giggled and took off for the kitchen in a run.

ↁ

Amanda heard laughter and awoke from a beautiful dream about her baby's first Easter. Aunt Ellie had made him a cute little basket.

She laid a hand on her stomach. She would have rather spent the day with the rest of the crew out at the ranch, but she should not miss a doctor's appointment. After that scare with Braxton-Hicks, she really wanted to be sure everything was all right. Tugging the nightshirt down over her belly, she padded barefoot to the kitchen, where the smell of bacon was already wafting through the house.

"Good morning." She knuckled sleep from her eyes.

"Today is the day!" Gracie exclaimed.

"For what?" Amanda teased.

Gracie rolled her eyes. "Ah-mannn-duh!"

"Oh, I forgot, this is the ranch day when you and Lisa ride in a stage, right?" Amanda winked at Jamie.

"Yes, and see the animals. And we're having pancakes for breakfast with bacon and sausage. And when is that baby coming out of your stomach anyway?" Gracie finally stopped to draw in a breath.

"In about four weeks," Amanda said.

She was about used to Gracie asking so many questions, but that one took her by surprise. Still, she was glad that she'd answered honestly and not stammered around trying to find something right to say.

Amanda made a cup of decaf and took a sip. "Now my eyes are open. What can I do to help?"

"Get a pound of sausage out of the fridge and start it to cooking," Jamie said.

"For gravy or patties?" Amanda asked.

"Patties. We're having pancakes, bacon, and sausage."

"Sweet Lord!" Kate said from the doorway. "It's going to take a year for me to lose the weight I'm gaining."

"It beats the devil out of those green things you were drinking when you got here. Besides, with your height and build, I'd be willing to bet that you never gain a pound no matter what you eat." Amanda poured a cup of coffee and handed it to Kate.

"Never have, but then I've never tested it like I'm doing now. What can I do?"

"Set the table," Jamie said.

"We're eating on the deck," Gracie said.

"Since it's outside, shall we use the good plates or the plastic ones?" Kate asked.

"The good ones," Gracie said. "This is a special day and I'll help you."

ℰℴ

Amanda carefully arranged eight sausage patties in the cast-iron skillet while Jamie did double duty frying bacon and flipping pancakes on the grill. Amanda's thoughts went to the last time that she and Conrad made breakfast together in that same kitchen. That morning they'd had eggs Benedict, and afterward he'd taken her to the bedroom for one last bout of sex before they'd gone home from the honeymoon.

She'd thought that Conrad was the reward for turning her life around. She'd had a rebellious streak right out of high school. For a year she'd hung out with the wild crowd and frequented the bars around Wichita Falls, mostly country honky-tonks where she could always pick up a cowboy to take home for a one-night stand. Then one morning she awoke to find her cash and credit cards gone, right along with her laptop, her phone, and every piece of jewelry that she owned.

It took a lot of courage to go to Aunt Ellie and tell her what had happened, and it took hours of phone calls to get everything taken care of and reported. She'd lost what dignity she had left when she couldn't identify the cowboy to the police—when she didn't know if he was tall or short, had dark hair or light, or if he was young or old. Aunt Ellie put her back in church the following Sunday morning.

"Do you think that we get punished for our past sins?" Amanda whispered.

"Did you repent of them?" Jamie flipped two pancakes onto the platter and poured two more to cook.

"With many tears and lots of humiliation," Amanda said.

"Then they are forgiven and forgotten," Jamie answered.

Amanda frowned. "Why do they keep coming back to haunt me?"

"Who is haunting you?" Kate asked as she came back inside. "Gracie says she is going to watch the birds until we bring out breakfast."

"We were talking about sins and whether we get punished for them," Jamie said.

"According to the preacher at my church in Fort Worth, if we are truly repentant, then God forgives and forgets," Kate said. "Why?"

Amanda drained the sausage patties on a paper napkin before shifting them over to the platter with the bacon. "I was wild. I partied too much, drank too much for sure, and had lots of one-night stands before I got myself straightened out. I thought God had forgiven me when I met Conrad. But now I wonder if he wasn't punishing me with Conrad."

Kate stole a strip of bacon and blew on it to cool it down before popping it into her mouth. "Then he was punishing all of us. What sin did you commit, Jamie?"

"You first?" Jamie grinned.

"Before or after Conrad?"

"Before," Amanda said. "But I can't see you committing a sin."

Surely the great Kate didn't ever do anything that resembled sin. Hell's bells! She hadn't even divorced Conrad when he told her that he was cheating with other women.

"I can't see you taking home one-night stands, Amanda." Jamie giggled.

"Well, I did, and the last one sure opened my eyes." She told them about what had happened and how embarrassed she'd been. "Aunt Ellie made me start going to church with her again, and I finally figured out I was punishing my mother for abandoning me by acting out like that."

"You have to show ID to buy a beer now. I can't imagine how young you must have looked then," Kate said.

"I had a fake one from the time I was sixteen, like every other kid in school." Amanda flipped the sausage over. "But you were about to tell us what you did that you'd feel like Conrad was punishment."

"I was too busy for one-night stands, but I did have a couple of relationships in college. One with a married professor," Kate said.

"No!" Jamie almost dropped the pancakes she was moving from griddle to platter. "I can't even imagine it. Was he old and bald headed?"

"You are joking, right?" Amanda whispered.

Kate held up two fingers and then crossed her heart. "It's the truth. He was about thirty. It was his first year as a professor, and I was twenty-one. When I found out that Conrad had two more wives, I figured it was my comeuppance."

"But then what?" Amanda asked.

"I truly repented and said I'd never do that again. Still, I wonder about it." Kate picked up a plate and headed toward the deck with it. "And you, Jamie?"

"I was very, very good at five-finger discounts," Jamie whispered on the way outside.

"What made you stop?" Kate asked.

"Mama Rita. She went through my bedroom one day when I was at school. It was my senior year, and I had enough scholarships and grant money to go to college. And there were enough pretty things in my closet and my jewelry box that no one would ever know I was a poor girl from inner-city Dallas."

"And?" Amanda asked.

"She put every single thing I'd stolen into a big black garbage bag and put it in the charity donation box down on the corner. She said there was no way that I could remember where it came from to take it back. And then I got the lecture of a lifetime."

"Which was?" Kate asked.

"If I got caught, all my college money would be revoked and I'd be lucky to get a waitress job. Then she made me go to confession and tell the truth, and believe me, what I had to do was not easy. For the whole summer, I had to clean the church every Saturday for penance."

"So you are Catholic?" Amanda said.

"Mama Rita is. I went with her, but after Gracie was born I didn't always go to church with her. Sometimes I went to a Methodist church down the block from me. And when I found out that Conrad was a thief of sorts, I wondered if it was my punishment for past sins."

"Mama, look!" Gracie yelled from the railing. "There's a bunch of baby ducks out there on the lake."

Amanda could hardly believe what they'd said. *There's bad things in people who are basically good and good things in people who are bad. When my baby is born, I'll just have to search for the good memories of his father to tell him about.*

గ్రా

When everyone had left that morning, Kate poured a cup of coffee, carried it out to the deck, and called her mother. "Do you have a few minutes to talk?" she asked when her mother answered.

"I don't like working without you here." Teresa's tone was still grouchy. "I would have never made the suggestion that you take time off if . . ." She stopped.

"If you thought I'd really stay this long, right?" Kate finished the sentence for her. "You figured I'd come up here and get bored out of my mind and be back in the office in a week at the most," Kate said.

"Yes, I did," Teresa said curtly.

"I like it here." Yesterday's church hymn played through her mind as she shut her eyes tightly for courage. "I want to take a year's sabbatical."

"Don't you joke with me this morning," Teresa said.

"I'm serious as a heart attack. I want a year off," Kate said.

She didn't only want it. She needed it.

"You are not a priest," Teresa said.

"Folks other than the clergy take a year off every now and then. You said the murder thing surrounding me right now could ruin my reputation, and I need some time."

"I swear, you sound and act more like your father every day that you live. I've tried and tried to make you tough and ready to take over the business, but I'm . . ."

"I told you so." Kate laughed.

"What?"

"You're working around to saying the words, so spit them out. Maybe you should repeat them about a dozen times for future use so we don't have to go through this whole thing again."

Silence on the other end of the phone.

"Mother?" Kate held the phone out to make sure her battery wasn't dead.

"You can't talk to me like that," Teresa hissed. "I'm your boss."

"And you are my mother, but I'm forty-four years old and a grown woman. Just say the words and then we can get on with our conversation," Kate said.

"I don't say that every time we talk," Teresa argued.

"I can count on the fingers of one hand the times when you didn't. Mother, did you ever want to be anything other than what you are?"

"What kind of fool question is that? And don't change the subject."

Kate flopped back on the bed and stared at the ceiling. "Did you ever want to be a nurse or a teacher or maybe even a stay-at-home mother?"

"I did not." Teresa said each word distinctively. "I wanted to grow up and run this business just like my mother did and like you will be doing before long. What has come over you? Surely to God you weren't serious about selling the company. Do you realize how long it's been in our family?"

"Since the oil boom days, which makes it almost a hundred years," Kate answered. "It started out as Texas Oil, and then it was—"

"I don't need a history lesson," Teresa snapped.

"I've hauled hay here, and a few days ago I spent the day driving a tractor. It made me wonder if I chose the profession I'm in or if you chose it for me."

"I told you that a trip to that backwoods place was a mistake," Teresa fumed.

"And there it is." Kate chuckled. She could imagine her mother pacing the floor in her office, her eyes narrowed and her forehead wrinkled as she tried to figure out a way to manipulate Kate into coming home early. "It's probably the single smartest thing I've ever done. A bit unorthodox, having friends that were married to the same man at the same time I was, but all the same, I've made friends in the short time I've been here. Real, honest-to-God friends who don't give a shit if I have money or if I'm poor as a church mouse."

"Those other women, either one of whom could have killed Conrad, are not your friends," Teresa said.

"There are more people in this town than Amanda and Jamie."

"I'm hanging up now, and Katherine Elizabeth Steele, you had better get your head on straight," Teresa said.

The phone went silent, and Kate tossed it to one side. "Way I figure it is that my head might be on straighter than it's ever been, even if I do forget where I'm going." She finished off her coffee and headed down the hallway with plans to get dressed and go to the ranch to help get things ready for Gracie's big day.

Chapter Twenty-Two

Kate found herself pretending that she really lived there on the ranch and that this whole day had been her idea. She waved when Hattie and Victor arrived, and Waylon hurried out to help them carry things into the house. Before she could go pitch in to help, Paul drove up with Lisa and they jumped out, bouncing around like rabbits. Right behind them were Gracie and Jamie, and it didn't take her long to get out of the van and grab Lisa's hand.

The feeling inside Kate's heart was a good one, even if it wasn't real.

"I love it here," Lisa yelled. "Daddy, we need a place just like this, and there's the stagecoach in the backyard. Can me and Gracie go see it?"

"Of course you can, but stay right close to it. Don't wander off out of the yard."

Lisa and Gracie joined hands like always and ran around the side of the house.

This was what it could have been like if she'd married someone like Waylon. What was it that poem said about two paths? The author had chosen the one least traveled. She wished she'd done the same—forsaken the road that her grandmother and mother had paved and taken the dirt one with all the rocks and potholes.

❧

Jamie was so aware that Paul was walking toward her that she didn't know what to do. Should she stop right there or meet him? In only half a dozen long strides, he was in front of her, that brilliant smile lighting up the whole countryside around them.

"Was Gracie dancing with excitement all morning?" Paul asked.

"Oh, yes. She watched the clock hands, and every five seconds she wanted to know how much longer it was until we could leave." Jamie started toward Victor's car to help carry a third huge container into the house.

"I'll get that," Paul said.

"Take that one around the house and to the stagecoach. We're strapping it down on top," Victor yelled as he came out of the house. "What we carried inside is a snack that Hattie is putting out on the screened porch. It'll take a while to get back to the creek, and the kids will be too excited to eat the first hour."

Jamie waited until Paul had gotten out of sight and headed straight for the porch, where Kate sat with a big, cheesy grin on her face. "Okay, spill it. Was this really Waylon's idea?"

"Classified, but I can tell you that it wasn't Paul's, so you don't have to worry about him stalking you or planning to con you out of something," Kate answered. "You do look cute today. I haven't seen that sundress and those sandals. Did you get all dressed up for someone special?"

"That classified thing can work both ways. We like being around each other, and we have some of the same interests. It would be real easy to be friends. But Kate, we both know this other thing should be settled before either of us even takes baby steps into a relationship, whether friendship or serious."

"Hey." Kate put up her palms. "You are preaching to the choir."

"Just sayin'," Jamie said.

Too bad saying didn't always convince the person who was doing the talking.

Hattie poked her head out the door. "Y'all come on in here and call in the young'uns. I've got a little sack with a juice box and a cookie for them to eat in the stagecoach. That much won't ruin their dinner."

∾

Kate's heart hurt for Hattie. Her grandchildren and Victor's lived so far away that they couldn't have a day like this with them. Did Teresa ever look back and wish that Kate's baby had survived so that they could pass the company on down to her?

I am the end of the line, Kate thought. *There is no one past me. I'd never thought of that.*

So what's the difference if you sell it now or if it's sold and the proceeds go to the charity of your choice when you are dead? her father's voice inside her head asked.

"I'm glad that I planned this," Waylon whispered behind her, close enough that she got a whiff of his shaving lotion and the warmth of his breath tickled the soft skin on her neck.

"Jamie is onto Victor and Hattie," she said.

"Did I hear my name?" Jamie asked.

Paul's grin deepened the few crow's-feet around his eyes. "You did hear me mention your name. I was telling Victor that I'm glad you decided to stay in Bootleg."

"Saved by the bell," Waylon whispered.

"Thank goodness," Kate said.

"They sure look like they're having a good time out there." Waylon tapped Kate on the shoulder and pointed toward the stage. "I'd thought about a make-believe stagecoach robbery, though I was afraid it would scare the girls. Instead I've got unloaded BB guns for them to do their own pretending."

"Thank you for not loading them. They might . . ." Paul reached for a second sandwich.

"Shoot their eyes out?" Waylon laughed.

"You got it, partner." Paul nodded.

Victor brought empty plates into the house to throw in the trash. "Are we about ready to get this show on the road?"

Paul nodded. "Do you think you can handle those wild cowgirls in the coach?"

"If I can't, I bet Hattie can," Victor answered. "She can blow the rattles off the tail of a diamondback at thirty paces with nothing but her little pistol."

"Oh, hush!" Hattie beamed.

"You can shoot?" Kate asked.

"You can't?" Jamie asked Kate.

"No, but I'd love to learn."

"Then I'll teach you if you stick around Bootleg," Hattie said. "But for now, I think we'd better join those girls out there in the stagecoach. I bet they're ready for them guns. Y'all did bring extra clothing for them, right? They'll most likely get wet in the creek."

"Yes, ma'am, I did." Jamie nodded. "Let me help carry one of those food bins out to the coach so this big adventure can get underway."

"We brought a lot. Kids go through a lot of food around the water," Victor said.

Waylon gathered up a couple of BB guns that had seen lots of wear from the far corner of the porch and carried them out to the stage. Kate, Paul, and Jamie followed right behind him.

Lisa's big blue eyes popped out. "We get guns?"

"Got to protect the land from varmints and outlaws," Waylon said.

"You think you can shoot straight, Gracie?" Jamie asked.

Gracie narrowed her eyes until they were barely slits in her little round face. "Yes, Mama, and if one of them bad guys chases us, I'll shoot him."

Victor and Hattie came out with the packed bin between them. Two pink cowgirl hats rested on the top. Gracie's eyes twinkled when Victor handed one to her.

"Hats and guns. We really are cowgirls." Lisa settled hers on her blonde hair.

Gracie set her hat back on her head. "We are the baddest cowgirls in the whole state of Texas."

"Yes, you are." Hattie climbed up into the stage with them. "And me and Jamie and Kate and Victor expect you to protect us."

"I won't let nothing hurt you," Gracie declared. "Look, Mama. I'm a real cowgirl. Someday I'm going to live on a ranch like this and wear this gun every day and be just like Waylon."

"Well, now." Jamie nodded. "That is a mighty fine goal."

Kate giggled as she climbed into the stagecoach. Someday she'd like to do the same thing, only maybe without wearing a gun every day.

Whoa, hoss! she thought and then laughed under her breath. Not one time in her life had those two words ever gone through her mind.

Waylon and Paul climbed up on the top while Hattie, Jamie, and Victor settled themselves inside with the children, who were already poking their guns out the windows.

"Y'all ready in there?" Waylon yelled.

The girls gave a shout.

Jamie and Kate sat on one side of the coach. Victor and Hattie took the other seat. Gracie kept watch on one side while Lisa had her BB gun poked out the other way.

"It's rougher than riding down Main Street," Hattie said.

"It's fun." Gracie raised her voice above the sound of the wheels and the horses. "I love it."

Kate agreed with Gracie. It was fun, even though it was hot and the ride was rough.

"How far are we traveling?" Jamie asked.

"To the back side of the property by the creek. It's about a mile, and Waylon is going to drive slow, so maybe thirty to forty-five minutes," Victor answered.

"I see a bandit," Lisa hollered and pointed out the window.

"Where? I'll shoot the dirty dogs and feed them to the coyotes," Gracie growled as she pulled the trigger on her gun and made popping noises with her tongue each time.

"Good Lord, Gracie, where did you hear that?" Jamie asked.

"From John Wayne movies. The babysitter let me watch them while she made out with her boyfriend on the porch." Gracie spoke above the noise of the horses and the rattle of the wheels. "Lisa, there's some more on your side. Shoot 'em before they get Kate. They'll kill her for sure because she can't even cook, and they'll steal my mama because she makes good fried chicken."

"I'm glad you cowgirls are here to keep me safe." Kate gasped with a smile she tried to hide.

"You really can't cook?" Paul asked.

Kate shook her head. "Never found the need to learn until I came here, and Jamie and Amanda are so good at it that I still don't feel the need."

"Surprising, isn't it?" Jamie said. "I thought she could do anything, too, until I got to know her and found out that she doesn't even own a superwoman cape."

By the time they reached the picnic area, the path was strewn with imaginary bandits, dirty rotten coyotes, and one or two dozen snakes. When Waylon brought the coach to a stop, Gracie blew on the end of her gun.

"We made it, guys," Lisa said. "We'll be safe here. We can leave our guns in the stagecoach."

"Not me!" Gracie said. "We need to take them with us. There might be a bear out there."

Waylon climbed down from the top and opened the stage door on Kate's side. He held his hand, and she put hers in it. A sweet little shot of heat flushed her cheeks.

"You girls did a fine job of protecting us. Miz Gracie, may I help you out of the coach?" Waylon asked.

She jumped out into his arms and then wiggled free and yelled, "Look, there's water! Lisa, come on over here to this side. We've got a swimmin' pool! Nobody told me about this!"

"It was a surprise," Jamie said.

"Water's cold, so y'all might want to just wade around and look for minnows," Waylon told them.

"Hey, Mama, can I get in the water up to my knees?" Gracie yelled from the shore, where she'd taken off her sandals.

"That's about how deep the creek is," Waylon said to Jamie. "It's spring fed and cold as ice so they won't get in that deep."

"Yes, you can, but stay where I can see you," Jamie yelled back.

"We've got guns, so if y'all see any bears you call us and we'll come runnin'," Lisa hollered.

"If I could go back in time, I would have a houseful just like them," Waylon told Kate.

"So would I," Kate answered.

Kate helped Hattie spread a quilt out under the drooping limbs of an old willow tree not far from the clear, trickling creek. Then Victor and Paul brought the food down from the top of the stagecoach and they set out a picnic fit for a queen. The girls romped through the water shooting bears behind every rock and blade of grass until Lisa said something to the Gracie and the bears were forgotten.

"Is that fried chicken, Daddy? We ain't had that in a long time," Lisa said.

"Not since Sunday at the church potluck," Paul said.

Lisa nodded. "That's a long time."

After they ate, Hattie brought out a couple of old books and moved the children over to another quilt that she'd arranged under the shade of a big pecan tree. "I thought I'd read to you while your dinner settles," she said. "You can't hunt bears or get in the water for a little while after you eat."

"Is that *ABC*?" Lisa yawned.

"Camel on the ceiling. C-C-C," Gracie answered.

Hattie sat down, and Lisa cuddled up next to her while Gracie claimed the other side.

Somewhere in the middle of the book, Gracie had laid her head on Hattie's lap and fallen asleep. Lisa was asleep before that. Without disturbing either of them, Hattie arranged a couple of pillows against the trunk of the tree, leaned back, and shut her eyes.

Kate pulled her phone from the hip pocket of her shorts and snapped a picture and then one of Jamie and Paul chatting beside the stagecoach. And one more of Victor with his cowboy hat pulled down over his face and his arms crossed over his chest. She was looking for Waylon through the camera eye when she felt him behind her. She slipped the phone back in her pocket and resisted the urge to turn around and kiss him.

"Walk?" he asked.

"You would have made a good father, Waylon," Kate said when they were fifty yards down the edge of the creek.

"Thank you. I like kids, but like I said before, I wasn't ready when the time was right, and now the time has passed."

"You really think so?" She pulled off her sandals and set them on the edge of the quilt. "With the right woman, you could still have a houseful of kids."

"I can't imagine that. I think I'll just enjoy Lisa and Gracie and be their surrogate uncle. Are you fixin' to wade in the water?"

"I am." She nodded.

"It's been years since I've got my feet wet in the creek." He tugged off his boots and socks, rolled up the legs of his jeans, and took her hand in his. "Shall we step off into it together?"

"One. Two. Three." She counted and then put her foot in the water. "Sweet Lord, Waylon! That water is really icy. How did those kids stand it so long?"

"They were hopping around and having such a good time that they didn't even notice." He chuckled. "This little creek is always clear and cold. It will cool you right down."

"I am definitely a tenderfoot." She moaned as she took baby steps into the water.

"Not any more than I am. I haven't gone barefoot in years. I have a big favor to ask," he said.

"Yes, you can kiss me." He tipped her chin up with his fist, and she looked deeply into his eyes. Her hands snaked up around his neck, and the temperature of the cold water around her calves felt as if it shot up forty degrees.

By the time the kiss ended, Kate was sure the water was boiling. No one had ever made her feel like he did. Timing was wrong, right along with everything else, but she liked this detective—a hell of a lot.

"I feel like I've known you my whole life." He smiled. "The favor is that when this is really settled, you'll go out with me."

"Like on dates? Even if I'm in Fort Worth? A long-distance dating thing?" she asked.

"Sounds crazy, but we might make it work," he said.

"Everything else in our world has been crazy this summer, hasn't it, so why not?" she said.

CHAPTER TWENTY-THREE

Kate envied Jamie the right to carry a sleeping Gracie into the house that Monday evening. She took in her backpack and watched Jamie strip her out of her clothing and tuck her between the sheets in nothing but her underpants.

"Wine?" Kate asked.

"Love some." Jamie nodded.

When they reached the kitchen, Kate got two glasses and Jamie opened the refrigerator for the wine.

"Paul?" Kate asked as Jamie poured.

"Waylon?" Jamie raised an eyebrow.

"I could like him, but long-distance relationships don't always fare so well," Kate answered. "You, on the other hand, will be living right here in the same town with Paul. He is handsome, he's honest, and he's a sweet guy and a great father."

"It's only two hours from here to Fort Worth." Jamie led the way to the deck.

"But how far is it to Huntsville or whatever prison I could end up in?" Kate asked.

A whimper made them both forget their conversation.

Kate quickly crossed the deck to the far side. "Amanda? What's wrong? Did you get a bad report at the doctor's?"

"No," she sobbed.

"Is it your aunt?" Jamie pulled a chair across the wooden floor to sit beside her.

"No, it's a girl."

"What girl? Who did something to make you cry?" Kate sat down on the end of the chaise lounge.

If someone had hurt Amanda's feelings, then they'd better get ready for a fight with Kate. Amanda was naïve, but she was pregnant and her hormones were all out of balance and she sure didn't need extra stress.

"The baby is a girl, not a boy, and I wanted a girl. I don't know anything about boys, and now I feel guilty because I didn't want a boy." Amanda blew her nose loudly, tossed the tissue into the trash, and reached for another one. "I'm a mess all over again."

"Gracie will be so excited," Kate said.

"I know, but I'd made up my mind to love a little boy and to work hard and not let him be like his father, and now I don't even know how to put it in words." Amanda dabbed at her eyes. "God answered my prayers and all I can do is cry."

Jamie laid a hand on her knee. "That's what pregnant women do in the last couple of weeks. Don't feel guilty."

"Are they sure it's a girl?" Kate wanted to do her version of Gracie's happy dance.

"She showed us very plainly that she is a girl and she has a lot of hair and she's gorgeous." Amanda nodded. "Are you sure all this is normal, Jamie? Did you cry and cook all the time?"

"I did both and cleaned closets," Jamie answered.

"Her name is Rachel," Amanda said.

"That's pretty," Kate told her.

Rachel and Gracie. The two names were perfect for a couple of sisters.

"I'm glad we're changing our names tomorrow. I want her to be a Hilton from the day she's born, and I'm not putting a father on her birth certificate." Amanda tipped her chin up in a determined gesture. "Tell me about your day. No, don't, or I'll get all weepy because I couldn't be there."

A phone rang.

Jamie checked hers and shook her head. Amanda picked hers up from the arm of the lounge and shook her head.

Kate didn't recognize the tone or the number, but it was definitely her phone.

"Hello," she answered.

"I'm so glad you answered, Mrs. Steele. The judge who will be presiding over the cases of you and two other women and a child has had a family emergency. The only time he can see you will be at eight o'clock in the morning. I'm sorry for the inconvenience, and if you want to reschedule, we can do that. We have a date open four weeks from tomorrow or on out past that," a woman said.

Kate glanced at Amanda and made a snap decision. "We will be there. How long will it take in the courthouse?"

"Fifteen minutes if he agrees. Longer if you have to talk him into it," the lady answered. "We just learned of the emergency. Sorry I couldn't give you more time."

"It can't be helped, I'm sure. Have a nice evening," Kate said.

"What can't be helped?" Amanda asked.

"We're going to Dallas tonight. Instead of seeing the judge at one o'clock tomorrow afternoon, we're seeing him at eight in the morning. With the traffic in the downtown area, we'd have to leave a three o'clock in the morning, so we might as well drive down to my house and spend the night there," Kate said.

"You've got to be joking." Amanda groaned.

"I have a perfectly good house! I'll arrange for a car to take us to and from the courthouse so none of us have to drive. We'll take my car down there. Just pack a bag and we might even have time for a swim before we go to bed," Kate said.

"Are you sure?" Jamie downed the rest of her wine.

"Very, and pack your bathing suits. Gracie will probably wake up on the way, and I'm sure she'll love a swim."

Amanda smiled for the first time that evening. "Me, too! I love to swim and I've got a maternity bathing suit. This will be a real treat. Thank you."

"Living in Bootleg is one thing. This will be in the middle of all your neighbors," Jamie said.

"So? Are you ashamed to be seen with me?" Kate teased.

"Hell, no!" Jamie answered. "I was thinking it might run the other way."

"Hell, no!" Kate echoed with a grin. "Let's get ready and go take care of business. I'll call for takeout food on the way. Y'all decide what you want."

"Sounds fine to me," Amanda said.

Gracie didn't wake up until they were on the outskirts of Fort Worth and had barely gotten her eyes open when Kate parked in the garage of a big two-story stone house. "Is this a castle?" she whispered.

"No, it's my house," Kate answered. But hey, if Gracie wanted it to be a castle, then Kate would gladly let her be the princess who lived there.

❧

Gracie stood in the middle of Kate's elaborate living room, eyes big as saucers, trying to take in the whole place at once. Where her daughter felt awe, Jamie was more than a little intimidated by the sheer size of the house. She'd realized that Kate came from money and had lived a life way above Jamie's pay grade as a teacher, but this was surreal.

"Where do I sleep?" Gracie finally asked.

"My bedroom is upstairs, along with two others. Y'all can take your pick of whichever one you want," Kate said. "They are pretty much the same."

"Did Conrad sleep in either of them?" Amanda whispered.

"He liked the master suite on the ground floor," Kate answered. "We'll unload all this food in the kitchen and open up the containers."

Amanda dropped her suitcase on the floor. "I'm so glad we opted for Chinese. I've been craving it for a couple of days."

"After we eat, can I see his room?" Jamie whispered.

"Of course, but why?"

"Final closure." Jamie shrugged.

Kate pointed down the hallway. "It's the last door on the left. Mother and I cleaned it out before I went to the cabin. Unless she stored other stuff in there, it's empty."

"Thank you," Jamie said.

Amanda had already started removing containers and chopsticks from the plastic bags and was setting them on the table when Jamie and Kate arrived in the kitchen. Jamie set the sweet-and-sour chicken in front of Gracie before she went hunting through the boxes for her spicier chicken.

"When I get done eating, can I explore the castle all by myself?" Gracie asked.

Jamie glanced at Kate, who nodded. "If it's okay with your mama, I don't care if you go on an adventure. Just yell real loud if you get lost so we can send the prince to find you."

Gracie giggled. "You'll have to come find me, Mama. We don't have a prince in this castle. We didn't bring Waylon with us."

"So you think Waylon is a prince?" Kate asked.

"Yep, and you are a princess. He's going to rescue you from this castle and take you to live on the ranch with him."

"What makes you think that?" Jamie asked.

"It's my story, Mama." Gracie sighed.

Jamie didn't voice it, but she felt as if she'd been admitted to a castle, too.

"That's right," Amanda said. "And I like her story."

Gracie finished her food, broke open the fortune cookie, and handed it to Jamie. "Read it to me, Mama."

Jamie straightened out the bit of paper and read, "You will find new things in your future."

"What does that mean?" Gracie asked.

Jamie planted a kiss on her daughter's forehead. "It probably means that you will make even more new friends in Bootleg when school starts."

Gracie sighed again, this time with more drama. "I thought it meant I'd find a hidden treasure in this castle."

Kate ate her last grain of rice and tossed the container in the trash compactor. "It's not really a castle."

"It's her story," Amanda reminded them. "Go and find the treasure, darlin' girl. And bring it back for us to see."

"But you only have about thirty minutes, and then it's bedtime for you, little girl. We have to get up really early and go to the courthouse and you need to be all smiles." Jamie kissed her on the top of her head.

Minutes later they heard her opening doors on the second floor.

"I want to see his room, too," Amanda said.

Jamie pushed back her food. "Want to go with me?"

"Why don't we all go together?" Kate led the way across the foyer and to the last room on the left. She opened the door and stood back to let them go inside first. "It's just a room with a nice closet and a big bathroom. I bought this house after we were married because I loved this room and the view of the pool." She pulled open the drapes to show them the backyard.

"So this isn't where you lived before you married him?" Jamie asked.

"I lived in a small house, not much bigger than the cabin, and I loved the coziness," she answered. "Do either of you feel anything about this room?"

Amanda walked over to the sliding doors leading out to the patio. "I don't want to sleep in here, but it's just a big empty room."

"I'm done." Jamie turned and left the room.

"Did it help?" Kate asked.

Jamie folded her arms over her chest. "It did."

"How?" Kate and Amanda followed her back to the kitchen.

"It wasn't just me that he couldn't love. It was any woman. We were all just a game to him. Like a hunter chases down a white-tailed deer. Marrying us was equivalent to shooting us. Now I know it wasn't because I couldn't make enough money or wasn't pretty enough or good enough in bed. It wasn't me or you or Amanda." Jamie picked up her suitcase and headed up the stairs. "I'm glad you invited us. It's really, really over now, or it will be after tomorrow morning."

"I'm not sure I understand," Amanda said.

"He lived here. He lived in my house, which you were paying for," Jamie said. "And he lived in your little apartment. Nothing satisfied him or brought him happiness. He craved the hunt."

"And look what it finally got him," Amanda said. "I'm ready to get in that pool and pretend that we are on vacation. What are you going to do with this house after the summer, Kate?"

"Sell it," she said without hesitation.

Amanda awoke with a start the next morning. She scanned the room and tried to figure out what she was doing in a five-star hotel. Then it all came back to her in a flash. She was in Fort Worth. Today she would go to the courthouse to get her maiden name back, putting the final touch on what had happened in the last month.

She hefted her round body out of the bed and drew the drapes back. Jamie and Gracie were sitting beside the pool having leftover Chinese for breakfast. Amanda dressed in the same outfit she'd worn to the funeral, a pair of black leggings and a flowing black top with a hankie hem that dropped to her thighs. She pulled her red hair up in a twist and secured it with a few bobby pins, applied a minimum of makeup, and repacked her suitcase. She took it with her so she wouldn't have to climb the stairs again.

Kate was foraging in the cabinets when she reached the kitchen. "There's oatmeal but no milk. I'll take us all out for breakfast as soon as this is over."

Amanda shivered. "I'm too nervous to eat anyway. The idea of standing in front of a judge gives me the jitters."

"My legal department is sending a lawyer. For the most part, we'll only have to answer a couple of questions, if that." Kate threw an arm around Amanda's shoulders and drew her even closer. "Look at us. Jamie has on her cowboy boots, I'm wearing high heels that are pinching my toes, and you have on your fancy flip-flops."

"Just like the day we arrived at the cabin."

"And we'd all rather be barefoot out on the porch, wouldn't we?"

"Or down by the lake with our toes in the edge of the water." Amanda smiled.

"That's where we'll go soon as today is over and we do some shopping," Kate said.

Amanda took a couple of steps to the side. "I'd like to go to the discount stores and look for things for my baby girl. I don't have a thing for a girl, not even something frilly to bring her home in."

"Of course," Kate answered. "We can go wherever y'all want, but please let me pay for our food today."

"Done." Amanda would gladly let Kate shell out the money for food, since it would take a chunk out of her bank account to buy baby things.

Kate glanced at the clock. "The driver will be here in five minutes. If you'll call Jamie and Gracie in from the pool, I'll make sure everything is ready for me to lock the doors."

"Are you really never coming back here to live, Kate?"

It was hard to think about owning a place like this and wanting to live in something the size of the cabin. But then on second thought, a huge place like that would be pretty damned lonely.

"Probably not. I'll live in a hotel until I find an apartment or small house that I like."

"Or maybe you'll stay in Bootleg?"

For the first time, Amanda didn't want any of them to leave the cabin. She felt safe and comfortable with all four of them living together. And besides, she needed Jamie for when the baby came and Kate for her quiet strength.

"I'll cross that bridge when I get to it. Right now I have to get us to the courthouse on time," Kate answered.

☙

Kate might appear calm on the outside in her cute little business suit and high-heeled shoes, but she was a nervous wreck on the inside. Time for a modicum of closure on the whole marriage thing.

The courthouse ruling took less than fifteen minutes for all three. They walked in with the same last name and came out with their different maiden names, and just like that, it was finished.

The firm had sent a seasoned lawyer, Mary Beth O'Bryan, who had made short work of the whole process. "I knew it would be easy. The judge wanted to get out of town and his plane leaves at ten, so he had to get through this in a hurry. Would you mind if I ride with you back to your house? There are a couple of things we need to discuss, and this will save time for both of us. It's all about Conrad, so I don't suppose you mind talking in front of the other two?"

"I'm good with you riding with us and with talking to you in front of them," Kate answered.

When they'd settled into the six-passenger van, Mary Beth opened a briefcase and took out a file. The gray-haired woman adjusted her glasses and introduced herself to Jamie and Amanda. "I'm one of the lawyers in the legal department of Kate's firm. We have notified the church in Bootleg of their windfall found in the bank deposit box and let them know that they will most likely own the cabin where you are staying, though it will have to go through probate. They are not interested in selling it, but they will lease it to any of you on a yearly basis for enough to pay the taxes and insurance on the place. That comes to about four hundred dollars a month, and at the end of the first year they will renegotiate if things aren't done by then. Their pastor is nearing retirement, maybe in two years, and they are hoping to use the cabin as a parsonage if they hire a new pastor with a family."

"We'll take the lease," Kate said. "Cut them a check for an entire year's rent."

"And you will be responsible for upkeep and for the utility bills?" Mary Beth asked.

"Agreed." Kate nodded.

"So we'll split everything three ways?" Amanda asked.

"How about I pay the rent for the year? Amanda, you take the water bill, and Jamie, you pay for the electricity? If we have a maintenance problem like plumbing or decide to paint the place, we will discuss the split on that then," Kate said.

Amanda frowned and shook her head. "That doesn't seem quite fair. You'd be taking on the biggest chunk."

"Let me do this for the first year until y'all get on your feet," Kate said. "We'll take it back to the table in a year when we have to renegotiate the lease anyway. Jamie?"

"Thank you," she said. "Just hand me the electricity bills from now on and I'll pay them."

"Now on to Conrad's stuff. He didn't have an apartment or house somewhere else. He had five hundred dollars and change in his personal checking account, and when his outstanding bills and taxes were paid up, he had about that in his business account. Both have been closed. Where do you want the money sent?"

"Split two ways. One check in Amanda's name and one in Jamie's. It's not much, but it will help with baby expenses and school clothes for Gracie this year," Kate said.

"Again, thank you," Jamie said.

"Any questions about all that?" Mary Beth asked.

"My house has both our names on the deed," Jamie said. "I want to sell it, but what happens now?"

"Where are you financed?" Mary Beth already had her phone out.

When Jamie told her, Mary Beth made a phone call, asked a few questions, and smiled when she hung up. "Were you aware that you bought insurance that stated in the event of your death, or his, the house would be paid for in full? You need to send them a copy of the death certificate and they will process the paperwork at that time."

"You mean the house is totally paid for now?" Jamie asked.

"That's right. Conrad is dead, so it is paid for as soon as they get the death certificate." Mary Beth nodded.

"Would you take care of all that for her, please?" Kate was every bit as happy as Jamie with the news.

"Be glad to. Anything else?"

"His van?"

"He still owes ten thousand dollars on it. The police have released it, and it's at the company parking lot. What do you want to do with it, Kate?"

"Sell it for enough to pay it off or take a loss on it. I don't care. I don't want to see it again," she answered.

"Then I think that's all of it. Other than if you've given any thought to your mother's retirement."

"Yes, I have, but I haven't decided what I'm going to do about it yet. I still have four more weeks, right?"

"Actually, you have until the last day of this year." Mary Beth closed the files and put them inside her briefcase. "And here we are, at your house. I'm glad that we've gotten everything cleared up and can move forward. I'm sorry that the murder hasn't been solved and that it's hanging over your head. Right when you should be taking over the business." Mary Beth shook her head slowly. "It's not a good thing."

Kate knew that it was ruining her reputation a day at a time, but right then, she was far happier with Jamie's news than with the worry of her own problems. "I know, Mary Beth, but it is what it is and we can't change it."

Jamie stuck out her hand and shook Mary Beth's a long time. "I can't believe I don't have to make house payments. Thank you."

"You are very welcome." Mary Beth smiled.

"What are you going to do with it now?" Amanda asked. "Rent it out?"

"No, I'm putting it on the market to sell," Jamie said.

The car came to a stop in front of Kate's house, and the driver opened the door for them. "Y'all have a nice day, Miz Kate."

Kate had never hugged Mary Beth before, but she slipped an arm around her shoulders and squeezed. "Thank you for everything."

Mary Beth's smile warmed her heart. "It's my job."

"Still, I want you to know you are appreciated." Kate crawled out of the car behind the rest of her crew. "How's the family, Lucas?"

"Doin' well, ma'am. Grandson graduates from college at the end of the summer. We're right proud of him. He'll make a fine Fort Worth policeman."

"I'm sure he will," Kate said. "If you are Mother's driver today, tell her that I missed seeing her."

"I'll be sure to do that." Lucas tipped his hat toward her and turned back to the vehicle to drive Mary Beth to hers.

Later, she'd call her mother and tell her the courthouse news. She would have liked to see her that day, but with Teresa, business always came before family. And as she'd told Mary Beth, it was what it was and some things never changed.

Kate turned around and motioned toward her car. "Now let's go inside the house and get our luggage and load up my car. Then Amanda can find the nearest IHOP on the GPS and we'll get some breakfast."

"French toast for me!" Gracie wiggled her shoulders.

It took only a few minutes to load the car, and Amanda poked buttons on the GPS system. "I can't believe that it was over so quick," Amanda said.

"Me, either," Jamie agreed. "We weren't in there more than twenty minutes."

"Fifteen, to be exact," Kate said as she started the engine.

"Just like that"—Amanda snapped her fingers—"I am now a Hilton again. My baby will always be a Hilton. Thank you, Kate, for getting the ball rolling for us."

"I never knew that you had such a big name, Kate," Jamie said.

"Let me introduce myself. I am Katherine Elizabeth Truman, but my friends all call me Kate."

Jamie smiled. "Pleased to meet you, Kate. I'm Jamillia Juanita Mendoza, and all my friends call me Jamie."

Amanda nodded seriously. "I'm Amanda Christine Hilton, and I'm just Amanda."

"Well, I am Grace Elizabeth Ruth—what's our name again, Mama?"

"Mendoza."

"Okay." Gracie took a deep breath. "I'm Gracie Mendoza, and Mama only calls me by all my names if I'm in trouble."

"I'm honored to meet all of you." Kate followed Amanda's directions to the nearest IHOP. She and Gracie shared a middle name. That did make the little girl partly hers, now didn't it?

They shopped. They ate. They laughed. They argued. And at the close of the day, Kate drove them all the way home and parked in the driveway at the cabin just as the sun dropped below the horizon.

Poor Gracie greeted their arrival with a tiny snore. Jamie eased her daughter out of the car and carried her inside. Amanda started to get out but grabbed her stomach with a wince.

"I'm fine." Amanda smiled. "It's just been a big day. Thanks again for everything, Kate. I'm going to have the best-dressed baby girl in Bootleg, Texas."

"Hey, it's amazing how far the dollar can be stretched at those places y'all took me to. And you are very welcome. It made me feel like I was really a part of something when you and Jamie let me buy a few things," Kate told her.

"Do you feel like because you have money that we . . ." Amanda paused.

"Sometimes having money is as hard as not having it. That doesn't make sense, but it puts me at a disadvantage with folks who don't have as much as I do. I never want to make either of you feel like . . . well, you know. It makes me so happy to do things for y'all and for Gracie, but I don't want . . ."

Amanda laid her hand on Kate's arm. "I know what you are trying to say. I can never do for you financially what you do for me, but if you ever need anything I can provide, all you have to do is ask."

"That means more to me than anything that money could ever buy." Kate's voice cracked.

"Don't you dare cry, because with my hormones on a roller coaster, I'll start bawlin' like a baby if you do," Amanda said. "Let's take all those bags inside. We can go through them tomorrow, but right now I want to prop up my feet and watch television until I fall asleep."

"You get your feet up. I'll bring in the bags." Kate went around to the back of the car and opened the trunk, handily hiding her face in case tears decided to escape. She was taking out packages when her phone rang. Her mother's picture came up on the screen. She backed up against the vehicle, kicked off her high heels, and wiggled her feet in the grass as she answered. Teresa would have a hissy fit if she could see her daughter at that moment, but the damp grass felt so good that Kate didn't care.

"Mary Beth tells me everything is done. She sent a check to the church for a year's rent and has talked to the funeral home. They sent a courier over to the bank with a copy of the death certificate for Jamie," Teresa said. "How does it feel to be Kate Truman again? Did it help to close the books on the past?"

"No, but spending the day with Jamie and Amanda did. We're about to get this whole thing talked through and settled." Mercy, but she did love the soft green grass under her bare feet.

"Talk faster. I'm ready for you to come home," Teresa said. "I'm sorry I wasn't there for you in court today. I had some meetings that couldn't be postponed and I couldn't miss."

"I understand." Kate meant what she said. Her mother would never change, so she'd have to learn to love her just the way she was. "We were in and out of the courthouse in less than half an hour. No more than fifteen minutes before the judge. It took longer to drive there than to actually get the decree signed." The phone beeped under her ear. "Got another phone call, Mother. Can I call you back?"

"Not necessary. I'm walking out the door to go to dinner with the potential buyer. I'll call you tomorrow," Teresa said.

Kate touched the screen and said, "Hey, Waylon."

"Hello, Miss Truman. How did things go today?"

"They went great. I figured out that I don't like high heels anymore and that I do like the feel of damp grass under my feet," she answered.

"That's a step in the right direction. You ready to drive a tractor tomorrow? The weatherman says it's going to be another scorcher," Waylon said.

"I'll be there." She smiled.

"I miss you on the days when I don't get to see you." He dropped his voice to a deep drawl that sent little waves of heat through her body.

She eyed the expensive shoes lying in the grass. "I'd almost put those high heels back on for a kiss right now."

"You don't have to do that, darlin'. There will be plenty of kisses waiting on you tomorrow when you get to the ranch."

"I'll hold you to that." She flirted, and it felt good, even if it was just because she'd had an emotional day, out of character for her.

"Good night, gorgeous lady," he said, and the phone went dark.

She hummed all the way into the house, where she dropped the first batch of packages in the living room and went back for more. When she'd brought the last of them inside, she found Jamie and Amanda sitting on the sofa. Jamie had poured two glasses of wine and one of water with a wedge of lemon.

"I'd brought movies with me to watch when I left a month ago. None of them are new, but they are some of my favorites. Have you seen *Something to Talk About*? It kind of seems fitting for tonight," Jamie said.

"I heard about it, but isn't that really old?"

"It is, but I think you'll like it," Amanda said.

"Then hand me that glass of wine and let's get started." Kate figured good wine and company would outweigh even a crappy movie. But it wasn't, and by the end she agreed it was the perfect movie for the evening.

Chapter Twenty-Four

At the end of the next afternoon, Kate was so hot, tired, and sweaty that she simply kissed Waylon on the cheek, told him she'd see him the next morning, and headed for the cabin. Big raindrops hit when she parked, and by the time she made it into the house, it was pouring so hard that she was drenched. Maybe that would break the heat.

"Well, you look like a drowned rat." Amanda laughed.

A loud crack of thunder rattled the windows, and the rain came down in sheets, blowing hard against the house. "I swear, that one parted my hair," Jamie said nervously. "August is showing July that it is a thing of the past."

"I'm going to take a shower. Did y'all save any leftovers?" Kate kicked off her shoes and headed down the hallway.

"I made chicken Alfredo, and there's still some in the skillet on the stove," Jamie said. "Amanda cleaned today and made two loaves of bread and a chocolate pie."

"You think we can keep her in this nesting phase for a little longer?"

"It would be nice, but when the baby comes and it's up all night, nesting ends," Jamie answered.

Kate shut the bathroom door and adjusted the water. The warmth beating down on her back felt wonderful right up until the electricity blinked once and then went off completely. Whatever water was in the small tank wouldn't last through their showers if she didn't rush, so she hurriedly rinsed the shampoo from her hair. She fumbled around for towels, wrapping one around her body and another around her head in the dark. When she opened the door, she went toward the flicker of light in the living room. Jamie must have found the candles.

"Got any more of those?" she asked.

"No, but there's a flashlight in the kitchen drawer that you can use to get dressed," Amanda told her. "What a time to get those stupid false labor pains again. I'm going to go lie down on my left side like they told me to do. It's early yet, but after a day of cleaning, I feel like I can sleep until morning."

"Good night, then," Kate said.

"I'll take that flashlight when you are done with it," Jamie said. "Gracie and I are going to turn in, too, and I'm going to use the light to read books to her."

"Take it now. The candle will throw off enough light for me to find my nightshirt," Kate told her.

With the wind sounding like a freight train coming down the rolling hills and the rain pounding on the roof and against the windows, she couldn't read, not even on her Kindle. Finally, she decided to call her mother, but there was no service. Next week she would check into buying a generator, because she was taking the sabbatical even if it pissed her mother off to the point that she fired her.

She fell asleep thinking about being there for the baby's birth and for Gracie's first day of school in the new place. At first she thought that she was dreaming, but then the screaming that had awoken her got louder. She sat up in bed so fast that her head spun in the semidarkness.

Then she recognized Amanda's voice yelling out her name. She stumbled across the hallway to find Amanda sitting up in bed and panting.

"This is the real thing. My water just broke. Call an ambulance. I don't want to try to go to Wichita Falls. Just call the one from Seymour."

"No phone service," Kate said.

"What's happening over here? Oh, my God!" Jamie asked. "Oh, no! Is it time? I'll get dressed. We'll have to drive her to Seymour."

"How close are the pains?" Kate asked.

"Another one right now. Maybe a minute," Amanda said.

"We'd better hurry, Kate. You drive. In a pinch I can deliver the baby on the way." Jamie raced across the hall, throwing off her night clothes on the way.

Kate was so nervous that she headed out the door in her nightshirt and bare feet and had to run back inside to hurriedly dress in jeans and a T-shirt and slip on a pair of sandals. "You ever delivered a baby before?"

Jamie appeared out of her bedroom, fully dressed with Gracie in her arms. "One time I helped Mama Rita when her neighbor's daughter went into labor like this. I mostly just watched, but I could do it if I had to. My van or your car?"

"Your van. It's bigger," Kate said.

Jamie threw a blanket over Gracie and headed outside in the wind and rain. "I'll get her situated and then come back and help with Amanda."

What should have been a ten-minute trip took thirty minutes because of the driving rain and Kate's inability to see more than one foot in front of the vehicle at any time. It didn't help when she missed the turn to the hospital and had to go around a block to get back to it.

"I—need—to—push!" Amanda screamed as Kate pulled up beside the emergency room doors.

Kate turned off the engine and slung the door open in one motion before she headed toward the big doors in a run. "Hold on, Amanda. I'll bring help."

The lady behind the desk covered a yawn with her hand. "Fill out the form and I'll need your insurance cards and—"

"I don't have time for that. My friend is in the car and starting to push. Her baby is coming right now and we need help," Kate yelled.

"Okay, settle down." The woman picked up the phone and pushed a button. "I need a wheelchair and a nurse right now."

An older lady pushing a wheelchair arrived in less than two minutes, but it seemed like an eternity to Kate, who paced the floor the whole time. She shot a knowing smile toward Kate, one that said babies took a lot of time, so don't get your panties in a twist. When she returned with a sweat-covered, screaming Amanda, she was doing double time and hollering at the check-in woman to tell the on-call doctor to hurry.

"I want Kate and Jamie to go with me. I can't do this by myself," Amanda squealed.

"I'll come and get them as soon as we get you on a bed and check you, I promise," the nurse told her as they disappeared through double doors.

"Me, too? I want to be there to see my baby sister," Gracie said.

"After the baby is born, you can go see it all you want," Jamie said. "When they call for us, I'll stay with Gracie and you go."

"We'll take fifteen-minute turnarounds." Kate nodded. "That way Gracie can stay updated all the time."

"Look at us." Jamie plopped down in a chair in the waiting room. "We are drowned rats."

Kate smiled. "At least we have on shirts and shoes. They can't refuse us admittance."

Gracie held up a bare foot. "I don't have on shoes."

"But you are under twelve years old, so the rules don't apply," Kate said.

The doors opened, and the nurse that had taken Amanda away stepped out. "She's going straight to delivery. The baby is crowning and the doctor is on the way. She's yelling for Jamie."

Jamie stood up and tucked her wet hair behind her ears. "That would be me."

"Then you need to come with me."

Kate looked up at the big digital clock hanging on the wall. In fifteen minutes it would be two thirty, and then it would be her turn to go help with Amanda. Cold sweat popped out on her forehead, and her hands went clammy. She had no idea what to do. Jamie had had a child, so she had some inkling of what happened in the delivery room. Kate had never even seen kittens born, and that video of a birth she'd seen in college was more than twenty years ago.

The time came and went and another five minutes passed. Kate's mind went into overdrive. Amanda had died back there and Jamie was trying to get a handle on her composure before she came out and told Gracie. Another ten minutes went by, and suddenly the doors opened.

Jamie was smiling so big that she could have been posing for one of those stock photos they put up in the dentist's office. "It's a girl for sure, and she's here. Six pounds even and eighteen inches long. Doc says she's about three weeks early, but everything looks good."

"Red hair?" Kate asked.

"Oh, yeah. Y'all can come back and see Amanda, but the baby is in the nursery. You can see her through the window, though, Gracie."

"I can't hold her or kiss her on the forehead tonight?"

"You can tomorrow. Doc says since she's a little early, they'll keep Amanda until a day or two at the most and then we can take her home." Jamie talked as she led them down the hallway to the maternity area. "Then I'm sure Amanda will let you hold her."

When they reached Amanda's room, they found her holding the new baby next to her chest. A pink blanket was wrapped around them both, and Amanda's face glowed. "Look, it's called skin-on-skin bonding. As soon as they got her cleaned up, they brought her back to me. She's perfect. I counted all her fingers and toes. Come on over here, Gracie, and look at your little sister."

Joy filled Kate's soul for Amanda and for Gracie. The sisters would always have each other.

"What are you waiting for, Kate?" Amanda asked. "I didn't have time to get invitations ready for this party. Come and meet Lia Beth, named after you two and Gracie."

Gracie crawled up on the bed beside Amanda. "I like that better than Rachel."

"Fits her better, doesn't it?" Amanda grinned.

Family does not have to be blood, and sisters do not have to be born of the same parents, the voice in Kate's head said loudly.

"I'm honored," Kate said as she crossed the room to meet her niece.

CHAPTER TWENTY-FIVE

Is it Monday's child that is fair of face?" Kate asked as she rocked Miss Lia on Saturday evening. "Jamie, how does the rest of that thing go?"

"I don't remember, but I do know that a child born on the Sabbath is fair and wise and good in every way, because Mama Rita told me that when Gracie was born on Sunday," Jamie yelled from the kitchen.

"Well, this baby was born on Thursday," Kate said.

"Thursday's child has far to go," Amanda said from the sofa. "I looked it up already."

"What does that mean?" Gracie was busy coloring a new picture for the baby not far from Kate.

"It means she will be beautiful and make lots of friends," Kate answered. "And that means that she is going to be like her older sister."

"Wow! Even though she has red hair and I've got black, we're going to be alike?" Gracie asked.

"Oh, yes, you are," Jamie said. "And now supper is ready, so go wash your hands."

"Roast and potatoes?" Gracie asked.

"You got it, kiddo, but only after you wash up." Jamie pointed to the bathroom.

Amanda got up from the sofa where she'd been resting. "I'll take her so you can go eat."

"You go first and let me hold her awhile longer. I had a midafternoon snack, so I can wait awhile." Kate smiled.

Amanda eased up off the sofa. "I'm glad she didn't weigh nine pounds. I wouldn't be able to walk for a month. And I'm very happy they didn't make me stay in the hospital another day. Whatever they brought on the supper tray wouldn't be as good as Jamie's pot roast and hot biscuits."

Kate started humming when the baby whimpered, and she quieted right down. "She likes music."

"I listened to it a lot when I was carrying her," Amanda said. "Aunt Ellie said it was good for a baby."

Listening to the chatter at the supper table, Kate realized that she did not want to leave Bootleg. She didn't want this baby or Gracie, either, to grow up and only know her as the aunt who came on holidays or sent money in a Christmas card. She wanted to be a part of their lives, to go to church with them and be there when they went out on their first dates.

I don't want to just be a part of their lives with pictures on the mantel and seeing them a few times a year, she thought. *I need to be involved with everything, or I will regret it when they are grown. Time slips past quickly.*

Kate sighed when someone knocked on the door. She wanted to explore this idea of a drastic life change a little longer. Carrying the baby in one arm, she crossed the living room floor and slung open the door to find Hattie and Victor with big grins. Victor held up an enormous gift bag and stood back while Hattie pushed her way past him into the house.

"We came to bring the baby a present. Y'all just keep your seats out there in the kitchen," she called out. "I'm going to steal this baby from Kate and rock her a spell. She needs to get to know me real good so she'll be comfortable with me when her mama goes to work."

Kate waited until Hattie was settled in the rocking chair before putting the baby in her arms. "She's a good baby. When Amanda finishes her supper, she'll come in here and open the present."

"Thank you!" Amanda called out. "I hope I'm not being rude, but I am going to eat first and open later. This is too good to let it get cold."

"I understand. Take your time," Hattie said. "I'm good right here. She's a beauty, with this mop of red hair."

"You think it will stay that color or all fall out and grow in dark like Gracie's?"

"She'll be a redhead, mark my words." Hattie began to hum a lullaby. "This is what I've missed about having my grandkids live so far away. I can't just pop in and see them for a little while and then go home."

Kate touched Victor on the arm. "Come on in the kitchen and have a glass of tea or some pot roast if you haven't eaten."

"I'm not sure I can get away from staring at this little princess," he said. "You looked pretty good with her in your arms."

"It felt good, but there's no use wishing for miracles," Kate said.

He followed her into the kitchen. "I've eaten, but I might have one of those biscuits with some honey."

"Sit down and help yourself," Jamie said. "There's plenty of everything if you change your mind. And Kate is a natural when it comes to babies. Most people in her position wouldn't be that comfortable with one."

"In my position?" Kate put a thick chunk of roast on her plate and covered it with gravy. "What does that mean?"

"That you haven't been around kids," Amanda answered for Jamie. "And that you are a career woman, not a mothering type. But I got to say, if any woman could have it both ways, I believe you would be able to do it."

"Do what?" Waylon poked his head in the door after a brief knock.

"Be a mother and run a business both," Amanda said. "Come on in and see Lia Beth."

Waylon removed his hat and laid it on the coffee table. "In my opinion, Kate could run a ranch, plus an oil company and a houseful of kids all at the same time."

"Where's my Supergirl cape?" Kate laughed. "Truth is that I'd trade it all if I could have a baby."

"There's other ways to get one than birthin' her," Amanda said. "There's adoption."

Kate shook her head. "That's a possibility, I guess, but my age might be a hold up for adoption."

"Forty is the new thirty." Jamie chuckled. "Or you could buy a dozen."

"Now that might be a possibility." Kate laughed with her. "Except Waylon tells me that's against the law."

It was the perfect time to tell them all in one fell swoop that she was taking a year to sort things out. She had no idea what she'd do, other than keep working part-time at the ranch. But she wanted to hold the decision close to her heart for a few days, be selfish with it and wait until that perfect moment to tell them and Waylon. Tonight was all about Amanda and the new baby, and she didn't want to steal their thunder.

Waylon held out his arms toward Hattie. "It's my turn to do some rocking."

"I'm an old woman," she protested.

He wiggled his fingers. "I bet Victor hasn't even gotten to hold her yet, has he?"

"No, I have not," Victor called out from the kitchen. "But you go on. I can take her away from you easier than I can get her away from Hattie."

"Oh, all right!" Hattie handed the baby to him. "You could have had a dozen of them if you hadn't been so busy chasing bad guys."

"Can't do a recall on that decision. Besides, you met my ex-wives. Which one would you pick to be a mother?" Waylon asked.

Hattie shook her finger at him. "Neither one. They were both too self-centered to ever have children."

"And there you have it." Waylon sat down and stretched his long legs out in front of him.

"Here, you can come and sit beside me, Gracie." Hattie patted the sofa. "Tell me what you think of your new sister."

Gracie snuggled up next to Hattie. "I thought she'd be big enough to play Barbies with me when she got here, but Amanda says that first she has to learn to crawl and then walk and talk and that all takes time. I guess I like her, but about all she did all day long when we got her home from the hospital was eat and sleep."

"You did that when you were a baby, too," Hattie said.

"Mama told me that. It don't sound very exciting, does it?"

Kate listened to them with one ear, but she couldn't take her eyes off Waylon. There was something extremely sexy about a big, muscular man with a tiny newborn in his arms. His eyes sparkled when he stared down at her, and when she wrapped her little fist around his forefinger, he absolutely beamed.

"What?" He looked up and caught her staring.

"You look pretty good with a baby in your arms, too," she answered.

"Every little girl needs an uncle to spoil her and teach her to ride horses," he said.

"Yes, she does," Amanda said. "We'll be christening her at the church as soon as we can take her out of the house. I want you and Kate to be her godparents."

"What about Jamie?" Kate stammered.

"I've talked to her about it. If something happens to me, she'd be glad to help you two out, but she has Gracie, and you two don't have any children."

"I'd be honored," Waylon said.

"Me, too," Kate said.

That solidified her decision right there. She was Lia's godmother, and she needed to be close by to help Amanda with her upbringing. Plus, Waylon would spoil her too much, and Kate needed to keep an eye on him.

No one saw her swipe a tear out of her eye or knew the peace that settled around her like a warm blanket on a cold winter night when she finally came to grips with the decision she'd been fighting for days.

Chapter Twenty-Six

The job had consumed Waylon for more than twenty years. From beat cop to detective had been a journey that had cost him, but there was no use in looking back. Good memories linked him with three different partners in that busy room through those doors. He finally pushed into the room to the nods of his fellow detectives and smiles from his partner and the new woman who was officially taking his place at the end of the month.

"You can't tell me you aren't going to miss this." Larry grinned.

"You could still work for another twenty years," Christina said.

Waylon set three cups of coffee on the desk. "It's time for me to go home, and I'm happy with the decision. So you think my phone call last week spooked the florist?"

"Oh, yeah," Larry said.

"And he's willing to talk?"

"He's scared out of his mind, but he says he'll only talk to you. He's got a sign on the door saying he's closed this week due to a family emergency. Says for you to come to the alley door. What did you promise him when you talked to him that second time after we'd visited with Estrella Gonzales?"

Waylon handed each of them a coffee and sipped at his. "A way out."

"Well, then let's go take it to him."

Half an hour later, three empty coffee cups lay in a plastic bag in the backseat of Larry's unmarked vehicle behind the Red Rose Florist. A little round man with a bald head and wire-rimmed glasses poked his head out and motioned them inside before they even knocked on the door sporting a gang's spray-painted graffiti. He'd flipped on the overhead lights in his office, but the rest of the place was dark.

"I'm Detective Waylon Kramer. This is Detective Larry Johnson and Detective Christina Miller. We talked on the phone. I understand that you have something to say to me," Waylon said.

"You said that I could be held as an accomplice if I withheld information. Before I say a word without a lawyer, I want your word that—"

Waylon held up a palm. "You didn't think it was important, did you, Mr. Drummond."

He shook his head. "Of course I didn't, or I would have told you earlier."

"And then you remembered and you called me immediately, right?" Waylon wanted to pinch the man's head off for wasting his time, but more than that, for the misery he'd put Kate through by not coming forward at the beginning of the investigation.

Mr. Drummond's head bobbed up and down several times. "That's right. You see, Conrad was a very good customer. But the past few months, I got nosy and saw that he was signing the card with a different name. I figured he was sending the weekly roses for one of his buddies who had affairs all the time, like he did."

"How long had he been a customer?" Larry asked.

"Fifteen years, I'd say. The first lady he sent flowers to worked at Truman Oil Company. I'm the florist, so I don't ask questions. I just send them wherever he says." He ripped a tissue out of a box and wiped his hands. "There were lots more through the years, but his last few times I noticed that he signed 'Carl' to the card instead of 'Conrad.'"

"We know he used that name sometimes, so this isn't anything new," Waylon said.

"Let me finish," Mr. Drummond said. "So after a few weeks my protector"—he made air quotes around the last word—"came into the store and wanted to know all about Carl, the man in the picture that they showed me."

"We asked you about gangs weeks ago," Larry said.

"Didn't you hear me?" Mr. Drummond's beady little eyes bugged out. "Protector. *Protection money.* Murder in my shop. They shoot people for less than talking to the cops. I've been scared they'd kill me for even letting you know about Estrella."

"Go on," Waylon said.

"Stickler—that's the name of the gang leader—asked me if that was Carl in the picture with his sister. I told him no, that was Conrad."

"And?" Waylon asked.

"That's when I recognized the woman. It was Katrina Gonzales, the young bathing suit model that you see on the billboards around town," he answered.

"Go on," Larry said.

"Katrina is Estrella and Stickler's baby sister. She's not in the gang business, and they protect her like a mama bear with a new cub. My bet is that they checked into Conrad Steele and Carl Swanson, found out they were the same man, and you can do the math on the rest."

"They found out about his three wives and his other life," Christina said.

"And the dozens of other women he'd sent flowers when they came back and made me pull out my files." Mr. Drummond nodded again. "They've been back in a couple of times a week since that day, and my protection money doubled. I don't need a blueprint to show me that they *will* figure out that I told you about Estrella, and when they do, I'm as dead as Conrad."

"So you want to go into wit sec?" Larry asked.

"I do not," he snapped. "I'm retiring. Have a flight to a place where you can't bring me back, and I won't be using this name. I'm tired of all this gang crap. I'm only talking to you because of those three wives. It's not fair to them to suffer for what they didn't do. I saw that article in the newspaper and I felt guilty. I want to leave here with a clear conscience."

"One more question. Was it Stickler who killed him, or did he have it done?" Larry asked.

"There are six nanny cams scattered around my shop—I hide those so all people see are the surveillance cameras. Here are the flash drives from inside them. It was family, so Stickler and Estrella took care of it." He handed them an envelope. "I was hiding behind the counter and I didn't see a thing from the time the shooting started, but these will help you."

"Thank you," Waylon said. "That's good information. Enjoy your retirement."

The man followed them outside, locked the door, and got into a green SUV. Waylon quickly wrote down the license number and then tucked his notebook back into his vest pocket.

"You going to let him leave?" Christina asked.

"Take a look at these right now and then I'll decide." Waylon pulled several flash drive sticks from the envelope and put them into her hands. She quickly pulled a tablet from her purse and plugged the first one into it.

A quick run-through showed a male and female with their backs to the main surveillance camera, but the nanny cams caught their faces clearly. Their masks were pulled up so the last faces Conrad saw would be theirs. Then there was gunfire. The masks came back down in front of the surveillance cameras, and they walked away, leaving Conrad on the floor with yellow roses still clutched in his hands.

"Can we identify them with that?" Waylon asked.

"Oh, yeah," Christina said. "We couldn't see them on the normal camera, but this is pure gold."

"We couldn't lock anything down until now," Larry said. "Let's call in for a couple of warrants and go pick them up."

"Where?"

"At their bar down south of town. That's where the whole gang hangs out," Christina said. "They'll be there. The king and his sister don't leave the castle unless it's important."

"And you know this how?"

"I paid my dues on the street," Christina answered. "So now that we're getting the case closed, how long are you sticking around for, Waylon?"

"Until the end of the week. I want to see these two behind bars. And I need to clean out my apartment. Lease is up on September 1."

"You won't quit. Detective work is in your blood." Larry laughed.

"Watch me." Waylon smiled.

Christina's dues paid off, and they snagged both Estrella and Stickler in the bar right where she'd told them they would be. They lawyered up before they were even in the interrogation room, but it was over. Kate's name was cleared, as were Amanda's and Jamie's.

He called from his apartment that evening, and she answered on the fourth ring.

"Sorry, I was rocking the baby. What have you found out?"

"It's over," he said simply.

⁊

Kate hit the button to put the phone on speaker and sat down on the sofa with the baby in her arms. "Are you serious? For real, it's over?"

"Probably be on the front page of the metro papers in the morning." He went on to tell her about Katrina Gonzales. "Conrad's lifestyle caught up with him. He saw a money deal. The gang saw a con man."

She'd expected a great surge of adrenaline to shoot through her veins when she finally heard the news, or maybe a few emotional tears, but nothing happened except that the baby burped up milk on her shoulder.

"Are you sure?" Kate asked. "They are behind bars and they confessed?"

"No confession, but the lawyer is already begging for a deal. Seems they have some information about a drug cartel that the feds have been after for years."

"Will they go free?"

"Oh, no, but they might get the death penalty off the table or their sentences reduced by a few years. Estrella is a cocky little witch. She'll run the whole Gonzales business from behind bars. Aren't you happy?"

"Yes, Waylon, but I'm in shock that it's over. 'Thank you' seems like so little."

"Just doin' my job," he said. "I thought I'd be home on Friday, but I need to stay over until the middle of next week to get everything finalized."

"You'll be home a week from Sunday for the christening, won't you? They're having a baby shower along with the potluck. As godparents, we will need to be there," she said. "This isn't a dream, is it?"

"No, it's real, and you are free to do whatever you want." He chuckled. "I'll call you tomorrow and every day I'm gone."

"I'll miss you," she said.

"I'm glad. Good night, darlin'."

He'd said *home*, not back in Bootleg or Mabelle or at the ranch. Waylon was coming home for good, and she'd made up her mind to live in Bootleg. Things were sure enough looking up.

With a towel around her red hair and wearing a white terry robe, Amanda padded out of the bathroom. "That felt so good, and thank you for watching her so I didn't have to hurry."

"Sit down," Kate said as she pulled a tissue from the box on the end table and wiped away the baby's spit-up.

"Why?" Amanda stopped in her tracks.

"Because I'm going to deliver good news, and you can't dance around like a wild woman when I do."

Amanda eased into the rocking chair.

"It's over. They caught Conrad's killers." Kate told her the whole story.

"Katrina Gonzales is that new swimsuit model, isn't she?" Jamie came in through the deck doors with Gracie behind her.

"Can I take my Barbie dolls in the tub with me?" Gracie asked.

"Go ahead and get her in the tub, and then I'll tell you," Kate said.

Kate told the story again when Jamie returned.

"The last tabloid news I saw on Katrina was that she was sporting a gorgeous antique engagement ring, but it didn't show the ring. I wonder if he gave her the same ring he gave me," Jamie pondered.

"I can't believe that he was already engaged when we'd only been married six months," Amanda said. "And to a gang member's sister. Was he losing it?"

"He saw dollar signs, not bullets," Jamie said.

"Well, I hope she has better luck with that ring than I did. Maybe she'll hock it and buy herself something nice with the money. This time it wasn't seven years in between." Amanda dried her hair and tossed the towel onto the coffee table.

"Who knows how many times he was married and divorced between each of us?" Kate said. "So your ring went missing, too, Jamie?"

"Oh, yeah, not long after we were married."

"And yours, Amanda?" Kate asked.

"About two weeks," Amanda answered. "I felt so bad about it, but Conrad was real sweet. He said that he should have had it sized down to fit my finger before then so it was his fault. He even said he would replace it, but he hadn't gotten around to it."

Jamie unfolded a lawn chair and sat down. "How about you, Kate?"

"It disappeared a couple of weeks after we got married. He said it had sentimental value because it was the ring that his father gave his mother. I felt horrible that I'd lost it, until a couple of years later when he told me that he'd taken it back because I wouldn't give him a divorce."

Jamie raised her hand. "I'd be willing to bet we all had Iris's ring from her first husband and that his new fiancée got the same ring."

"That son of a bitch," Amanda growled. "I'd take my wedding band off and throw it in the lake if I was wearing it. I had to remove it when pregnancy made my hands swell. I'll get rid of the thing when I bring the rest of my stuff to Bootleg."

"Home—that reminds me," Kate said. "The murder is solved. We are all free."

"I like that," Amanda said. "But I'm kind of glad that this has all happened. I came looking for closure, and I got it. But I also found myself. I like this town and these people, and I'm glad that we don't have a stink on us. Do you guys feel like it's not as big a deal as it was a month ago?"

Kate glanced at Jamie.

Jamie pushed up out of the chair. "Yes—same story again, but different reasons. I like the future I see here. Let's have a glass of wine to celebrate. You haven't put your two cents in yet, Kate. Are you staying or going?"

"Staying," Kate said. "I've got some things I need to work through that have nothing to do with Conrad. Right now he's probably more history to me than he is to y'all."

"Yes," Amanda and Jamie said at the same time.

❧

Kate had gone to bed with damp hair the night before, and now it was sticking up and out in so many directions she could have modeled for a punk rock band. She ran a brush through her hair, drew it up in a ponytail, and got dressed. When she looked into the mirror again, the same Kate stared back at her, but this one was far different than the one who'd left Fort Worth more than a month ago. That corporate lady would never have been caught in denim shorts and a neon-green T-shirt with a picture of a multicolored unicorn on the front. Gracie had picked it out when they'd gone shopping after the court date, and wearing it made Kate smile—every single time.

She padded to the kitchen in her bare feet and poured a cup of coffee, picked up a leftover breakfast burrito from the stove, and carried both out to the deck. Wednesday morning, five minutes till eight thirty. She'd made an appointment with her mother's assistant for a fifteen-minute block of time to talk to Teresa.

At fifteen seconds before the time, Kate dialed the number. Her mother picked up at exactly eight thirty. "Okay, Kate, your vacation time is over on Friday. Your name has been cleared. You don't have any common sense when it comes to men and that will hurt your business a little, but it won't ruin you if you go forward with determination to show your worth. It's time to come home."

"Where is home?" Kate asked. "Is it where you hang your hat or where you park your checkbook?"

"Don't mess with me," Teresa warned.

"Okay, I'll shoot straight. Either I get a year off, without pay, of course, or my resignation will be faxed to you in ten minutes," Kate said.

"You are serious? What are you going to do? Drive a tractor for a living?"

"Maybe. That does sound exciting." Kate pictured herself walking across a plowed field hand in hand with Waylon.

"I'm not giving you a year off, and if you resign, I'll sell this company and you won't get a dime of the money." Teresa's icy tone left no room for argument.

"I've never been poor. It might be an interesting adventure." Kate could live for years on the interest from her own investments. She didn't bother to remind her mother that she owned thirty percent of the stock in Truman Oil.

"I mean it, Kate. I'm not backing down one inch."

"Then you'd better call Red Dirt and see what their offer is, or else get ready to sit on the throne awhile longer. I'm not coming back to Fort Worth."

"Send me the resignation." Teresa hung up on her.

Ten minutes later, Kate watched her two-line resignation with her signature at the bottom go through the machine in her bedroom. When it finished, she took a deep breath and let it out slowly. There were no regrets, and she felt freer than she had in her whole life.

∽

"What does a godmother wear to a christening?" Kate asked, standing in the living room wearing nothing but her underpants, bra, and a short silk robe.

"Are you nervous about the godmother thing or about seeing Waylon as a totally free woman?" Jamie asked. Waylon had finally tied up all the ends in Dallas and come home the night before.

"Don't go judging me until you walk a mile in my high heels."

"High heels, hell!" Jamie laughed. "You aren't that girl anymore, darlin'. You are a barefoot country girl now, so embrace it. It's an August Sunday in Texas, so wear one of those cute little sundresses and sandals."

She looked down at her bare feet and unpolished nails. She had taken the time to remove the last remnants of polish and promised

Gracie that they would do each other's toenails when Gracie decided on just the right color.

"I'm wearing fancy flip-flops," Jamie said.

Amanda held up a foot. "My feet still aren't skinny enough yet to get into my regular shoes. Which reminds me, Aunt Ellie is bringing a truckload of my things today. I told her to sell the furniture because we don't need it."

"Don't you want a bigger bed?" Kate asked.

"I'm fine with the one I have. I shared the one in the apartment with Conrad and don't ever want to see it again. She's packed up my prebaby clothes and my other things, and the apartment lease is up on the first day of September, so now I don't have to go up there and deal with it."

"And you, Jamie?" Kate asked.

"House is for sale. I'm leaving the furniture in it, because the Realtor says that it helps sell the place. When papers are ready to sign, we can decide if there's anything we want out of it," Jamie answered.

"Are we ready? Y'all take forever!" Gracie sighed. "I haven't seen Lisa in four whole days and she hasn't even met my baby sister."

"Give me five minutes." Kate slipped her feet into a pair of sandals that matched a bright floral sundress with thin straps over the shoulders.

Waylon waited for her at the front of the church and walked inside with her hand tucked in his. His touch after two weeks made her want to drag him off to the hay barn instead of to a church pew, but today was the christening and she'd have to be good for a little while longer. The service lasted three minutes longer than eternity, but finally the preacher wound down and called Amanda, Jamie, Gracie, Kate, and Waylon to the front and the christening began. Kate tried to listen as he explained the duties of godparents, but she kept shifting her eyes and her thoughts to Waylon. The wink he shot her let her know he was also having trouble paying attention.

The ceremony ended, and as everyone in the church gathered around Amanda and the baby, Waylon maneuvered the other way and draped an arm around Kate's bare shoulders. His breath warmed her neck as he whispered, "You sure we can't sneak out of here?"

"We are the godparents. We have to stay."

"A drive afterward?" He kissed her earlobe.

"Definitely." She nodded.

She'd begun to think the party would never end and the congregation would never stop talking, but at three o'clock, Hattie pulled her to the side. "Why don't you and Waylon sneak out the back door? I can see he's getting antsy to talk to you in private, and I bet it's got more to do with you than that nasty murder business."

Kate made her way around the crowd and tapped Waylon on the shoulder. "We've been given the green light to leave this party."

"Well, halle-damn-lujah!" He looped her arm in his and headed toward the door. "Let's go before the thing turns red and stops us."

Luckily everyone was either involved with the new baby or visiting about whatever gossip was new in town, because no one even tried to start up a conversation with either of them on the way out to the churchyard. The hot August sun burned brightly and there wasn't even a hint of a breeze, but it didn't take the truck long to cool down once they were underway.

"Where are we going?" Kate asked.

"Anywhere you want to go," he answered.

"To the lake, where I can put my toes in the water and then curl up in your arms under that willow tree."

"A wonderful place." He grinned and made a turn to take them in that direction.

He parked beside her car and held her hand all the way down to the dock. Waylon was one of those cowboys who knew how to hold hands with a woman to make her feel special. Not too tight so that he was in control and she had no say-so over anything. Not so loose as to make her feel like he'd rather be anywhere else in the world other than beside her.

When they were settled down under the shade of the willow tree, he draped an arm around her shoulders, brushed her hair back, and kissed her. "I missed you so much this week, but I am officially just a Texas rancher now. When are you going back to Fort Worth?"

"I'm not. I'm looking for a job. I'm real good in a hay truck, and I can turn a tractor on a dime at the end of a field. Know anyone who might need a woman with those skills?"

"Are you teasing me?" Waylon asked.

"No, Mother is not happy, but she'll come around. She's decided to sell the business since I'm staying in Bootleg."

"Why did you decide to make such a drastic change in your life? You had a fantastic financial future and a good life."

"That was only existing. What I've chosen is living, and it's far better."

"In that case, I could use a good woman on the ranch." He grinned.

Epilogue

One year later

The whole crew, including Hattie and Victor, waited in line that Saturday afternoon at the festival in Bootleg.

"We're going to pass on the ride. I'm afraid it will scare Lia," Amanda said.

"Well, both of us are still aboveground," Victor said. "So we're taking our traditional ride and then we're going to have funnel cakes."

The ride stopped and all the people got off, then the man who took the money let the next bunch fill up the buckets.

Kate looked at the three kids and all the adults. "How are we doing this?"

Johnny, Waylon's right-hand man, kissed Amanda on the forehead. "You go help with the children. Me and Lia Beth will be fine right here. You'll be able to see her the whole time. She loves the music, so I know she'll be good. Besides, Victor and Hattie always ride together and"—he lowered his voice to a whisper—"something big is going to happen, so Kate and Waylon need to be together, too."

"Okay, then, I'll ride with Lisa. Gracie can ride with her mama," Amanda said.

"Thank you," Kate said. "Last year I promised Waylon that I would ride with him at this festival."

"And Paul and I will get to ride together that way," Jamie said.

"Y'all are so welcome." Amanda grinned.

❦

Kate buckled herself into the seat and thought about the last year. There had been lots of changes since the three women had decided to stay in Bootleg. Paul and Jamie were married over the Christmas break. They built a house out on twenty acres next to the Double Back Ranch and the little girls were regular visitors to the ranch.

Kate moved in with Waylon in the fall and never looked back. Teresa sold the business, but Kate had no regrets about that, either. She'd thought about building a bigger place on the ranch, but she and Waylon both were comfortable in the cozy little house. Besides, there was plenty of room for when Gracie and Lisa had a sleepover.

Johnny and Amanda had been dating for six months now, and she spent more time in his trailer than she did at the cabin. She'd told Kate just last night that he'd asked her to move in with him. That meant the cabin would be completely vacant in the next couple of weeks.

In some ways that made Kate sad, but then she thought of all the happiness that had come from there and the fact that a new preacher could be living in it within a year, and the good outweighed the sadness.

"Hey, darlin', penny for your thoughts." Waylon drew her close to his side as the ride started.

"You can have them for free. I was going back over the past year," she said. "It's been a good one, even if it did start out on rocky ground." She smiled. "You told me last year to save you a spot. We couldn't ride together then, but we can now."

Waylon buckled himself in and slung an arm around her. "You remembered."

"Of course I did," she said.

"Any regrets?"

"Not a single one," Kate answered.

"We've lived together for almost a year now. That's long enough for you to pass judgment on ranch life, right?" Waylon asked.

"I wouldn't be living there if I didn't like it and love you," she said.

"Then"—Waylon pulled a little velvet case from his pocket—"Katherine Elizabeth Truman, will you marry me?" He popped it open to reveal a lovely sapphire-and-diamond ring.

"Yes," she said without a second's hesitation.

He put the ring on her finger and then kissed each knuckle on her hand. "Blue for your eyes. Diamonds because they last forever, like our love will."

Neither of them gave a damn who saw their long, passionate kiss. They were on top of the Ferris wheel when he pulled away and she threw both hands into the sky.

"I'm engaged!" she squealed, and everyone on the Ferris wheel applauded.

Acknowledgments

Dear readers,

The first days of summer are pushing spring into the history books here in southern Oklahoma. You will be getting to know the characters in *The Barefoot Summer* in the cold winter months, so wrap up in a quilt and sip on a cup of hot chocolate.

I'm sitting in front of the computer putting the finishing touches on this story and not wanting to tell these characters good-bye. They've all been voices in my head for weeks now, and we've gotten to know one another really well. I've watched them grow from enemies to friends to family in spite of the crazy situation they were tossed into in the middle of a funeral. It's my hope that when you finish the last words in the book, you feel like they are real people and not just characters.

As always, it takes a village to turn an idea that filtered through my head into a book. And for that I'm humbled and grateful to the many people who have paved the way from beginning to end. To Montlake Romance, my sincere thanks for continuing to buy my works and have faith in me. To my editors, Anh Schluep and Krista Stroever, I love you both to the moon and back. To my team at Montlake—those amazing people who work on final edits, cover ideas, and all the promotion—big old Texas-size hugs to each and every one of you. To my agent, Erin Cartwright Niumata—having you on my side is a blessing that I never take for granted. A big thanks to my husband, Mr. B., for all the reasons he knows so well.

To my readers . . . you are truly appreciated beyond what words can say. Thank you for reading my books, for the reviews you write, for discussing them in your book clubs, for passing them over the backyard fence to share with your neighbors, and for continuing to support me. I really do have the most awesome friends, family, and fans in the whole universe.

Until next time, happy reading!

Carolyn Brown

About the Author

Carolyn Brown is a *New York Times* and *USA Today* bestselling author and a RITA finalist. Her books include romantic women's fiction, historical romance, contemporary romance, cowboy romance, and country music mass-market paperbacks. She and her husband live in the small town of Davis, Oklahoma, where everyone knows what everyone else is doing—and reads the local newspaper on Wednesday to see who got caught. They have three grown children and enough grandchildren to keep them young. When she's not writing, Carolyn likes to sit in her gorgeous backyard with her cats, Chester Fat Boy and Boots Randolph Terminator Outlaw, and watch them protect their territory from crickets, locusts, and spiders.